Del

Delphi in Space
Book Four

Bob Blanton

Cover by Momir Borocki
momir.borocki@gmail.com

Delphi Publishing

Copyright © 2019 by Robert D. Blanton

Cover by Momir Borocki

momir.borocki@gmail.com

https://www.facebook.com/StarshipSakira/

Table of Contents

1 What A Break

"Well, at least we can take a break," Marc McCormack said. The news had just announced the end to the standoff between Delphi city in the Cook Islands and the US. Marc was looking forward to some downtime. He, his brother Blake, and his daughter Catie had been going non-stop since Marc had discovered an alien spaceship off the coast of Hawaii. They had formed MacKenzie Discoveries and were trying to introduce the technology from the Sakira in a slow, controlled fashion, but things kept happening that were forcing them to accelerate their timeline.

"Captain, North Korea has launched a missile," ADI said. ADI is the digital intelligence that runs the Sakira, Marc's alien spaceship.

"Admiral Michaels, I need you to leave the room."

"Why, what's going on?" the admiral demanded. The admiral was a new member of MacKenzie Discoveries and not yet privy to the secret of the Sakira.

"Please leave the room!" Marc said. The admiral got up and left in a bit of a huff.

"ADI, bring up a plot of the missile's trajectory. And what kind of missile is it?" Marc asked.

"It appears to be a Hwasong-15, one of their long-range missiles," ADI replied. "I have plotted three possible trajectories; I have them projected on the table."

Catie, Marc's thirteen-year-old-daughter, rushed around the table to look at the trajectories. "Do we have a satellite close enough to knock it down?" she asked.

Blake joined them at the table, while Samantha Newman, the company lawyer, and Marc's girlfriend, just sat where she was and held her head in her hands. "You had to say *take a break*," she moaned.

"Tempting fates. You should know better," Blake said with a chuckle. He leaned over and started examining the map in detail. "All three trajectories show the missile heading for the US," he said.

"Why did you kick the admiral out?" Catie asked.

"I'm not ready to share the satellites with him," Marc said. "ADI, do we have a targeting solution? And which are the closest Oryxes?"

"Captain, it is too early for a targeting solution. I should have one in eight minutes," ADI said. "Oryx Three and Oryx Seven are in orbits that intersect the trajectories I have mapped. However, neither of them can reach the missile before its reentry."

"Jason and Carrie," Catie provided the names of the pilots. "Use Jason, he's the better pilot."

Marc nodded his head in agreement. "ADI, redirect Jason to the intercept point."

"Yes, Captain."

"Where is the earliest possible targeting solution?"

"Captain, the missile's current trajectory indicates that it is targeting Los Angeles. The earliest targeting point is in the southern Bering Sea. I've highlighted it on the map."

"It's north of Great Sitkin Island, Alaska, USA," Blake said. "That's part of Alaska."

"Wow, I didn't realize that Alaska goes so far to the west," Catie said. "It looks like the intercept is north of it above international waters."

"ADI, probability of success?"

"I am already moving a satellite into a better position," ADI said. "Probability of being able to hit the missile is ninety-five percent. I need your objective before I can predict the probability of success."

"Give me the probabilities for destroying the missile, for disabling or destroying its rockets, for destroying the warhead, and for disabling the payload so that it burns up on reentry."

"The probability of destroying the missile is sixty percent. The probability of disabling the rocket is ninety-eight percent. The probability of destroying the warhead is eighty percent. The probability of disabling the warhead by rupturing its reentry vehicle is eighty-six percent."

"Okay, give me the probability of disabling the rocket and then rupturing the reentry vehicle."

"Disabling the rocket first raises the probability of rupturing the reentry vehicle to ninety-six percent," ADI said.

"Great!" Marc said. "ADI, execute that plan. Where will the reentry vehicle land?"

"That would depend on whether the warhead explodes," ADI said. "If it doesn't explode, it will land within a two-hundred-mile radius, the center of the area is seven hundred miles west of Seattle."

"Time to targeting position?"

"Five minutes."

"Time for Jason to reach the targeting position?"

"Eight minutes."

"Why send Jason if he can't get there in time?" Catie asked.

"FUD," Blake answered for Marc. "Fear, uncertainty, and doubt. He doesn't want anyone to know how the missile was destroyed, preserving the secret that we have satellites in orbit."

Marc nodded his head. "Best-case scenario, everyone thinks it was a malfunction. I want Jason close by so the US will pick up something on radar close enough to have done something. He could have fired a missile," Marc said.

"What about the warhead?" Blake asked.

"I don't think there is one," Catie said.

Marc's head did a little stutter at her pronouncement. "Why not?"

"I think they're testing the US intercept capability," Catie said, "and they want to raise the fear factor in the US to gain more leverage in the negotiations."

"How does launching an unarmed missile help there?"

"They can destroy it before it gets to the US," Catie said. "Say it was a mistake. The US won't launch a counterstrike before it hits, it's only one missile after all."

Marc gave a slight nod. "So, by destroying it early?"

"We mess up their strategy," Catie said. "They can't have two launches too close together and still claim some kind of mistake."

"And the US reaction?"

"You should get Admiral Michaels back in here," Samantha said. "This is more his area of expertise."

Marc nodded in agreement. Samantha went to the door and invited the admiral back in. Admiral Michaels had been the head of Naval intelligence until the president fired him in a pique of anger. Then fearing for the safety of his family, he had joined Marc in the Cook Islands.

"Admiral, I apologize for earlier," Marc said. "But you have to accept that there are certain things that we are not yet ready to share with you."

The admiral nodded his head and waited for Marc to go on.

"It appears that the North Koreans have launched a missile at the United States," Marc explained.

The admiral shook his head in shock. "How could you know . . . Doesn't matter. What do you need from me?"

"We believe we can shoot the missile down before it reaches its peak," Marc continued. "We're trying to gauge the US response."

"They're obviously trying to take advantage of the confusion surrounding the president and Admiral Morris," Admiral Michaels said, "but firing a missile doesn't make sense."

"Catie believes that the missile is unarmed and that they will have it self-destruct before it reaches US territory," Marc added.

"Ah, that makes more sense," Admiral Michaels said. "If the US shoots it down before it passes the Aleutians, they say it was simply a test, if the US doesn't shoot it down, they trigger the self-destruct and announce that there was a targeting error during the missile test. If

—

they get by the US defenses, it would really ratchet up the tension in the US and give them more of an edge in the negotiations."

"Okay, so what will the president's response be?" Marc asked.

"You said you were going to shoot it down, when and where?"

"Before it reaches its peak altitude," Marc said. "We'll hit it just north of Grand Sitkin Island. It should break up and crash about seven hundred miles west of Seattle."

"That's close," Admiral Michaels gasped. "What about the payload?"

"We expect it to burn up during reentry," Marc said.

"Okay, so the North Koreans will claim it was a test launch and that . . . ," Admiral Michaels said, then he hesitated as he tried to decide what would happen next.

"They'll say it was a success," Catie interjected. "Taking out the launch vehicle will look like a successful separation, and then it just burns up as planned."

"You are probably right," Admiral Michaels acknowledged. "So that leaves the president ratcheting up his rhetoric. But if he knows better?" The admiral gave Marc a questioning look.

"We don't know how much they're going to be able to see or determine."

"If he knows or suspects that you shot it down, he won't announce that to the public," Admiral Michaels said.

"Captain, the missile's rocket has been destroyed. I am targeting the reentry vehicle now," ADI said.

Marc held his hand up as ADI provided the update, "Include everyone and repeat, and include everybody in the rest of the reports."

ADI repeated the message, and everyone paused, waiting to hear about the reentry vehicle.

"The reentry vehicle has burned up and broken apart," ADI announced. "The debris was scattered in a two-hundred-mile area that is six hundred miles west of Seattle."

"As you were saying," Marc indicated that the admiral should continue.

"I think the biggest issue will be what he will do about you if he suspects you shot it down. That would significantly raise your threat profile as far as he's concerned. But after the last debacle, he's limited in what he can do. Minimally you should expect the CIA to put a lot more effort into trying to infiltrate your position here."

"So, we're basically back to normal," Marc said with a chuckle.

"I guess you could say that."

2   Board Meeting – Sept 2nd

"I hope everybody had a good weekend and got a chance to relax after all the excitement of last week," Marc said as all the board members gathered in the boardroom. "Please, have a seat, and we'll get started."

"I still think we should have gotten a day off," Blake said. "How many times do you have to avert a disaster to get a day off?"

Marc laughed, "The world keeps marching along. Let's discuss where we are after last week's drama. Admiral?"

"With the help of ADI, I've reached out to my friends in the White House," Admiral Michaels said. He was referring to the fact that ADI could connect his Comm to any cellphone without leaving a trace. "They tell me that the president is still fuming. But they say he is resigned to the fact that seizing Delphi City is no longer an option."

"That's certainly nice to hear," Samantha said. "What is he saying about North Korea?"

"They did see your Oryx fly by," Admiral Michaels said. "But it was too late to have shot the missile down. They're assuming it was coming to see what was going on. The consensus is that the missile had a normal separation and that the reentry vehicle failed due to flaws in the North Korean design."

"I think that is good news," Marc said.

"They are wondering how you would have seen the missile launch," Admiral Michaels said. "That is something I'm wondering myself."

"Well, a little wondering is good for the soul," Marc said. "For now, we continue forward with our plans. I would like you to think about what we could do to permanently resolve the instability caused by North Korea. What do you think about the situation vis-à-vis our families?"

"I would recommend keeping them outside the US for a while longer," Admiral Michaels said. "I know we would all like to think we can trust the government not to take advantage of our loved ones, but your new technology threatens too many interests."

"I agree," Marc said. "I just hoped it would be different. Sam?" Marc nodded to Samantha, giving her the floor.

"We have to reschedule the press conference about the clinics," Samantha said.

"Do we really have to?"

"Hey, the world keeps marching," Blake said, laughing at Marc's discomfort.

"Okay," Marc said. "Schedule it and let me know."

"It's already scheduled for Friday at two o'clock," Samantha said, giving Marc a bright smile. "Moving on, we have completed negotiations for the Moroccan automotive plant. Herr Johansson will start construction next week."

"Thank you. Kal, how is security going?" Kal was the ex-Marine who Blake had recruited to run security for MacKenzie Discoveries.

"Our police candidates are doing well," Kal reported. "The first four rotated back last week. As I explained before, they'll work here until the next class starts, then go back. But it gives us some community-type police to handle the normal day-to-day stuff."

"Good!" Samantha said.

"The rest of security is going well. Now that we're off Manuae, it's a little easier. Much better control of access and one less place to worry about. We're patrolling the airport on a regular basis now. We send a fresh group on the catamaran every time it makes a trip to Arutanga, and it picks up the off-shift guys on its way back."

"That's a long overnight shift for them," Blake said.

"We send two shifts; they break it up into two four-hour shifts," Kal explained.

"Looks like you have things covered," Marc said. "Blake?"

"Construction is running smooth," Blake said. "I've handed off a lot of the management of the day-to-day to Hakim Mostafa; he ran a construction company back in Syria. He's picked it all up quickly. We only need to meet once a week."

"Sounds like a perfect match," Marc said.

"It would be a perfect match if only he drank," Blake quipped.

"I suspect it is a perfect match because he doesn't drink," Samantha said. She laughed as Blake gave her a silent comment with his hand.

"You're probably right," Blake agreed. "Anyway, the airport is coming along. We're completing the sections along the side, adding warehouses, hangars, and some office space as needed."

"Sounds like you could pick up some more work," Marc said.

"NO! Why is the punishment for doing a good job always more work?" Blake asked with a sigh. "I was planning on doing an investigation of how to set up a distillery here so we could make our own scotch."

"I'm fine with you having a hobby, but we have a lot of projects to manage," Marc said.

"You say that now, but wait until someone decides to embargo our alcohol," Blake said.

"I think I'll fall back on the age-old custom of smuggling," Marc said. "The Lynx is the perfect ship for that. Speaking of the Lynx, Catie, how are we doing?"

"Now that we have enough superconductor matrices," Catie said, "I've started making more Lynxes. We're still using the standard engines so they won't be able to make orbit, but we can refit them later. We're going to start building the Oryxes in the space station next week. We're going slow so we can iron out the process first. Besides, we don't have a big enough crew up there to run a full production process. We've sent four Lynxes out for certification, two to the Kiwis, one to Mexico and one to France."

"I assume Sam insisted on France making it to the top of the list," Marc said.

"Yep, she even has some friend over there who's supposed to help expedite the certification."

Marc laughed at his girlfriend's efforts to get them a vacation in Paris without having to spend a day traveling to get there.

"Last but not least, our asteroids are here," Catie continued.

"Asteroids," Admiral Michaels said. His voice almost squeaked, and he sprayed his last sip of scotch across the table.

"Oh, I guess there's no use hiding that from you," Marc said. "We acquired three asteroids that we will be mining for the materials we need on the space station."

"How did you manage to acquire these asteroids?" Admiral Michaels asked.

"Not ready to share that yet," Marc said, "and the existence of the asteroids is to be kept secret."

"Of course," Admiral Michaels said, shaking his head.

Samantha leaned over and patted his hand. "Just be glad they're spreading the shock out," she whispered.

"Way to bury the lead," Blake told Catie. "Where are they?"

"They have entered orbit about one hundred degrees ahead of Earth. We'll start slowing them down now until we can get them to about two degrees ahead of Earth. That puts them at a little over seven hours away for an Oryx at one-G acceleration," Catie explained.

"Can an Oryx accelerate that long?" Blake asked.

"We'll have to add a particle accelerator to the engine," Catie said. "We planned on doing that when we designed them. Now that we have microgravity manufacturing, we can make them and retrofit the engines. By the way, that means we need to invent a particle accelerator." Catie gave her father a bright smile.

"Oh my," groaned Admiral Michaels.

Samantha reached over and patted the admiral's hand again. "It does get better," she said. "Until then, you'll need to rely on Blake to pour you a glass of scotch."

Blake immediately got up and grabbed his bottle of 15-year-old Glenlivet and a few glasses. He poured one for the admiral and himself, then looked around for any other takers. Samantha asked for a splash, the rest declined.

Marc shook his head at Blake's antics. "Anything else?"

"Yes, we need to move a few of the fabricators up to the station. Then we'll be able to make the special parts we need like the small power plants and particle accelerators. We'll need to make them that way until we come up with a way to manufacture them on a larger scale."

"I'll take care of it," Fred said.

"Okay, Liz, you're up. I'm glad you're waiting until after your update for a glass," Marc said. Liz was the second ex-Marine who Blake had recruited to provide security and help out at MacKenzie Discoveries. She was a chopper pilot and a Krav Maga master. Besides all her other duties, she doubled as Catie's personal bodyguard.

Liz smiled at Marc and indicated to Blake how much she wanted. "We will finish up the hub for Delphi Station next week," Liz said. "We're already manufacturing the superconductor matrices at the station. We're also manufacturing the polysteel panels that we're using to finish out the interior. We need to paint them; we'll use the same compound that ADI gave us for coloring the walls here in the city."

"Are we going to let people change the color in their personal space?" Samantha asked.

"I don't know," Liz said. "It's tough on the air-purifiers."

"Cer Liz," ADI said. "We can use local circulation filters when people paint. It will capture the fumes, and we can recycle the material."

"Thank you, ADI, that will help," Liz said. "The big news is, our fusion team is actually ready to build a reactor. They believe they have solved all their problems."

"How did they take care of the heat issue?" Catie asked.

"My understanding is, they are using liquid gallium to move the heat from the containment vessel to a set of coils. Those coils will then heat the water, turning it into steam to run the turbines. You'll need to talk to Dr. Tanaka if you want a better answer than that."

"Isn't gallium a metal?" Blake asked.

"Yes it is," Liz answered. "Apparently it melts at thirty degrees C. And, it can handle the extreme heat without turning into a gas. Everything is kept at ten atmospheres of pressure. Very complex, so if you want more, talk to them."

"No, that's good enough for me," Blake said.

"Okay, and last but not least, we're getting ready to extrude the inner ring. We're going to need to install a treatment plant as soon as we can," Liz said. "Currently we're using the systems on the Oryxes to handle all the waste, but we're approaching the limit of what we can do with them."

Catie raised her hand.

"I'm assuming you're volunteering," Marc said.

"Sure, I'll get Tomi on it, and Natalia wants to study environmental science. I want to give her a chance to see if she's going to like it," Catie said.

"I'll trust you to take care of it. Now other assignments," Marc said. "We have some applications from people who want to start businesses here on Delphi City."

"I'll take that as long as Catie will help me," Samantha said.

"Sure, sounds like fun," Catie said.

Marc nodded his approval. He had wanted to give the assignment to Catie so she would get more people-based experience. Samantha taking the lead was perfect, she would make a good coach for Catie.

"Thank you," Marc said. "Now that our asteroids are getting close, we need to start up the mining operations for them. We need to find miners; hopefully, we have some people with mining experience. That way, they're not too overwhelmed with having to do it in microgravity and in vacuum. Blake, can you take that?"

"Absolutely," Blake said. "That actually sounds like fun."

"Liz," Marc continued. "How about getting someone started on the particle accelerator Catie wants."

"Already added it to my list," Liz said.

"Then that wraps the meeting up for today," Marc said.

Samantha motioned for Catie to follow her to her office.

"We should talk about the business applications," Samantha said while they walked down the hallway.

"Sure," Catie said. "Thanks for including me. I'd like to learn about this stuff. You and Daddy didn't set me up, did you?"

"No, but with his reaction, you'd have thought we did."

"He did seem happy."

"ADI, please send us the business applications," Samantha asked.

"They are on your Comm, Cer Sam," ADI said.

"Thank you," Samantha said. "Let's see what we have. A Lebanese restaurant, a Jamaican restaurant, a hotdog stand, and a clothing store."

"A clothing store!" Catie said, completely surprised that someone would want to start one up in Delphi City. Almost everybody either ordered online or made their own. "That will be interesting."

"Why don't you take the clothing store and the Jamaican restaurant," Samantha said. "I'll check out the hotdog stand and the Lebanese restaurant. If you need help, just text me. We can review things on Friday."

"Okay," Catie agreed. "I'm surprised you didn't take the clothing store and give me the hotdog stand."

"I think we'll give a more impartial review of their business plan this way," Samantha said with a small laugh. "These are the first people who have asked to start up their own business. We'll have to decide how to handle the leases and select the locations."

"We have set aside areas for commercial districts," Catie said. "I'm not sure about a hotdog stand, though."

3   Business Plans

Catie was meeting with the Shammas family in their home. She had
invited them to her office, but they had requested that the meeting be
in their condo.

"Would you like some tea and sweets?" Mrs. Shammas asked.

"Some tea would be nice," Catie answered as she took the seat on the
sofa that Mr. Shammas was indicating. "So tell me about this clothing
store you want to open."

"Nezha wants to sell some clothes that she makes," Mr. Shammas said.
"She thinks that the young people here in Delphi City would like to
buy suits that look like the ones the pilots wear."

"You mean our shipsuits?" Catie asked.

"Yes," Mrs. Shammas said as she entered with the tea. She poured a
cup for Catie and her husband and then sat down next to her husband.
"Our son and daughter both begged me to make one for them. I made
them one each, now all their friends are asking for them."

"Even the girls?" Catie asked, surprised that Muslim girls would wear
anything so tight as a shipsuit.

"She is only seven," Mrs. Shammas said. "But I am sure that even the
older girls will be wearing them. This generation is so daring, and it is
so safe here. Let us show you. Hanifa, Salim, come here and show Ms.
McCormack your suits."

Two children came out of the back bedroom wearing shipsuits. They
were made of spandex but were a remarkable likeness for the shipsuits
that the pilots wore when going into space. They fit snugly, although
not with the same tightness of the real shipsuits that had to provide
pressure to compensate for the vacuum of space.

"Those are so cute," Catie said. "And so realistic. You have even made
the boots."

"My friend, Sania, made the boots," Mrs. Shammas said. "She makes
many different types of footwear. She will have a booth in our store."

"Do you think there will be enough demand to keep a business going?"
Catie asked.

"Oh yes, I would not be able to make them so fast. And your pilots wear them all the time, they even wear them to restaurants and bars," Mrs. Shammas said. "That means the children will be wearing them all the time, so they will need more than one pair."

"They are comfortable," Catie said.

"Of course, you are a pilot also," Mrs. Shammas said. "I'm surprised you are not wearing one now."

"My father would have a fit," Catie said.

"Oh, he cannot be such a prude," Mrs. Shammas said.

"Oh no, not because of that. He would be upset because I wasn't wearing proper business attire while I was having a meeting," Catie said. "When I was flying, I wore mine all the time. I haven't been flying for a while."

"Yes, one must project the proper image," Mr. Shammas said. "At home, Nezha would sell them at the local market, but we don't have one here."

"A local market," Catie said. "Like they have on Rarotonga?"

"Yes," Mrs. Shammas said. "The women have arranged to set up a small market in someone's condo each week, but it doesn't work too well."

"Someone should have come and asked," Catie said. "We can make arrangements for a market. I assume you're referring to an open-air market with booths."

"Yes, so that you can choose which days you come."

"Is it important that it be outside?" Catie asked. "We could use one of the smaller warehouses and set something up inside. That way, it would be permanent."

"Being outside helps to draw a crowd," Mrs. Shammas said. "People see the booths, and they stop to shop. If it was inside, how would they know? Besides, at first, we would only open the market during the weekends."

"You could advertise," Catie said. "What about if it were inside, but you could set up a few booths on the outside so that people would see that you were open. You could change which products you show outside based on how well they draw people in. And I think we can figure a way that works for only having it on the weekend."

"That would be wonderful," Mrs. Shammas said. "But wouldn't it be expensive to use a warehouse?"

"I don't think it would be too bad, certainly less expensive than everyone opening a small store," Catie said. "I'll make you a deal. You arrange with your friends to hold a community market; I'll give you the space for free for the first three months. If at the end of that time, you think you can afford to pay rent, we'll negotiate a reasonable rate. I'll supply the tables; you'll need to supply everything else. If that doesn't work, we'll come up with another plan."

"What about taxes?" Mr. Shammas asked.

"Ohh," Catie moaned. "I'll take care of taxes for the first month. During that time, we'll work out how to handle them."

"Excellent," Mr. Shammas said. "And you will let us know which warehouse?"

"Yes," Catie said. "I already have in mind the one we'll use, but I need to check with some people first. I'm sure we can have everything ready for next weekend."

Catie decided that the warehouses were too far away from where people lived to really work for a community market, so she decided on some of the unused manufacturing space instead. The space she chose was at the edge of the residential section, right across from one of the larger parks. She thought it would lend itself to people congregating and making an outing of going to the market. She was interested to see how things turned out next weekend.

The next day, Catie went to meet with the two men who were planning to open a Jamaican restaurant. She was meeting them at the site she thought was the best fit for the restaurant. It was in one of the condo complexes where the ground floor had been designated as retail space.

"Good day, gentlemen," Catie said as she opened the door to allow the two men to enter. "I think this would be a good location for your restaurant. Of course, I will be happy to consider other options if you don't like it. It's located right next to an office park, and although many of the offices are empty now, that should change over time. And this is one of the more desirable condo complexes since it's the farthest from the airport."

"We like it," the first man said. "I am Kenyon Deogene, and this is my brother, Jaylin."

"I'm pleased to meet you," Catie said; she smiled at the Caribbean lilt to his voice.

"We are pleased to be making your acquaintance, too," Kenyon said. "Now what would be the rules if we lease this location?"

"You are responsible for modifying the interior to suit your needs. You will have to use one of our construction teams, but you pay their wages for the time you use them. We'll provide the materials for any walls or windows," Catie explained. "The first three months of the lease are free, then you have to pay four thousand dollars per month."

"Is there a minimum duration for the lease?" Kenyon asked.

"No," Catie replied.

"This seems unusual," Jaylin said. "No deposit, no fixed term, and we only pay to have the place altered."

"That's correct," Catie said. "Basically, your startup cost is the fixtures and the labor to set everything up. We're looking for businesses to succeed, so we want to help. If you fail, we'll keep the alterations you've made and offer the space to another restaurant. We assume you'll be buying the fixtures on credit, so we don't expect them to stay."

"I'm liking this place," Kenyon said. "Do you have a bank we can talk to about borrowing money to set up our place?"

"I can take care of that for you," Catie said. "Do you have any collateral?"

"Not much," Jaylin said, "I only have my two hands and the twenty thousand dollars we've managed to save and bring with us."

"I'll tell you what," Catie said. "You make me and my friend dinner tonight, and if we like it, we'll loan you the money."

"You bring your boyfriend to our place," Jaylin said. "We'll impress you so much, you'll be happy to loan us the money."

"It won't be my boyfriend," Catie said. "I'll be bringing her," Catie said as she pointed to Natalia. Natalia, Catie's bodyguard and friend, was sitting in the background trying to be inconspicuous.

"You have our address," Kenyon said. "We'll see you tonight at seven o'clock."

"We'll see you then," Catie said as she let them out.

"Why did you include me in the dinner?" Natalia asked. "I could have waited outside for you."

"I know, but you're always having to follow me around, I figured it was only fair that you get some benefit out of it," Catie said. "Besides, you told me you like Jamaican food. You'll be a good judge of their food quality."

"Hello, Ladies," Kenyon greeted Catie and Natalia at the door; he had dressed like a waiter. "Right this way."

He led them to the dining room, which was set up just like a restaurant. "Your table is right here. May I offer you something to drink? We have wine and beer. We also feature Papaya juice, lemonade, and refreshing ice tea."

"I'll have ice tea," Catie said.

"I'll have the same," Natalia added. Once Kenyon left to get their tea, Natalia leaned over to whisper. "They're doing this just like we were in a restaurant."

"I think it's clever," Catie said. "What better way to impress us. And it gives me the perfect opportunity to talk to you about your job."

"My job?" Natalia asked, sitting back and wondering if she'd been doing something wrong.

"Yes, you said you wanted to study environmental science, and an opportunity has come up. I wondered if you were interested in it."

"I've only been studying for ten weeks, isn't it a little early to talk about a job?" Natalia asked.

"There's nothing like on-the-job training to complement your studies," Catie said. "At least that's what Daddy always tells me when he gives me a new job."

"Here you go, Ladies," Kenyon said. "Your ice tea and some coconut shrimp for an appetizer. This is a homemade honey-mustard sauce. It's a bit spicy, but I'm sure you'll enjoy it." Kenyon stepped away from the table.

"Those coconut shrimp look delicious," Natalia said.

"They sure do, and remember I get half," Catie said as she scooped some of the sauce onto her plate.

"Half? Hey, I have to take in a lot of calories to keep this body fit," Natalia said, making a point of her two-hundred-pound frame.

"Then you'll just need to eat more veggies," Catie said. "Now about that job. It's developing the waste treatment plant for our high-altitude residence."

"Oh, you mean *the space station*," Natalia said, only mouthing the words for *space station*.

"Yes, you remember Tomi," Catie said. After Natalia nodded, Catie continued, "He's going to be the main designer, but there is a lot of work to do, and then there will be starting it up. He's made it clear he's staying grounded, so someone needs to be on the job site to test things out."

Catie had grabbed three of the six shrimp and was working on her second while Natalia was thinking.

"So how hard can it be," Natalia said. "He already has one down here, won't he just copy that?"

"There's that whole half-g thing to deal with, plus it has to be designed to be able to handle microgravity for short periods of time," Catie said. "Then we have to design the whole air and water purification scheme."

"Don't you already have a design for this?" Natalia asked. "You know on the Sakira."

"Not really the same thing," Catie said. "We're talking about a system that can handle three- to five-thousand people. The Sakira's system is for five hundred."

"Would that mean I would need to live up there?" Natalia asked.

"At least part of the time," Catie replied. "I plan on living up there, and I know Daddy is going to move up there as soon as some cabins are ready. The first system only has to handle a few hundred people, but it needs to prove out the design."

"Ladies, are you ready for your salad?" Kenyon asked as he removed their now empty plates.

"Yes, we are," Catie said.

"Those shrimp were delicious," Natalia said.

"No dodging the subject," Catie said. "What do you think?"

"It sounds like a lot of work and a lot of stuff I don't know anything about," Natalia said.

"But you'll learn," Catie said. "ADI can structure your coursework so you're studying what you need for the job and fill in the rest when you have time. That's what I do."

"But you're a lot smarter than I am," Natalia said.

"I don't think you give yourself enough credit," Catie said. "And ADI agrees with me. She says you're doing really well in all the work she's assigned you."

"But she's taking it easy on me," Natalia said.

"No, Cer Nattie," ADI said. "I am not taking it easy on you. Your studies are harder than they would be at a university because I don't give you anything you already know."

"See," Catie said. "Now promise you'll think about it. Besides, it will give us stuff to do together."

"Sure, I'll try," Natalia said. "I know Tomi, ADI, and you will keep me out of trouble."

"Your salads, Ladies," Kenyon said as he placed the salad in front of them. "It is our house salad with greens, pineapple, mangos, and tomatoes. The dressing is our special mango vinaigrette."

"Delish," Catie said. After Kenyon returned to the kitchen, she continued with Natalia. "We also need to figure out what the best plants are to grow up there. We have to have a greenhouse and hydroponics setup that is even better than what we have here."

"Now that part I can do," Natalia said. "I like helping you with the farming here."

"Are we going to use the farming sections for air purification?" Natalia asked.

"We'll use it to convert the CO_2 to oxygen," Catie said. "But we'll have to really filter the air afterward. We don't want anything getting into the air system and growing. I read a book where they got mushroom spores into the air system, and it really messed things up. We have to avoid anything like that."

Natalia laughed, "That would be terrible," she said. "But you're going to have stuff on people's clothes and things like that."

"The farm areas have to have airlocks, and the workers will need to change into a jumpsuit when they go in. I think we may even need them to wear a respirator like they do in a hospital. That way, they can't breathe in some spores in the farm area and then breathe them out in the main area."

"That does sound complex," Natalia said. "Oh, here comes the main course."

"Finished with your salads?" Kenyon asked.

"Yes, we are," Catie said, leaning back to provide room for Kenyon to remove her salad plate.

"And for our main course, we have grilled jerk chicken marinated in our signature jerk spices and sauce with a fresh cabbage, broccoli, and carrot medley. Also, a small order of fried plantains and some rotis."

"What are rotis?" Catie asked.

"Jamaican flatbread, very much like the Indian flatbread you may have had before," Kenyon explained.

Catie and Natalia talked a bit more about the work, but most of the time they concentrated on eating the meal. When they finished, Kenyon came back to clear the dishes.

"I hope you have saved room for dessert," Kenyon said. "We are serving a traditional Jamaican Black Cake, it's a dark, rich fruitcake that you're going to love."

"Oh," Catie groaned. "Only a small piece, please."

"You can give me the rest of hers," Natalia said.

"Would you like some coffee with your dessert?"

"Please," Catie said; Natalia nodded in agreement.

After Kenyon served their desserts and coffee, Catie decided to give him the good news. "If you'll send me the info on what you need to borrow," she said, "I'll work up the loan papers. I think we're charging three percent."

Jaylin was listening at the kitchen door and came rushing out to thank Catie.

"We will make you proud of us," he said.

"If you can serve food like this, I'm sure you'll be a success," Catie said. "That is, if your customers don't all explode from overeating!"

As they were leaving the Deogene condo, Natalia asked Catie, "Since when do you guys have a bank?"

"We don't," Catie said. "Can you believe it. I don't understand how we missed setting up a bank. I'm going to bring it up at the next board meeting. We should have a credit union at least."

"So, who's going to loan them the money?"

"Oh, I will," Catie said, "unless we get the bank set up first."

"Aren't you running out of money?"

"A little," Catie said. "But ADI has been managing my investments for me, so I'm making it back. Where do you have your money?"

"Bank of New Zealand," Natalia said. "But I'd move it to your credit union if you open one."

4   Catie's Surprise

Everyone was gathered at the entrance to the new park Catie was unveiling. She'd been keeping it a secret, and even Blake had avoided flying over it to see what was behind the walls Catie had erected to keep her secret. Now there was a curtain covering the fifty-meter entrance that Catie had the community gathered at.

"I want to thank everybody for coming," Catie announced. She saw Sophia looking anxious to get the details so she could get it into the Delphi Gazette right away.

"I hope all of you love Delphi City as much as I do," Catie continued. "The thing I miss about Manuae and Rarotonga is the beach. I know the kids would love to play in the sand, and I also have heard some of the adult residents complain about having to ride the ferry to Manuae or Rarotonga to go surfing or wave boarding. It is a bit strange to live on an island city in the middle of the ocean and not be able to do those things. As you know, this is going to be the central park for the city once it is complete, and as a central park, I felt it needed to be special, so here it is. Our very own ocean beach," Catie said as the curtain was pulled away.

Catie led the way through the now open entrance and into the park. "I give you Kealoha Beach, after our head of security and surfing aficionado, Kal. The lake you see is seawater," Catie continued. "It is surrounded by real beach sand and has a wave machine that creates waves that are just right for a bit of surfing or wave boarding." As she said that she pointed at Kal who was surfing on a wave coming toward them. He expertly rode the wave all the way into the shore.

"It's not as challenging as some of the waves around the islands, but it does give you a good ride," Catie continued. "We can make the waves bigger, but then they tear up the beach. That requires a lot of cleanup afterward, so we won't do it very often, but it would allow us to hold surf competitions."

Kal came running up the beach, dropping his surfboard as he hit the grass area. He continued running until he reached Catie. "That was one nice ride," he said as he gave Catie a big hug. The children in the crowd ran to the water and started splashing around in it. Two security personnel quickly took positions in the lifeguard towers to watch over them. There were several groupings of buckets and shovels strategically located, which were quickly found by the younger children, and sandcastle building commenced immediately.

"This was quite an undertaking," Marc said as he hugged his daughter.

"It was," Catie said. "But I think it'll be worth it. Uncle Blake has set aside those three blocks on the east side for a hotel. We're hoping we might actually generate a bit of tourist trade."

"How are you planning on doing that?" Samantha asked.

"Well, we are kind of unique. A floating city," Catie said. "Plus, we're going to do some things to encourage our artistic residents to express themselves so there will be a nice shopping experience. We also have some amazing restaurants going in."

"Yes, add virtually zero crime, and you might have something," Samantha said.

"Yes, and we can set someone up to do snorkeling and scuba charters on the Mea Huli. We might even get someone to bring their own boat here and start up a business like that," Catie added.

"How long has Kal been in on it?" Blake asked.

"Just a couple of weeks. I needed a surfer to help me tune the wave generator," Catie said.

"How do you keep the water clean?" Liz asked.

"It's continuously exchanging with the ocean below us," Catie said. "About twice its volume gets exchanged every day. It's set up to do a fast exchange late at night when nobody's around."

"Are you sure nobody will be around?" Liz asked.

"Well, we turn the wave machine off at night, and Kal's security will be checking it. I don't think we really care if people come down at night," Catie said.

"I can guarantee you that there will be teenagers here at night partying," Kal said. "We should put in a fire ring so they can have a fire. It'll be just like home."

"Oh, I never thought about that," Catie said.

"That's because you haven't been a teenager long enough," Blake said. "As teenagers, your dad and I used to go to the beach to party whenever we could."

"Kal, I think you'll want to assign extra security here at night," Marc said. He laughed as he thought about some of the parties he and Blake had gone to.

"Oh, you were bad boys, were you?" Samantha teased.

"I think we should have a beach barbeque to celebrate," Marc said, quickly changing the subject.

"I've got a hibachi and fixings right over there," Kal said as he pointed to a section of the beach with one of his security personnel standing watch.

"Squirt, you thought of everything," Blake said.

"If you don't stop calling me Squirt, I'm going to bar you from the beach," Catie said to her uncle as she slugged him in the shoulder.

"Come on, Squirt, I'll show you how to cook shrimp on the barbie," Blake said.

5 Press Conference

"Good day, ladies and gentlemen," Marc said. "We at MacKenzie Discoveries have invited you here today for an important announcement. Members of our board will be available after the press conference for further interviews. Now let me begin by saying that we know there have been many rumors about us having a treatment for Alzheimer's disease. I'm here today to tell you that the rumors are mostly true. We do have a treatment. It has completed ten months of trials with dramatic success. The data from the trials will be available in the handout after the conference."

Marc waited while various reporters jumped up, trying to ask questions.

"Please let me finish the announcement, then I will take your questions."

Marc had to wait for another minute before the reporters gave up shouting out questions. They finally figure out he wasn't going to answer any, no matter how provocative they were.

"Our trials have shown that ninety percent of the patients make a full recovery while the other ten percent make a significant recovery. We are currently opening a clinic in Tijuana, Mexico, and one here in the Cook Islands on Rarotonga," Marc continued. "The clinics should be able to handle about five hundred patients per month and will open next week."

Marc gave in to the stampede of questions, deciding that the rest of the information would get out just as well during questions.

"You have a question," Marc indicated the woman who was practically jumping up and down as she waved her arm.

"How much are these treatments going to cost?"

"The price is five hundred thousand per patient, but . . . but we are charging on a sliding scale based on the patient's ability to pay."

"How can you justify such a huge amount of money for a medical procedure?" the reporter jumped in with a second question.

"It costs over fifty thousand dollars per year to take care of an Alzheimer's patient, plus it is a terminal disease. We feel the charge is warranted, and remember we do have a sliding scale."

"How will your scale work?"

"It will be based on the patient's assets and income and the income statements for the previous ten years," Marc said.

"Why ten years?"

"We don't want people who have been able to set up a trust, shall we say, to protect their income, to get a better deal than the person who has worked for his entire life and has never built up enough assets to take advantage of such financial vehicles."

"Why only two clinics?" another reporter shouted.

"I'm going to take that question," Marc said, "but from now on if you shout out a question, I'm going to ignore you. Please wait until you're called on. Now to your question, sir, we have plans for more clinics, but we need to iron out the process first."

The reporter waved his hand, giving Marc a desperate look.

"I assume you have a follow-up question?"

"I do, where will you open the other clinics?"

"We are planning on one in the Bahamas to help serve the Americas. One in Casablanca, Morocco, and one in the city of Neum, Bosnia, to serve Europe. And one in Chittagong, Bangladesh, for Asia," Marc said.

The reporter was just beside himself, wanting to ask another question.

"I'll give you one more," Marc said.

"Thank you. Why those cities, or more specifically, why those countries?"

"One of the missions of MacKenzie Discoveries is to help balance the income disparity around the world. We felt those cities would benefit the most from the added income generated by the clinic. They will also benefit from the increase in tourism that will come as families accompany their loved ones to the treatment centers."

Other reporters started waving their hands and calling for attention.

"Yes, the lady in the blue suit," Marc said, pointing at the reporter.

"Why not simply release the treatment and charge for the medication?" she asked.

"Several reasons," Marc said. "First: I don't trust the drug companies to provide the sliding scale that we will. Second: it would take too long to get approval from the FDA and other oversight agencies. And third: there are proprietary technologies used in the treatment that we don't wish to share at this time."

The reporter signaled that she wished to ask a follow-up question.

"Your follow-up."

"Yes, how can we be sure the treatment is safe?"

"We have one hundred case studies from our trials," Marc said. "We also have twenty case studies from earlier trials for a similar treatment. Due to confidentiality and privacy issues, we cannot release them to you; however, no patient in those trials has had any adverse effect for twenty years after the trial."

The reporter was clearly not happy with the answer.

"I'll give you another," Marc said with a smile.

"But without agency oversight, how can we trust you?"

"You don't have to," Marc said. "The treatment is voluntary. But I will say that my daughter's great grandparents received the treatment. And I received it before that to prove to myself that it was safe. Those are all the assurances we can provide."

"Next question. You in the green kaftan."

"Thank you. If you locate the clinics in those remote cities, won't that affect the patient's ability to pay?"

"The cost of the treatment includes travel for the patient and one family member. The clinics will have double rooms so the family member can stay with the patient. It takes two to three weeks for the full treatment, depending on the patient."

Marc nodded, indicating that she could ask her follow-up.

"You're saying that if my grandparents need treatment, you will pay for them to travel to the Bahamas?"

"I'm sure that if your grandparents need treatment, you and your family can afford to send them to the Bahamas," Marc's comment received chuckles from the rest of the reporters. "But to your point, if a family in Detroit with a modest income and minimal assets were to apply for assistance, we might charge them five thousand dollars for the treatment, and it would include travel and two to three weeks in the Bahamas."

"Next," Marc pointed to another reporter.

"This is going to generate billions of dollars per year," the reporter said. "How can you justify making so much money on these victims of such a terrible disease?"

"We are in this business to make a profit, and to make the world a better place. I can assure you that we will treat as many patients as we can, that's why we're offering the sliding scale. If the price becomes prohibitive, we will make adjustments," Marc said. "Next question."

"Can you tell us how the treatment works?" the reporter asked.

"I can give you the basics without revealing our proprietary secrets," Marc said. "Basically, it scrubs the plaque from your brain."

"But studies have shown that there is not a one-to-one correlation between plaque and the disease."

Marc chuckled, "Studies are difficult to assess. Studies have shown that there are people with plaque in their brains that don't have Alzheimer's. They have not shown the opposite, that people without plaque have Alzheimer's. We have found that the plaque is your brain's way of protecting itself from injuries. A concussion or an infection occurs, and your brain builds up plaque to protect that area. In a normal person, that plaque is eventually dissolved and removed, or at least the inner coating, the part closest to the neurons. An Alzheimer's patient is unable to dissolve the plaque, and it builds up. Eventually, it blocks the neurotransmitters, rendering that area of the brain inaccessible. Now, in some patients, as you have mentioned, the plaque is blocking unimportant areas of the brain. In others the brain has dissolved the plaque closest to the neurotransmitters, enabling them to operate beneath the plaque. Our treatment removes the plaque. The patient will continue to build up plaque, and in thirty or forty years, they might need a second treatment. We'll offer those for free."

The reporters continued to jockey for position and try to get recognized to ask another question.

"Please, submit any further questions in writing, and we'll try to answer them," Marc said. "Good day."

6   Miners

Blake was meeting Fred at the Rusty Nail. The bar used to be on the Sky Princess, but once they'd had extra space on the airport, they'd sold the Sky Princess and put the construction workers in housing there. The bar followed its patrons.

"Hey, Fred, how's it going?" Blake asked as he sat down and indicated to the barmaid that he'd have the same thing Fred was drinking.

"It's going," Fred replied. "I just finished my second flight for the day. I'm off tomorrow, so I thought I'd take the Mea Huli out and do some fishing, you in?"

"You buying the beer?" Blake asked.

"You cheap bastard," Fred said with a laugh. "You're worth millions, and you still want free beer."

"Hey, all my money is tied up in MacKenzie," Blake said. "Besides, you're worth a few million too, and yours is in the bank."

Fred shook his head, "It's always a game with you. Well, I'll buy the beer, you buy the gas."

"Ouch," Blake said. "Well played. You have yourself a deal." Blake looked around the dark bar, "There sure are a lot of pilots in here."

"We're running flights twenty-four-seven," Fred said. "After the second flight, we all can use a beer. That Catie is a harsh taskmaster.

"She keeps the planes making four flights a day. We have to hustle to unload them so she can get four hours every other day to have them inspected. She pulls each plane out for a twelve-hour inspection once a week," Fred moaned. "It keeps us hopping."

"Do we need a few more pilots?" Blake asked.

"Not for this rotation; if you only give a pilot one flight a day, they'll bitch about not getting enough flight time. If you give them two flights a day, they'll bitch about too much flight time."

"So, what you're saying is, pilots like to complain."

"That about sums it up," Fred said. "Now we're recruiting for the Oryxes that will fly the asteroid route. That's going to be interesting;

you're in space for two weeks, then you rotate down here for a week of R&R, or you can stay upstairs for the R&R if you like."

"I'm planning on moving to that," Blake said. "I like the idea of a week off every three."

"Like Marc gives you any time off. If you're not flying, you're working on one of his other assignments. You're recruiting miners now, right?"

"Trying to," Blake said. "Not sure we have any refugees with experience working in a mine. I've been asking around; haven't heard anything back yet."

"Damn refugees," a voice snarled.

The music had just stopped playing; otherwise, Blake wouldn't have heard it. He looked around to see who it was. One of the young pilots that had been working for about a month was avoiding his eye. Blake was pretty sure he'd been the one to say it. He got up and carried his beer over to the table.

As soon as he walked up, the pilot snapped to attention, "Sir, I apologize."

"Sit down, Lieutenant Norton, isn't it?" Blake said.

"Yes, sir," Lieutenant Norton said.

"Can the sir," Blake said. "You want a beer?"

"Yes si . . . , sure," Lieutenant Norton said.

"Now I know you're not some idiot who hates people, so tell me what's got you upset," Blake said.

"It's nothing," Lieutenant Norton said.

"I'm sure it's something," Blake said. "Come on, tell me. We're just two guys having a beer together. It will go no further."

"Well, sir, it's that everyone is always bending over backward to help the refugees. It's not that they don't need or deserve help; but nobody is bending over backward to help people who need help, but are stuck where they are."

"We're helping the refugees because we need people, they're good people, and we can find them," Blake said. "Maybe we would help these other people you're talking about, but we don't know who they are."

"That's just it," Lieutenant Norton said. "The news media makes a big deal about the refugee crisis, but they don't say anything about the crisis at home where good folks are losing their livelihood while having to watch their hometowns turn into ghost towns."

"Who are these people?" Blake asked.

"My kin back in West Virginia," Lieutenant Norton said. "They've been coal miners for generations. They started shutting the coal mines down eight years ago, and now just about everybody is unemployed. There just aren't any jobs around."

"Well, it just so happens we're looking for miners," Blake said.

"Yeah, but you're looking for refugees that used to be miners," Lieutenant Norton said.

"No, we're looking for miners who are willing to relocate here and are willing to go into space to do the mining," Blake said. "We just happen to have a lot of refugees around and are hoping they might have that skill. We really don't know how to recruit for this job."

"My kin would be happy to come here," Lieutenant Norton said.

"Are you sure?" Blake asked. "It's amazing how much pain a person will put up with before they're willing to leave the place they were born."

"My kin would move."

"I'll tell you what, we'll go visit your kin and see if they're willing to relocate. We'll hire anyone who wants to come here, and we'll pay them good money."

"How much?"

"As much as you're being paid," Blake said. "But let's not focus on the money. We want people who are willing to relocate, not people who want to make a quick killing and go home."

"Fine by me, when can we go?"

"As soon as you're packed. Catie tells me that we can fly the Lynx to Canada now, so we can be in Toronto in about three hours. Then we have to take a quick hop to where?"

"Spencer, Bogg's Field."

"Okay, call me when you're ready," Blake said. He picked his beer up and headed back over to Fred.

"I'll be ready in an hour," Lieutenant Norton called out.

"Damn," Blake said.

"What's the problem?" Fred asked.

"I'm going to miss that fishing trip."

"You're just trying to get out of buying the gas," Fred said, laughing at Blake.

"There is that," Blake said, "but I have to go talk to some miners in West Virginia."

Blake and Lieutenant Kirk Norton were sitting in Bettie's Diner in Pohawk, West Virginia. The place was filling up fast, as the locals were coming to hear about the job offers that Lieutenant Norton had posted.

"I think that's everybody," Bettie said. "Let's get this here show on the road. I want this placed cleared out in two hours so I can start serving dinner."

"We'll keep that in mind," Lieutenant Norton said. "Okay, folks, settle down, and we'll get started."

It took a few minutes for everyone to find a place. Several people got up and shifted to other seats to allow families to sit together.

"I know that you're all interested in hearing about the jobs, but I'm not talking until you're quiet," Lieutenant Norton said.

"Then what is that you're doing right now," a young man in the back shouted, "cackling?"

"Hilarious Herb," Lieutenant Norton said. "You all know me. I grew up here, my family has lived here for a hundred years. I know this is home to all of us, but it's not the home it once was. When I was a kid, this place was just tolerable. There were still four mines open, so there were jobs. Now, the only jobs seem to be police jobs rounding up the drunks and Oxycontin dealers."

"You got that right!"

"Yeah, why doesn't the government do something about that, then maybe we could get some business in here to help the town out."

"We've been saying that for years," Lieutenant Norton said. "I've found myself a great job in a great place, and I'm here to offer you the same. This is my boss, Commander Blake McCormack. His company, MacKenzie Discoveries, is looking for some miners, and I told him that I knew some folks who knew more about mining than anyone else."

"Yeah! Damn straight, we do!"

"The thing is, these mines are a long way from here. So if you want these jobs, you're going to have to relocate. And there are a lot of confidential things involved, so you will have to be sworn to secrecy."

"What's that mean?!"

"You wouldn't be able to write folks back here and tell them what you're working on and things like that," Lieutenant Norton said.

"Hell, you're fine, Wally. You can't write, anyway!" shouted a man in the back. The whole crowd laughed at the joke.

"Where would we have to relocate to?"

"It's called the Cook Islands," Lieutenant Norton said. "It's down by Australia and New Zealand. It'd be like moving to Hawaii."

"I'd move to the moon if'n I could afford to feed my family without assistance from the government!"

"We're hoping more of you feel that way," Lieutenant Norton said. "Now, this place is a small city."

"Oh no! we can't be living in no city!"

"For sure, you can't even walk around in a city without some foreign cab driver running you over."

"Hold on there, ya'll, I said it's a small city, but it's different than most cities," Lieutenant Norton said. "Why, we don't even have any cars."

"No, cars! You mean, ya'll drive trucks?"

"Nope, I mean no cars, no trucks. Well, we do have a few trucks to move stuff around and a bunch of golf carts, but they all belong to the company. Nobody can own a car."

"Then how do you get around?"

"We walk," Lieutenant Norton said. "Right now, the city is only about one-and-a-quarter miles on each side."

"Hell, Uncle Joe's farm is bigger than that!"

"I know it is," Lieutenant Norton said. "We have a small subway to get you around the city if you don't want to walk too far. I guess they might add some kind of taxi service or something so old folks don't have to walk too far to the grocery store."

"I told you there'd be taxis!"

"Shut up, Josh! Let the man talk."

"Now everyone lives in condos," Lieutenant Norton continued. "The basic condo is two bedrooms, but they can expand that depending on how big the family is. Your place would all be on the same floor, so no stairs."

"What about places for the kids to play?"

"Each condo block has a big inside area that's private for the condo. They'll put in a playground and a pool if there are kids. There are parks all around the place."

"What about the jobs, working conditions?"

"As I said, these folks don't know anything about mining, so they're counting on you to set all that up. They're not skinflints or anything, so they'll spend what it takes to make the mines safe. But the mines aren't that close to the city, so you'd be staying on the job site during the workweek, and coming home for your day off."

"What, one day off!"

"No, you guys have to decide how you want to split it up. They were doing four days on and three days off for the manufacturing guys. But you need to figure out what works best for you. They're just looking for forty hours a week."

"What about overtime?"

"Sure, you can work overtime," Lieutenant Norton said as he looked at Blake. Overtime was one of the subjects they hadn't covered on the way over.

"Overtime pays double," Blake said. "But we limit how much you can do. We don't want a bunch of exhausted workers having accidents."

"What's it like living there?"

"Like I said, it's a city, but you can go hiking on Manuae, that's the island it's next to. You can go fishing on the ocean, it's kind of like fishing on a lake. You have beer, a boat, and your buddies. After a few beers, you're not sure if you really want to catch any fish, but hey, they're good eating if you do. Commander Blake was complaining, on the way out here, about missing a fishing trip with his buddy."

"But what about hunting?"

"You would need to go to Australia or New Zealand to hunt," Blake said. "But that brings up another thing you need to know. There are no guns allowed in Delphi City."

"No guns! Are you out of your freak'n mind?"

"No, I'm not," Blake said. "Our police don't even carry guns."

"How do you protect yourself?"

"We have swat teams that are armed if we need them. They try to use stun guns instead of bullets, but they're all ex-military. But, since there is a no-guns law, things are really safe."

"Yeah, you don't have a gun, but the criminals do!"

"Nope," Blake said. "There are no guns, it's a floating city, you can't get a gun in."

"Bah! I could smuggle a gun in, it'd be like falling off a log."

"Don't think you could," Blake said.

"Wanna bet?"

"Sure, easy money," Blake said. "I'll give you a thousand dollars for every gun you smuggle in. And I'll give you passes for the first five times you get caught. The fine for trying to smuggle in something illegal is a thousand dollars."

"Hey, I'm going to be rich," Herb said.

"But what do we do if we want to hunt in this New Zealand place?"

"You rent a gun," Blake said.

"That's crazy!"

"Well, if there is something really special about your gun, we could store it for you," Blake said. "Then you could check it out when you go hunting. Can't imagine why you'd want the hassle, but your choice."

"What other rules does this place have? Things like you can't smoke in a restaurant and such."

Lieutenant Norton gave out a big sigh, "That is one thing you can't do. You can't smoke or chew tobacco."

"Where?"

"Anywhere," Lieutenant Norton said.

"Well, that'll never work."

"You guys know me. I started smoking behind the school gym when I was twelve," Lieutenant Norton said. "I haven't had a cigarette in six months. The doctor cured me of the desire in two days. After that, I never wanted another one, couldn't figure out why I ever smoked the things in the first place."

"I started out smoking behind the gym with Kirk! If they can cure him of smoking, they can cure anybody."

"Hell, if they can cure me of these things, I'll sign up. I'll be rich just from saving all that money. A pack and a half a day costs me a fortune. Besides, this damn cough is getting on my nerves."

"What about drinking?"

"Oh, there's plenty of drinking," Lieutenant Norton said. "I'm sure the doctor could cure you of the desire, but we have no shortage of bars."

"Good thing."

"Howie, you don't need to be drinking. Your liver has already booked a spot in the cemetery." The room broke out in laughter at that.

"What about health care?" an older woman asked. "You know I have to be able to get the medication for my diabetes."

"Mrs. Mueller, we have excellent medical facilities, and not only can they treat your diabetes, I believe the doctor might just be able to cure you of it," Lieutenant Norton said.

"Oh, that would be nice," Mrs. Mueller said. "Then, I could have a drink now and then."

"Not like you don't already sneak a drink now and then!"

"What would we do about our places here?!"

"You should keep them," Lieutenant Norton said. "Maybe the ones who don't want to move could make a little money keeping them up. Maybe a few of us could put in some hunting lodges and create some tourist trade up here."

"Boy, them hunting lodges takes some big bucks, where are we going to get that kind of money?"

"Commander Blake tells me they'll be paying the miners as much as they pay me. So you'd be able to save some money up, that is, if you don't drink it all."

"Well, I've heard enough. I have to talk to the wife, but I'm sure she'll be willing to go. We've got three kids, and we want them to have a future. You guys got good schools down there?"

"Yeah, do you teach in English?"

"Yes, we have great schools," Blake said as he stood up. "The language is English, and most everybody speaks some or is learning to. But I have to tell you the one thing that will get you kicked out is any racism or being mean to people because of who they are."

"I don't care who I'm working with as long as they can do the job, and I get paid enough to feed my family. I'm Jimmy Gaines."

"I'm happy to meet you," Blake said. "Let us know when you want to move, and we'll set it up for you."

"We could pack and be ready tomorrow," Jimmy said. "We don't got nothin', had to sell everything before the government would give us help."

"Jimmy's a good miner," Lieutenant Norton said.

"We'd be pleased to have you," Blake said as ADI flashed a green light on his HUD. She'd been doing background checks on everyone while the meeting was going on.

"Thanks, I'm going to go talk to my Suzie," Jimmy said. "I'll let you know." Jimmy nodded to Lieutenant Norton.

"How many people are you taking?"

"We can take sixteen people on the plane we have now," Blake said. "We'll come back or arrange travel for anyone else. We think we need at least twenty miners."

"What about their families?"

"We have lots of jobs, so bring whoever wants to come," Blake said. "We don't have any government assistance, but we can put anyone to work. We need people to work in manufacturing plants, stores, and our parks and gardens. We need airplane mechanics, construction workers, and probably jobs we don't even know we need to fill yet."

"What happens if you don't know how to do those jobs?"

"We'll train you," Blake said. "We'll find a job you can do while you learn or even on-the-job-training if you have some skills. We just need people who want to work."

"Hell, we all want to work, we just need jobs!"

"Okay, you folks go home and think about it," Bettie said. "Now clear out, I've got dinner to get ready."

"Anybody who wants to go or needs more information, we'll be here tomorrow morning at seven o'clock," Lieutenant Norton called out. "Bettie will put out a buffet for breakfast, Commander Blake is buying."

"How many do you think will come?" Blake asked.

"To the free breakfast, or to Delphi City?"

"Delphi City," Blake said. "I'm thinking we'll have a full house for breakfast."

"I don't think so; people here aren't ones to take advantage. For Delphi, ten or so," Lieutenant Norton said. "You're right, it's a big change to consider. Jimmy will come, probably his brother will too. Might get a cousin or two. You've got Herb wanting to win that bet, he's actually a good miner too. And Wally was sounding like he wanted to come and get cured of cigarettes."

"We'll see in the morning."

Blake and Lieutenant Norton arrived at Bettie's at a quarter to seven to get ready to greet everybody.

"Hello, boys, welcome back," Bettie said as they entered. "Don't mind these gentlemen, they always eat breakfast here. I won't put them on your tab."

"We're interrupting their routine," Blake said, "the least we can do is buy them breakfast."

"That's right neighborly of you," one of the older guys said as he held up his cup requesting some more coffee.

Jimmy Gaines was there with his wife and three small children. They were eating a tiny breakfast.

"Hello, Jimmy," Blake said. "Aren't you guys hungrier than that?"

"We're just fine. I don't want to impose on you; we'll be paying our own way," Jimmy said.

"I can understand that," Blake said, "but, you're an employee of MacKenzie Discoveries now, and this is an official company function. So I can't have you paying for breakfast, now can I? Besides, we need you sharp so you can tell us who we should hire."

Jimmy's wife elbowed him in the side. "Thank you, Commander, we appreciate the hospitality. This is my wife, Suzie."

"Hello, Suzie, are you ready for a big adventure?"

"We sure are," Suzie said. "We're all packed and ready to go. How long is the flight? We've never been on an airplane before."

"It will take us an hour to get to Toronto," Blake said. "We'll change planes there, so everyone will get a chance to relax and stretch their legs. Then we'll get on the company plane and fly to Delphi City. That flight will take three hours."

"Three hours! Is that all it takes to get all the way down to Australia?" Suzie asked.

"Yes, we have a very fast jet," Blake said. "It's the fastest commercial jet there is."

"Land's sake. This is going to be exciting," Suzie said.

When Blake turned around, he saw a line of people pulling suitcases coming into the restaurant. He started counting, with kids he was up to forty-five when everyone was finally inside.

"Is everyone with a suitcase planning on coming with us today?" Blake called out.

"If you'll have us!"

"ADI, can we get another Lynx out here?" Blake asked.

"Yes, Cer Blake, I'm sending one now."

"We'll also need a pilot to fly the charter jet back here and pick these people up."

"Arranged," ADI said. "And I've also booked a pilot to return your Lynx for another load."

"Thank you, ADI."

"Okay, we'll figure this out," Blake shouted. "We can take sixteen people at a time. The first two loads will be this morning. It'll be an extra two hours for the second load. After that, there's another four-hour gap for the third load. If we need more, we can manage one every six hours."

"How long is the flight?!"

"There are two flights, it's one hour to Toronto, then it's another three hours to Delphi City," Blake called back. "We're making arrangements for a lounge in Toronto. You'll be able to wait there for the flight to Delphi City, or you can wait here, and only have a short layover in Toronto."

"Quit worrying about the small stuff! We need to find out who's going!"

"Why don't you all settle in and have some breakfast," Blake said. "We'll call up people to interview them. Then we'll make our decisions on who is a fit for our company and which flight they'll be on."

"Okay, Kirk and Jimmy, time to earn your money," Blake said. He set up his interview table next to Jimmy's family. "Who should we be taking?"

"Well, Paul Danvers is a good miner, and he's single," Jimmy said. "Then there's Herb, he's only got the wife and one kid. So you get two miners for four seats."

ADI flashed green okays for the two families.

"Kirk?"

"I agree with Jimmy," Lieutenant Norton said.

"So we have eight more seats to fill for the first flight," Blake said.

"Do you want me to go bring them over?" Suzie asked. "JC can watch the two little ones." She indicated the older child, a boy of about six.

"Why don't you do that," Blake said. He was a bit skeptical about a six-year-old keeping control of the other two, but Jimmy was right there, so he figured he could take the risk.

"Hanson is a real good miner," Jimmy said. "He used to be the safety supervisor in the Dayton Mine. They just have the two kids."

Blake got a green light from ADI on the other additions, so he gave Lieutenant Norton a nod on them.

"I don't know what JoAnn is doing here," Jimmy said. "She's single and has never been in a mine."

"Well, let's ask her," Blake said. He waited a few minutes while Lieutenant Norton and Suzie dealt with the first three selections. Then he had Suzie bring her over.

"Hello, JoAnn isn't it?" Blake asked as the young woman came over and sat down.

"Yes, it is," JoAnn replied.

"What are you looking for?" Blake asked.

"Well, I just want to get out of this here place," she said. "I figure I can cook for these boys. I'm sure the people you have down there are fine cooks, but I bet they've never heard of grits."

"Is that what you want to do, cook?" Blake asked.

47

"Well, I want to get out of here," JoAnn said. "I can cook, I did real good in school, but that was just high school. I don't know what else I could do."

"What do you do here?" Blake asked.

"I work check-out down at the market," JoAnn said. "There aren't many jobs, and that market is fixing to close any day."

"Okay," Blake said. "Sounds like we have grits covered for sure, and we'll see if there's something else you'd like to do once we get there."

"Thank you kindly," JoAnn said as she stood up and bobbed her head. Then she rushed over to Suzie and gave her a hug.

Two teenagers came up to Blake, looking very unsure of themselves. "Hi, I'm Devon, and this is my sister, Jaylee, the boy said. We're hoping you've got room for us."

"I'm not sure," Blake said. "How old are you?"

"I'm sixteen," Devon said. "Jaylee is fifteen."

"Where are your parents?"

"Our Pa died last year. Our Ma's on the Oxycontin, and she's a right mess. We're wanting to get away before she ruins our lives too. We'll work real hard, doin' whatever you tell us." Jaylee nodded her head vigorously in agreement.

"But you'd have to go to school," Blake said.

"We were hoping you didn't have any truancy laws down there," Devon said. "If'n we have to, we'll work nights. We just need to get away before the Oxy gets to us."

"Cer Blake," ADI said, "I would be happy to handle their education. They have a good background and do very well in school."

"But you're minors," Blake said.

"The law says we're old enough to travel on our own," Devon said. "I checked."

"He is correct," ADI said.

"Jimmy, help me out here."

"They're good kids," Jimmy said. "I'd take responsibility for them if you'll give them a chance."

"Okay," Blake said. "Don't make me regret this."

"We won't mister," Jaylee said with her first words. She gave Blake a hug then hugged her brother.

Blake messaged Catie and Samantha, apprising them of the situation and asking for some help when they arrived. Catie texted back that she had it covered.

At the end of the morning, they had twenty-one miners and sixty-two people, quite a few of them were small children. They also had four people who had nothing to do with mining, but just wanted out of Pohawk. At noon they loaded up the first plane and told everyone it would be back at three o'clock to pick up the next load. The last load would get picked up at six o'clock. They would have a short layover in Toronto before heading on to Delphi City.

Everyone was amazed at the luxury of the two aircraft, especially the Lynx. Blake was dreading what would be waiting for him when they got to Delphi City. He was hoping that getting the twenty-one miners would make up for the extra four people he was bringing.

When they landed at the city airport, it was eleven o'clock in the morning. The children had actually traveled well, so nobody was complaining about the lack of rest during the five hours of travel.

Catie met them and took charge as soon as the hatch opened. "I need JoAnn, Devon, and Jaylee," Catie called out. "We're putting you three to work right away. You're going to coordinate everyone's move. So here are your Comm units. Put the glasses on, they will act like a display, and you can read your phone without having to look at it. You use your eyes to pick the menu item you want, look at it then blink. I want you to start out by reading the text that is displayed in the HUD, that's what we call the display. Get on the cart, and we'll take you to the condos we've assigned you."

They all piled into the golf cart that Catie had waiting. There were four golf carts, each big enough for six people, sufficient to handle everyone and their luggage. Once they were in the cart, Natalia drove them to the condo. Catie watched as the three young people read the text; ADI was giving her a score on each one for how well the Comms would do interpreting their voices. By the time they reached the condo, the score was up to eighty percent.

"Okay, we're calling this Appalachia House," Catie said as the cart slowed to a stop. "I'm going to assign you your condos, then you'll need to assign everyone else their condos. The condos are two-bedroom units, so you'll need to pair them up for the bigger families. Use three if they need more than four bedrooms. We'll yank the kitchens out of the units you pair up and turn them into TV rooms. After you assign the condos, you'll need to do a walkthrough with each family and identify anything that they need. The condos come with pots and pans, dishes and basic furniture. But, if they need a baby crib, extra towels, sheets, special food, or clothes, you'll need to fill out the form on your Comm and send it in. We can get most of it here within an hour, but some things may take longer. Make sure that they have whatever they need for safety, or call me."

Catie led them up to the third floor, "I've assigned you guys the first three floors," Catie said. "There are seven more floors, but we'll let them fill over time. You're young, so you get the third floor. You don't need to fill the floors up, so leave room between families, so they don't feel too crowded. Do you guys have that?"

All three of them gave Catie a stunned look. "We think so," JoAnn said. "Will you help us do the first few families so we can make sure?"

"Not a problem," Catie said. "JoAnn, here's your condo, number three-twelve. Devon and Jaylee, you're down the hall in three-eleven. When they bring your bags, tell them your address, and the guys will carry them up here for you. Your Comms are the keys. The doors will automatically open for you and lock behind you."

Catie walked the three of them through the process on their own condos, then she stayed with them when they did the Gaines family. "You've got it, call if you need help. Our assistant, ADI, will be available until you're finished, just say 'ADI' and your Comm will connect her. Then just ask her whatever you need. If she can't help you, she'll contact me."

"Thanks," JoAnn said. "We won't let you down."

"I know you won't," Catie said. "Also, everyone needs to go to the clinic tomorrow for a physical. Schedule their appointments during the walkthrough. I'll text the Gaines family and give them their appointment now," Catie added as she and Natalia got on their golf cart and drove it back to the airport.

"I thought they were going to explode," Natalia said. "You barely gave them time to think."

"Get them busy before they figure out how scared they are," Catie said. "That's what Kal taught me. Besides, those three really need to feel useful, and ADI says they're smart."

"Well, they definitely don't have time to think about being scared." Natalia laughed as she thought about the three young kids trying to keep up with the litany of tasks that Catie had been throwing at them. "You are going to keep an eye on them, aren't you?"

"Sure, I'll check in on them, and ADI is going to monitor them closely," Catie said. "They'll do fine."

"We'll see," Natalia said.

"Hi, Uncle Blake," Catie said as they arrived back at the airport. "We're dropping off the cart then heading to the office. What are you going to do?"

"I'm going to go take a nap, then I'll be in later," Blake said. "I was supposed to be fishing today."

"Yeah, I heard," Catie said. "Fred went with one of the other pilots. He says you have to pay for the gas on the next trip."

"He did, did he?" Blake said. "Well, we'll see."

"Good day, Mrs. Mueller," Dr. Metra greeted her patient. "How are you feeling?"

"I feel fine," Mrs. Mueller replied.

"I see you have diabetes," Dr. Metra said. "We can take care of that; we've just developed a treatment that cures it."

"They told me that, but I didn't believe them," Mrs. Mueller said. "But I would love to be able to eat whatever I want."

"I'm sure the diet is problematic," Dr. Metra said. "Are you happy with your weight?"

"Do you mean, do I like being fat?" Mrs. Mueller asked. "I guess I'd rather weigh less, but I've always been fat."

"I see," Dr. Metra said. "I suspect that you're always hungry and always tired."

"That about covers it," Mrs. Mueller said.

"Okay, we can fix that," Dr. Metra said. "Would you like that?"

"I'm willing to give it a try," Mrs. Mueller said.

"Okay, I'll give you the first treatment now," Dr. Metra said. "You'll need to stay here for an hour to get the second half. Then we need you to come back in one week."

"Okay, what else is wrong with me?"

"Not much, we'll take care of a few minor issues, your arthritis for one," Dr. Metra said. "One last thing, you're only forty-five. Are you still having menstrual cycles?"'

"Yes, I still get visited by the curse every month," Mrs. Mueller said.

"We can eliminate those if you want," Dr. Metra said.

"What does that mean?"

"We'll give you a shot that will place a small stent on your ovaries," Dr. Metra explained. "It will regulate your hormones and eliminate the menstrual cycles."

"You can do that?"

"Only if you want us to. It will also prevent you from getting pregnant."

"I've had my four kids," Mrs. Mueller said. "I'm ready to be done with that. Give me the shot."

7   Board Meeting – Sept 16th

"This meeting is called to order," Marc said as he sat down at the head of the table. "Admiral, any news on your front?"

"My contacts say that the US is pressuring New Zealand to get the Cook Islands to seize MacKenzie Discoveries based on eminent domain. You have considered that, haven't you?" the admiral asked.

"Yes, I've been having nightmares about it," Marc said.

"What's eminent domain?" Catie asked.

"It's when the government decides that it would be in the best interest of the country if they just took what you own," Blake said. "They'll give you some money for it, but never what it's really worth."

"They can do that?" Catie asked.

"Yes," Marc said. "Sam, can you use your contacts to see how the prime minister is viewing it?"

"I'll start right away," Samantha said.

"Anything else, Admiral?" Marc asked.

"Except for that, it appears that things are quiet in the White House, at least as far as we're concerned," Admiral Michaels said. "They're still trying to figure out what to do with the North Koreans. Right now, the president's leaving that to the Secretary of State to figure out. The upcoming election is keeping him distracted."

"Is he worried?" Samantha asked.

"What politician isn't worried about re-election," Admiral Michaels said. "But he's feeling the heat. His popularity has been at a record low since he was elected, so he's trying to sow discord in the opposition."

"Typical," Marc said. "While we're talking about out-of-this-world things, Liz, why don't you give us an update on the space station?"

"Very funny," Liz said. "We're prepping the work so we can extrude the first ring. We're in desperate need of more material. We don't have enough lift capacity."

"Blake will update us on that in a moment," Marc said. "How is the outfitting of the hub going?"

"We're over fifty percent complete," Liz said. "We just need something to put there. We've got the polysteel plant up, the clear polysteel plant should be online next week. We've completed the production of our first Oryx with the particle accelerator in the engine. We'll be making one a week."

"How are our scientists doing?"

"They're going gangbusters on the fusion reactor. I offered up the particle accelerator project, and Dr. Nakahara jumped on it. He says he's bored with the fusion reactor work since it's just engineering now. So I gave it to him. We've set him up with a new lab."

"Did he give any indication of how complex it would be?" Marc asked.

"Not really, but he did say it should keep him occupied for a few months," Liz said.

"We should take heart that he didn't say a few years," Marc said. "Okay, anything else?"

"Dr. Zelbar is jumping on the superconductor project; he's handed off the clear polysteel to his wife. She's going to finish up all the proofs and run the experiments. I guess that's a good thing since we have a production plant running already."

"Good!" Marc said with a laugh. "Now we're in desperate need of the ability to manufacture more computer chips. Sam?"

"Since you mentioned it to me last week, I've done some research," Samantha said. "I've found a young company in Vancouver that was a big splash, built a big plant, and hired a bunch of people just to be hit with a huge patent infringement lawsuit. They've been struggling to keep afloat for the last eight months. They have a lot of talent; I think we might be able to bring them into the company."

"How much are you talking about?" Marc asked.

"I think it will take about three hundred million," Samantha answered. "There are four young engineers who are heading it. Smart people, but they got in over their heads on the patents."

"Would they join us or just sell out?" Catie asked.

"I don't know, but being the first to manufacture computer chips in space sounds like a great draw," Samantha answered.

"Why don't you set up a meeting with them," Marc said. "Take Catie."

"Got it," Samantha said as she gave Catie a wink.

"How's our car plant coming?"

"We reached out to Ayyour Dahmani, your friend from that little incident with Catie," Samantha said. "He's helped us push through the red tape. He and Herr Johansson have become good friends. They are estimating another six weeks before they can start production."

"Wonderful! Catie, what do you have?"

"We need to start a bank," Catie said.

Marc sat back and blinked a few times. "How did we miss that?"

"I don't know, but if we want to have businesses start up here, we have to be able to lend money," Catie said. "I'm going to do a personal loan for the Jamaican restaurant, but a credit union would be nice. And with ADI managing the investments, it'll give a better return than the Bank of New Zealand."

"Anybody know a banker?" Marc asked.

Samantha raised her hand sheepishly.

"Who?" Marc asked.

"Zane Parker, Linda's boyfriend," Samantha replied.

"Oh," Marc said. "I guess I've never paid any attention to him. What's he been doing since he arrived?"

"He's been teaching at the school," Catie said. "He teaches economics and social studies."

Marc smiled; he was glad that Catie was able to interact with her mother's new boyfriend without feeling awkward. "Okay, so who wants to approach him?"

"I will," Catie said. "It's my idea."

"Okay, you've got it," Marc said. "What else do you have?"

"The asteroids are settling into position; they're close enough that we can start sending the modified Oryxes out to them."

"Do we have pilots trained?"

Catie smiled.

"Besides you."

"We've been running a few of them through training on the simulator," Fred said. "It's not all that different than just making the orbital run."

"Okay," Marc said. "Go on Catie."

"We have the final certification from New Zealand on the Lynxes. Canada, Australia, Mexico, and France have all reciprocated contingent on an inspection of one. I'm sending one on a tour of all the countries. We've got Uncle Blake a tentative approval for his trip to Toronto, but they want to see a jet before they issue a blanket approval."

"Then we definitely want them to see one," Marc said. "Let me know when France gives us the green light."

"I have an alarm set on that one," Catie said as she gave Samantha a smile. "I'm also working with Natalia and Tomi to get the treatment plant for Delphi Station designed. Natalia really likes working on it, and they've been making great progress. Kal, that means Natalia will probably need a backup so she's doesn't have to chase after me all the time. That is unless you're going to let me off my leash."

"Not a chance," Marc said.

"I'll send one over," Kal said. "I just need to pick one who can deal with such a problematic protectee," Kal joked.

"Har, har."

"I'll have Nattie help me pick," Kal said.

"And the open-air market was a big success," Catie said. "All the booths did well, and we got lots of positive feedback on the merchandise quality and variety." Over the weekend, Catie had done a couple of passes through the community market to see how it was going. She was surprised at how many people were shopping. A third of the space was filled with booths, she thought that was a good start.

"Ah, Dr. Metra, thank you for joining us, I know you're busy," Marc said as Dr. Metra entered the room and took a seat. "Do you want to give us your update next?"

"Yes, please," Dr. Metra said.

"Catie was just updating us on the community market they held last weekend," Marc said.

"Some of my patients mentioned it," Dr. Metra said. "I think I'll go this weekend."

"I'll go with you, I missed it last week," Samantha said.

"Let me know what time, and I'll go with you," Catie said.

"Liz?" Samantha asked.

"I'll be with Catie. Nattie will be there too," Liz said.

"I'm sure you will all have fun," Marc said. "Dr. Metra, are you ready?"

"Of course," Dr. Metra said. "I've finished the physicals on all of your recruits from Pohawk. An interesting lot. Most of the men needed to be treated for one kind of lung disease or another. It seems coal mines are filthy places, and on top of that, most of them smoked. Another week of treatment should sort them all out. A couple of them could have done with a new liver, but I just fixed up the one they have."

Everyone at the table chuckled at Dr. Metra's humor, and all of them were surprised by it. She was spending a lot of time watching various TV shows to acclimate herself to Earth's culture better. Apparently, she'd settled on the British dramas and comedies based on the word choices.

"How about the children?" Catie asked.

"They're all very healthy," Dr. Metra replied. "The mothers opted for the hormone control for their children and for themselves. I have one interesting case with diabetes."

"Mrs. Mueller?" Blake asked. "She's the matriarch of one of the bigger groups."

"Yes, that's her," Dr. Metra confirmed. "She not only has diabetes but a serious weight issue. It appears they are related. I'm treating her for both of them. I'm very interested in how she responds to the weight-loss treatment."

"What about the diabetes?" Samantha asked.

"Oh, I'm interested in that, but I don't think I'll be surprised there," Dr. Metra said. "I believe we have several other people with similar weight issues, so I'd like to be able to offer the treatment to them if it works."

"Keep us posted on that," Marc said. "Anything else?"

"I had to convince a few of the parents to allow me to immunize themselves and their children," Dr. Metra said. "It's never been an issue before, but you should add that to your orientation material. We don't want to have non-immunized people wandering about."

"Why is that an issue?" Liz asked. "We can treat anyone who picks up a disease."

"We can when we know about it," Dr. Metra said. "Then, they need to be close to the clinic. But you are planning to have people running around up there a few days away from the clinic. We don't want tragedies to occur on one of those missions."

Liz's eyes went wide as she realized what that would mean, "No, we wouldn't. Sorry, I wasn't thinking."

"Okay, Blake, you're the man of the hour," Marc said.

"Thanks a lot," Blake chuckled a bit. "I'll get the obligatory airport update out of the way. We've completed all the decking, so all we have left to do is install a bit of infrastructure. Then we can add buildings as we need them. We've got the warehouses there, a unit of dorms for the pilots to rest up, a cafeteria, and a bar. I'm going to let it sort itself out for a few months before we do anything else."

"What are we going to do with the construction crews?" Marc asked.

"I'm scaling them back," Blake said. "We still have at least another quad ring to do around the city, that's eleven more quads. Plus, we have all the buildings we need to add in the empty lots, but there's no hurry there. About a third of the people we're letting go are asking to stay on and pick up some of the manufacturing jobs."

"That's good," Liz said. "If we need to ramp back up, they'll be right here."

"That's what I thought," Blake said. "Now, to our mining operations. As you all know, one of our pilots is from a mining town in West

Virginia named Pohawk. He took me there to recruit miners since most of the local mines have shut down. We came back with twenty-one miners and another forty-one people, a lot of them young children."

"It'll be a nice infusion of fresh blood for the community," Kal said.

"I'm glad you think so," Blake said. "One of the big sticking points was *no guns*. I have a bet with one of them that he can't smuggle any into the city. I'm counting on you to protect my money."

"Don't worry about it," Kal said. "It'll be a good test of our systems. I assume he's the one who tried to bring three handguns in his luggage."

"Yep, that's him. I gave him five free passes, so that's three of them used up," Blake said. He shook his head and laughed a bit. "We picked those up on the scanner in the cargo hold. Catie, those things work great, by the way."

Catie beamed at the praise. She'd added the scanners to the Lynx design to protect the jets from any bombs or other attempts to disable one. They'd become a plus for dealing with attempts to smuggle stuff into Delphi City.

"Okay, so we have our miners, now what?" Samantha asked.

"So now we have to figure out how to mine an asteroid. I'm having the first meeting with a couple of the miners on Thursday to go over the objectives. It'll be the first time we tell them about the asteroids. I'd like Catie, Natalia, and Liz to be there since they're the only ones with experience," Blake said. He spoke very slowly to emphasize that he'd been cheated out of doing the space mission.

"Oh, quit whining," Catie said. "Natalia and I would love to be there."

"Just give me a time and place," Liz said.

"Good, I'm looking forward to a report on the meeting," Marc said.

"I'm sure it will be entertaining," Blake said as he shook his head and chuckled.

"Okay, now for our last subject, how do we staff our space station?" Marc asked.

"It should be easy," Catie said. "Who wouldn't want to work on a space station?"

"Well, we can't exactly advertise," Marc said. "If you and Sam are successful with the company in Vancouver, that will give us a start. But we want to be selective about who goes up there. It's not quite the same as being here in the city."

"We can start with the people we have here," Kal said. "Quite a few of them will want to go up, I'm sure we'll be able to find good matches."

"Why don't we wait and see what happens with our Vancouver deal," Samantha said. "If it works out, then you'll have a good base. It's possible we could just recruit through referrals after that."

"Before we close, does anyone have an update that we've missed?" Marc asked.

"Not much," Fred said. "The fabricators are going up on the next Oryx, so you can start making a few parts."

"That's good, we're running out of things," Catie said.

"Our four police officers are starting to take over local patrols," Kal said. "The community seems to like seeing them around."

"That's good," Marc said. "You need to think about staffing the space station as well. And are we going to need more down here?"

"I'm going to recruit another four to go to with these four when they go back," Kal said. "We can always put them to work on other things if we don't need so many."

"Alright, back to work, people," Marc said to close the meeting.

"Hi, Mommy," Catie said as her mother answered the door.

"Oh, hi, Sweetie," Linda said. "Did I forget you were coming over?"

"No, I'm here to see Zane," Catie said. "I thought I'd just surprise you."

"It's a pleasant surprise," Linda said as she gave Catie a kiss on the forehead. "What do you need to see Zane about?"

"Work."

"Oh, you're here," Zane said as he came out of the kitchen.

"What are you two cooking up?" Linda asked.

"Well, I just made lunch," Zane said. "I don't know what Catie has going on, but she said she had a business proposition for me."

"She did, did she?" Linda asked. "Do I get to listen in?"

"Fine by me," Catie said.

"I guess it had better be fine with me then," Zane said. "Come on in. I told you I'd make lunch."

Linda and Catie joined Zane in the kitchen. He had them sit at the counter as he served up BLTs for everyone. "What would you like to drink?"

"I'll just have some water," Catie said.

"Me too," Linda said.

"Okay, waters all around," Zane said as he grabbed three glasses. "Ice?"

"Not for me," Catie said. Zane apparently knew how Linda wanted her water; he brought three glasses of water, no ice, to the counter.

"Now, what is this about?" Zane asked.

"Sam tells me that you're a banker," Catie said.

"I was," Zane said.

"You didn't like it?" Catie asked.

"Oh, I liked it," Zane said. "But you guys don't have a bank here. Almost everybody uses ANZ on Rarotonga."

"I know," Catie said. "But I think we need to have our own bank. A credit union."

"You do?" Zane said. "What about your father?"

"The board agrees with me," Catie said. "And since you're a banker, we'd like you to run it."

"And just what would that entail?" Zane asked.

"I don't know," Catie said. "That's why we're asking you to run it. I assume it's mainly about approving loans and stuff."

"And stuff," Zane said with a small laugh. "You make banking sound so glamorous."

"We already have an investment person," Catie said. "She's managing my money and MacKenzie Discoveries' reserve capital. But we need the person to manage the bank and deal with people."

"How would you capitalize it?" Zane asked.

"MacKenzie Discoveries would," Catie said. "We'll move fifty million into a separate fund for you. Then any deposits over that you would loan out or put into the investment fund our guy would manage. I think you're supposed to manage the reserve differently."

"That's correct, or at least you should," Zane said. "That's a pretty big capitalization for a small bank."

"We want to get more businesses to start up here on Delphi City," Catie said. "I had to make a loan for a restaurant just the other day because we don't have a bank. Besides, we have different objectives than ANZ Bank would."

"What's the difference?" Zane asked.

"Well, we don't really want to make money off the loans, we just want to enable the startups. That's why we're thinking of a credit union," Catie said. "We also have more control over how the new businesses will do since we control the competition."

"Do you think that's right?" Zane asked.

"I don't know," Catie said. "But if a business starts providing goods or services that MacKenzie is already providing, we would scale back what MacKenzie does and let the new guys take over the business."

"You would?"

"Yes, unless it was something we were keeping control over for another reason; in that case, we just wouldn't let the business get started."

"What if an existing business started branching out?"

"Same thing, if we didn't feel we needed to have control, we would let them take over."

"What if they started to overcharge their customers?"

"I don't know. How would they do that? People would just buy online or from Rarotonga," Catie said. "We have plenty of bars and restaurants."

"What about grocery stores?" Zane asked.

"Right now, we control all of them. We supply most of the fresh food and produce, and they import the paper goods, canned food, and things like that," Catie said. "If we started letting them go private, I assume we would make sure there was more than one company."

"What if one company starts buying out the others?"

"I think we'd tell them to stop it," Catie said. "Everything that comes into the city comes through us, so we should be able to force the issue if we think it's necessary."

"An interesting set of problems," Zane said. "How would I interact with the board?"

"You would come in to do reports to the board; you could make recommendations, and ask for policy changes then," Catie said.

"No seat on the board?"

"Not now," Catie said. "Maybe later, but we're still keeping it to a very tight group. I hope you're not offended."

"Not much," Zane said. "What does it pay?"

"I don't know; what should it pay?" Catie said. "We pay our pilots two hundred thousand per year."

"That's way more than I was making as the managing director of the bank," Zane said.

"That's okay," Catie said. "We're going to have special problems and special headaches."

"Then you've got yourself a bank manager," Zane said. "Where is this bank going to be?"

"I assume we should put it in the office block," Catie said. "Lots of stuff will just be online. The Comm units everybody has will let them manage their accounts and buy stuff. And if they bank with you, we'll deposit their money directly. So it's okay that it's a bit far."

"Two miles isn't that far," Zane said. "That's typical of a neighborhood bank."

"If you go by and look around, you can tell me which unit you want. The block is only about twenty-five percent built up, and most of the units are still empty."

"I'll let you know by tomorrow. How big a staff am I authorized?"

"You decide," Catie said. "We're not worried about startup cost, so tell us what you need."

"Deal," Zane said and extended his hand to shake with Catie.

Catie shook his hand and stood up to leave, "Bye, Mommy."

"My little tycoon," Linda said. Her eyes were damp with tears as she gave Catie a kiss to say goodbye.

8 What's an Asteroid?

"Thanks for coming," Blake said to Jimmy Gaines and Paul Danvers.

"Hey, you're the boss," Jimmy said.

"Anyway, I think you know my niece, Catie, and her colleague, Natalia. This is Liz, one of our pilots and a member of the board as well."

"Howdy ladies," Jimmy and Paul said. Paul put a little more emphasis into his greeting, and he smiled at Natalia.

"Let's get started," Blake said. "I want you to keep these discussions private for a while. I want to have most things worked out before we get everybody involved. Of course, we'll bring in additional expertise as we need it."

"Okay," Jimmy said. "What's the big secret? Just where is this mine you want us to work?"

"It's actually three mines," Blake said, "and they're not actually mines, they're asteroids."

"What the hell is an asteroid?" Paul asked.

"You know, one of those big rocks in space," Blake said. "We call them meteors when they fall to Earth."

"So you have some of them meteors that you want us to mine?" Paul asked.

"No, these are still in space orbiting the sun," Blake said.

"I know you're the boss and all," Jimmy said, "but do you really have to razz us like this? We can take a joke as well as any man, but we'd really like to get to work."

"Uncle Blake, let me help," Catie said. "Here, look at this." Catie turned on the big display and brought up a picture of the space station with the Earth in the background.

"What's that?" Jimmy asked.

"That's our space station," Catie said. "It's in orbit around Earth, and here's what it's supposed to look like when completed." Catie brought up the display of the station with all three rings. "It's really big, and it takes a lot of material to build it. That means we had to get some asteroids so we could mine the material in space instead of having to lift it all from Earth." Catie changed the display to show a picture of one of the asteroids with the six women posing for the photo. "That's us when we got this one. Right now, it's in orbit around the sun just ahead of Earth."

"Now this is just crazy talk," Paul said. Jimmy was just hugging himself and moaning quietly.

"This is an Oryx," Catie said as she changed the display. "They're the shuttles we use to get into orbit and to lift material to the space station. They can only be filled about twenty percent when they have to lift off from Earth. But we can fill them all the way up when we're just going from the asteroids back to the space station."

"You folks are serious," Jimmy said.

"Oh, yes. We'll take you up to the space station next week," Catie said. "That will give you a chance to experience microgravity and a chance to dispel any doubts you have left."

"What do you mean by microgravity?" Paul asked.

"The asteroids are so small that they don't have any gravity, or not enough to mean anything. So, when you're working on them, you don't have any weight," Catie explained. "Uncle Blake, do you want to take over?"

"No!" Blake said, "you're doing fine, I'm just here to take notes right now," he said with a laugh.

"We have a bunch of guys who are experienced working in microgravity now; they're the ones who built the space station. Liz did all the coordination of that so she'll have lots of details about what they had problems with while working in microgravity," Catie said. "The three of us did all the work to get the asteroids here, so we've got some experience in what you'll have to deal with."

Both Jimmy and Paul just shook off their shock and leaned forward. "Now how about you tell us about the problems you had getting them?" Paul asked.

"Well, the first issue was that you can't do anything without anchoring yourself down. Natalia tried to drill holes at first, but she would start floating off after a few seconds. We had to put small anchors into the asteroid so she could tie herself down."

"If you were floating off when you drilled, how did you drive the small anchors?"

"Our inertia was enough for that," Catie said. "Inertia is kind of like weight. If I tried to push you, your inertia would make it hard. Or if you're running, your inertia makes it hard to stop you," Catie explained. "I'm sure you've dealt with it when you were mining."

"Yeah, we called it momentum," Paul said.

"Momentum is your inertia when you're moving. Anyway, you can drive a small anchor in, counting on your inertia to keep you in place. If that isn't enough, you can use the thruster in your suit to push you down."

"Thruster?" Jimmy asked.

"A stream of air that pushes you," Catie explained. "Oh, I guess I forgot to mention the vacuum. As you know, there's no air in space. That means you'll have to work in a spacesuit. Uncle Blake will take you by the outfitter, and he'll make a few for you so you can go up with us on Thursday. Ours are really tight and flexible, nothing like you see the astronauts wearing on the news."

"Okay, so we got to tie ourselves down to the asteroid," Paul said. "What are we mining, by the way?"

"Two of the asteroids are mostly ice," Catie said. "One is frozen water, and that's what we want, the water. You may decide to just set up a way to melt the ice and pump it into the Oryx."

Paul nodded in agreement.

"The other one is frozen methane. To stay liquid, it has to be at minus one-sixty degrees C."

"That's natural gas," Jimmy said.

"Right."

"That stuff is explosive," Jimmy said. "It's a big safety issue in a coal mine."

"Yes it is, but there's no air. That way, it can't combust," Catie said. "You just need to be careful not to introduce any oxygen into the environment and not to melt it so much that turns into gas and floats away."

"And the third one?" Paul asked.

"That's a more typical mining job," Catie said. "It's mostly iron, which is what we need. It's hard like you would expect, so it takes a lot of effort to drill into."

"Okay, what do you want the iron to be like when we put it in that Oryx?" Paul asked.

"Right now, before we ship it up to the station, we grind it up and mix in a little oil," Catie said. "Then we can pump it like a slurry into the Oryx, and we can dump it into space where it freezes up into a ball."

"How pure does it have to be?" Paul asked.

"Purer is better," Catie said. "We'll purify it on the other end, but we don't want to be hauling a bunch of rock around if we can avoid it."

"Sounds like if we break it up into small bits and sift it, that would work?" Paul asked.

"Yes, but you'll need to figure out how to sift it without gravity," Catie said.

Paul scratched his head for a bit, "Hmm, wouldn't blowing it with air be the same?"

"I think so," Catie said. "The iron will have more inertia, so it won't start moving as fast. The light stuff will pick up speed right away. If you gave it a small crosswind, you might find it works better."

"Okay, we'll try that stuff," Paul said. "How long do we have to figure this out?"

"As long as it takes," Blake said. "We're in a hurry, but sometimes slow is fast."

"You got that right," Paul said. "Measure twice, cut once, my pappy always said."

The six of them spent another hour talking about what they might need, how things would work, even things as mundane as what they could eat when in space. Then Blake took the two of them to get measured for their spacesuits.

---

9   Space Experiments

"Liz," Catie pinged her friend over her Comm.

"I'm just about to head your way," Liz replied.

"No, wait. Can you bring me one of your shipsuits?"

"Sure, is something wrong with yours?"

"I don't know, but they won't fit."

"Did you try a different one?"

"Yes, I tried them all. None of them will fit. I haven't worn one for a few weeks, but what could have happened to them?"

"I've got one of my spares, I'll be right over," Liz said.

When Liz arrived, Catie was in a dressing gown examining her shipsuit. "Here," she said, handing Liz the shipsuit. "I don't know what's wrong with it." She took the suit Liz offered and went back into her room to put it on.

"It looks fine to me," Liz called through the door.

"Me too, but I can't get it up over my hips," Catie said. "Yours fits just fine," she added as she came out of the room.

"Well, mine are a little bigger," Liz said. "Turn around."

Catie turned around once and then stood, looking at Liz, who was trying to hide her grin.

"What?"

"Catie, there's nothing wrong with your shipsuit."

"Then why won't it fit?"

"You're growing up, you've got hips," Liz said as she started laughing.

"Knock, Knock," Natalia called out as she came into the condo. "What's so funny?"

Catie just stood there, looking at Liz furiously.

"Our Catie is becoming a woman," Liz said. "She's got hips now."

"Oh, turn around," Natalia said.

Catie just stood there, glaring at them.

"Come on girl, spin around for your Aunt Nattie," Natalia said. "It's about time you started filling out."

Reluctantly, Catie turned around.

"Oh yes, much more woman there," Natalia said. "How did you get your suit on?"

"She didn't," Liz said, "that's one of mine."

"Well, I'm going to have to keep an eye out for the boys," Natalia said. "They'll be chasing after her now." Natalia was laughing with Liz.

"It's not funny!" Catie said.

"No, it's not," Liz said. "What's funny is your surprise and the fact that you're not thrilled about it. I remember when I first started putting weight on my hips, I was thrilled. I was measuring them and my breasts every week to see how much they had grown."

"You too," Natalia said. "Catie, you look great. You should get an appointment with Dr. Metra to make sure all is okay, but it's perfectly natural. You are almost fourteen, after all."

"How big are they going to get?" Catie asked.

"Just look at your mother," Liz said, "Take off a few pounds because she doesn't exercise as much as you do, and that should be about right. Your dad's mother is about the same."

"Come on, let's go," Natalia said. "They'll be waiting on us."

When Catie, Liz, and Natalia boarded the Oryx, they heard Blake talking to the miners. "Are you guys ready for this?" Blake asked.

"As ready as we can be," Jimmy said. "Is this going to be like that vomit comet thing they talk about on TV?"

"I hope not," Blake said. "Everyone reacts differently."

"We haven't had that many people get sick," Catie said. "The pilot is able to ease off the acceleration slowly, so there's not an abrupt transition like on a rollercoaster."

"Well, we hope to do well," Paul said. "We don't want to embarrass our families by getting sick."

"Just keep a barf bag handy," Catie said. "What have you guys been doing to prepare?"

"We brought some tools," Jimmy said. "Blake, here, says we can practice on one of those blobs you talked about being up here."

"Oh, that's a good idea," Catie said. "It's close so you can go into the space station for a rest. They have a little bit of gravity there."

"We'll see," Jimmy said. "You guys coming up just to help us out?"

"We're going to help you get started," Catie said, "then Nattie has some experiments to run for her job."

"Oh, what job is that?" Paul asked.

"I'm working on getting us a functioning treatment plant up here," Natalia said.

"You mean like sewage treatment?" Paul asked.

"Yes, glamorous isn't it," Natalia said.

"Well, it needs to be done," Paul said. "What do you have to test?"

"We need to have something that can survive a few days of microgravity," Natalia said. "We have a reference design on Delphi City, but it can rely on gravity being there. We also want to recover more from it since we're so far away from everything."

"Sounds complicated," Paul said.

"Everybody, strap in," the pilot announced over the intercom.

"Hey, Jason," Catie said over the Comm.

"Hi, Catie," Jason said. "Do you want to come up front?"

"Sure, I'll be right there," Catie said. "Hi, how are you doing?"

"I'm doing great," Jason said. "I'm working on qualifying on the Fox now. But this is my day job."

The copilot indicated to Catie that he would be happy to move into the navigator's seat. Catie gave him a nod, and he moved, letting her take the seat next to Jason.

"I haven't flown for like six weeks," Catie said.

"That doesn't sound like you."

"I know, there's just been so much going on," Catie said. "My mom's here now so that's a bit of extra drama. And I've just had so many projects going."

"Sounds like you need a break," Jason said. "Mrs. Michaels is hosting another movie night next weekend. Are you coming?"

"My mom's going to make me go," Catie said.

"Oh, you had fun last time."

"I guess I did. Is Annie going to be there?"

"I think so," Jason said. "I never got a chance to thank you for letting me take her up."

"No problem," Catie said. "Glad to help. Nice takeoff there," Catie complimented Jason on his flying. "By the way, we've got a couple of newbies back there, can you really ease us into orbit?"

"Sure," Jason said. "I'd rather not smell vomit anyway."

"Me either," Catie said. "Thanks. I'm going to go back and work with Nattie, we've got some tests to run when we get up there."

"Okay, hope to see you at the party."

"Sure."

Catie worked her way back into the cargo hold. As she came out of the airlock, she saw that Natalia was sitting with Paul, and they were talking about her experience on the asteroid mission. Catie sat next to Liz, "They're working hard."

"What?" Liz said.

"Nattie's helping Paul get ready for his spacewalk," Catie said.

"Girl, get a clue," Liz said. "He likes her."

"What!"

"He likes her. He's been keeping her talking the whole time. No man is that interested in what someone else is saying unless it involves a little romance."

"You think so?"

"Earth to Catie," Liz said as she knocked on Catie's head. "Look at him, he's all goo-goo eyed."

"Well, I'm glad for her," Catie said.

"So, Jimmy, how do you like microgravity?" Catie asked while everyone was putting on their exosuit, the armor they wore over their shipsuit when they went outside.

"I can't say that I like it," Jimmy said. "But I didn't need that barf bag."

"We're all happy about that," Catie said. "How do you want to start?"

"Paul and I were talking about how we would mine the thing. Since it's almost all metal, we figure we're just going to break it up into small pieces and dump off the rocky stuff into some kind of pile. We can grind it up later to separate out the metal, but mostly we're thinking the metal is going to be in big chunks. You guys need to decide how big a chunk you're willing to take on your end. The bigger, the better from our point of view."

"I see," Catie said. "Well, we're going to have to separate out the nickel from the iron. There are two ways to do that: one is with acid; the other involves melting the metal and then using a big magnet to pull the iron to one side and out through a drain hole."

"I don't like the thought of using no acid," Jimmy said. "And if'n you're going to melt it, then you should be able to take big pieces. If we can fit 'em into the Oryx, then you should be able to melt them down."

"But if they're too big, you won't be able to get as much into the Oryx," Catie said. "There'll be all these big gaps."

"I see," Jimmy said. "You're saying you think transportation is the limiting factor."

"I think so," Catie said. "What do you think, Liz?"

"Sorry, I wasn't paying attention," Liz said.

"Jimmy is asking what we think the limiting factor will be on the iron, shipping it or mining it," Catie said.

"Well, up to now, it's been shipping it," Liz said. "We can only fill the Oryx to like one percent of its volume when we're loading iron."

"I'm guessing those gaps aren't going to be important," Jimmy said.

"I think you're right," Catie agreed. "I guess Liz and I need to figure out how to melt big chunks of metal."

"Why are we melting big chunks of metal?" Liz asked.

"We have to separate the nickel from the iron," Catie said. "That's one of the methods ADI recommended."

"If we're melting it, what about just feeding it into the plasma field?" Liz asked. "Will the nickel separate out like the sulfur does?"

"I'll ask Nikola," Catie said. "ADI?"

"Message sent," ADI said.

They spent an hour getting Jimmy and Paul comfortable maneuvering around in their spacesuits. Then they helped them move their equipment to the iron ball they were going to practice on. Then Catie, Blake, Liz, and Natalia sat back and watched the two men go to work.

Jimmy and Paul first drilled four holes with the auger, like the one Natalia had used on the asteroid mission. The holes were drilled at a shallow angle. To drill the holes, they anchored the guy who was going to run the drill, the driller, down with three small anchors. They tied him to the surface of the asteroid where each of his shoulders and the matching foot were tied to the two anchors closest to the hole. The third anchor was tied to the center of the driller's shoulders and was just behind him, so he was held tight to the surface. Then the driller started drilling with a small auger first. Once they had the hole started, they switched to the bigger auger, and the driller really leaned into it.

"Wow, those guys really know what they're doing," Catie said.

"Yeah, they make what we did on the asteroids look pretty amateurish," Natalia said.

"Yeah, four holes in like one hour," Catie said.

Then the two guys inserted a hydraulic rock splitter into each hole. They used anchors to hold the splitters in place. Each rock splitter had a three-piece nose made up of two cone pieces that formed a spike. A third piece was a smaller spike that would be driven down between the other two, spreading them apart. When they had all four splitters in place, they turned the hydraulic pump on, and the small spikes were forced between the two cone pieces. In twenty minutes, a big crack formed along the line between the four holes. They then shifted over to halfway between each of the holes and drilled another three holes. They moved the spreaders to each of the new holes, leaving the center one where it was. Then they turned the hydraulics on again. After another twenty minutes, a two-foot sheet of the iron ball broke off. "Wow, that was pretty nice," Catie said.

Jimmy and Paul gave everybody a wave, then they went back to work. They used the augers and spreader to break the sheet into manageable sizes, then moved them off the ball and let them float above it. Then they went to the vertical wall that had formed at the end of where the sheet broke off and repeated the process. Things went smoothly until they tried to do it a third time, then the hydraulic pump wouldn't work.

Blake signaled everyone to go back inside the Oryx for a debrief.

"Okay, that was really impressive," Blake said. "I assume you plan to just keep shaving the top of the asteroids off like that."

"That's the plan," Paul said. "But our pump busted, what do you think is wrong with it?"

"The hydraulic fluid froze," Catie said, "or at least got too thick to work."

"Oops, what do we do about that?" Paul asked.

"Just put a recirculation pump on the fluid line and a small heater to keep it warm. The manufacturer might even make them for working in cold environments," Catie said. "If not, it wouldn't be too hard to rig one up."

"That worked pretty slick," Liz said.

"Yeah," Jimmy said. "The real asteroid won't be as nice. It won't shear off nice and smooth like that did. But we should be able to deal with it."

"What are you gonna want us to do with the trash rocks we pull out of them?" Paul asked.

"I think we need to clean up after ourselves," Blake said.

"We can just put them in front of the three asteroids in the same orbit," Catie said. "When it gets big enough, we can use some oil to tie it together. Then we can either boost it back to the asteroid belt, push it into the sun, or haul it to the space station and use it for something."

"Isn't that like pushing the problem down the road?" Liz asked.

"More like pushing it ahead in the orbit," Catie said. "But we'll have lots of time to figure out what we want to do."

"What else did we learn?" Blake asked.

"We should use four-man teams," Paul said. "Two can break the sheet apart, while the other two keep shearing new ones off."

"I agree," Jimmy said. "We'll learn a bunch as we go. I'm also inclined to treat those ice balls the same way. Then we're not trying to melt things, then freeze them, or whatever. Rocks are easy to deal with."

"I'm good with that," Liz said. "Catie?"

"Hey, it's a place to start. If it works, we're done; if we run into issues, we'll replan."

"You guys ready to gather your equipment up and go home?" Blake asked.

"We sure are," Jimmy said.

"Okay, we'll see you guys," Catie said. "Natalia and I have some experiments to run. We'll be coming back down tomorrow." Catie could tell that Paul was disappointed that Natalia wasn't going to be riding down with him.

"I'm hanging out with them," Liz said. "I've got a few inspections to do to prepare for the first ring. Hoping I'm going to be getting lots of material to work with soon."

Catie and Natalia set six experiments up in the microgravity hub. The crew chief agreed to have someone monitor their experiments once they were done. It wouldn't be much work since Natalia had everything fitted with video cameras and instrumentation so that the experiments could be monitored remotely.

"Okay, Natalia, tell me what these are?" Catie asked.

"They're all identical boxes," Natalia said. "They have a membrane separating the air compartment from the water and sludge compartment. We've started the bacteria growing in the sludge compartment and some algae in the air compartment; the air is ninety percent oxygen. Now we want to see what happens in microgravity."

"Okay, so what's the difference between them?"

"Box A will just sit here," Natalia said. "Box B will get a little shake every two hours to stir things up. Box C will get shaken on the same schedule, but it has a little circulation pump that will create a current toward the bottom of the box. And Box D won't get shaken, but it will alternate the direction of the current every two hours."

"And the last two?"

"Box E will be like box C, but will also pump air into the circulation water. And F will do the same for the D design."

"I get all that, but what's the point?"

"We're trying to figure out the minimal energy required to keep the boxes active, that is, if any of them work," Natalia said. "But we're pretty sure we'll have at least one winner in the group."

"Okay, so why are we staying up overnight?" Catie asked. "It seems like we'll be done setting this up in a couple of hours."

"I want to see what the results are after twelve hours," Natalia said. "I might want to make some adjustments."

"Okay."

10   Vancouver Recruiting

"Welcome, Cers, as we at MacKenzie Discoveries like to say," Samantha said as the four founders of Vancouver Integrated Technologies entered the conference room at the Pan Pacific, Vancouver, British Columbia. "Cers is our non-gender-specific honorific. Please be seated, and I'll introduce everybody."

The four young technologists walked into the room and took a seat at the table. They glanced at Catie and gave her an awkward smile.

"As you know, I'm Samantha Newman, the general counsel for MacKenzie Discoveries. With me, I have two members of our board, Catie McCormack, one of our major shareholders and one of our lead technologists, and Liz Farmer, another of our technologists."

There were head nods and smiles all around.

"And from Vancouver Integrated Technologies, we have the four founders, Ray Fowler, Aaron Leach, Shelby Ramsey, and Bryce McMillan," Samantha said, concluding the introductions. "May I ask where your general counsel is?"

"I act as our general counsel," Ray Fowler said. "We can call for assistance if this gets beyond what I'm comfortable with, but we want to keep this meeting to just the founders if we can."

"I can understand that," Samantha said. "We often have the same concerns. Our board of directors is only ten people right now. It was only five for most of the first year."

"Thank you," Ray said.

"As I've explained during our initial conversations," Samantha said, "MacKenzie Discoveries is interested in acquiring a majority interest in your company. We would let you manage the operation; you'd be able to continue to headquarter here in Vancouver, but we would want you to open an operation in Delphi City to meet our special needs."

"How does that help us?" Ray asked.

"You get to stay in business," Samantha said.

Ray looked around at his partners. They all knew that they were hanging on by their fingernails, but were they willing to give up control just to stay alive?

"Let's hear her offer," Shelby said.

"I don't know if you're familiar with MacKenzie Discoveries," Samantha continued, "but we're a new technology company. Last year we introduced the new batteries and fuel cells that are setting the standard for those technologies. We're the majority stakeholder in Fuerza Motores, which I'm sure you know has become the leading supplier of both electric cars as well as electric scooters. By the way, the scooters were designed by Catie McCormack."

Catie got a few more glances; these carried more respect than the earlier glances.

"Our batteries and fuel cells are the driving force behind Tata's new line of electric and hybrid electric-fuel-cell trucks," Samantha continued. "We have also introduced the first commercial jet capable of doing Mach four. We arrived here today from the Cook Islands after a three-hour flight. And we recently introduced a treatment for Alzheimer's and dementia. I'll pause here for questions."

"All of that is interesting," Shelby said, "but we're an integrated circuits company. How would we fit in?"

"I'm glad you asked," Catie said. "I'd like each of you to put one of these on." Catie handed out four pairs of specs and four Comm units.

"Nice shades," Bryce said.

"Thank you," Catie said. "We call them specs. You'll notice a HUD if you look up. If you focus on a menu item and blink, it will activate. Go ahead and play with them for a bit," Catie told them.

Catie gave them five minutes to peruse the menu and play with the options.

"They're kind of cool Google Goggles," Bryce said. "Nice, but only a little interesting."

"I like that you're hard to please," Catie said. "Now I'm going to take control of your specs so we can expedite the demonstration."

Catie had their Comm units display a video she'd prepared. The video was in three-D and included surround sound music. It showed a flight through the Grand Canyon. "You will all see a set of controls in front of you; they should look like a steering wheel for a plane, the yoke if you fly. If you take hold of it, you can change your orientation and essentially fly through the canyon."

"More interesting," Shelby said after about five minutes of playing, "but, I'm still not sure what you bring to the game."

"Two more demonstrations," Catie said. "Will one of you please read the text on your HUD?"

Aaron started reading. He had a very pronounced Canadian accent. Catie watched the recognition score; when it reached eighty percent, she interrupted him. "Now just start dictating anything you want," Catie said. "The words that the Comm unit is not sure of will appear in yellow, the ones it has no clue about will be in red."

Aaron started dictating. He talked for three minutes, "Hey, that's pretty good," Aaron said. "I've only got two words in red and twelve in yellow."

"That's what we can do with our software on an Apple iPhone. Now I've made all your specs dependent to this Comm unit," Catie said. "I've copied the training data for your dictation over to it. Aaron, why don't you try again?"

Aaron started dictating again. "Faster!" Catie said. "What do you think of the results?" Catie asked Shelby as Aaron kept talking. "Don't worry about interfering with his dictation."

"It's almost perfect," Shelby said.

"Liz, how did you like flying the Lynx up here?" Catie asked.

"It was so cool. Going that fast and over the ocean. We got to see such a beautiful sky the whole way. That storm we passed through really made things interesting," Liz rattled on for a minute while Aaron continued to dictate.

"This is how I like to take notes," Catie said as she started typing on the tabletop. Everyone's Comm unit showed her fingers and the text that she was typing.

"Wow, now you have my attention!" Shelby said. "What's different?"

"These two Comm units are our custom design," Catie said. She picked up a small hammer she had sitting on the table next to her and pounded the Comm unit. She hit it three times.

"You're crazy!" Shelby said.

Catie tossed her the Comm unit.

Shelby examined it, turning it over in her hand, "Not a scratch, how is that possible?"

"Some more of our new technology," Catie said. "The glass is a special material that we call clear polysteel. The computer chip is custom made. We can only make them one at a time. We need you to help us make them in quantity."

"And before we can go on," Samantha interrupted, "we would need the nondisclosures signed."

"I assure you it will be worth it," Catie said.

It only took a few moments before they all agreed to sign the nondisclosure forms. Once they were signed, Samantha continued.

"First, let me explain what we can do to help," Samantha said. "We've done some research on your legal troubles, and as I'm sure you're aware, the claims against you are thin. With our research, we can help you push back on the infringement suits. Once your competition has been forced to realize you're able to fight back, we can announce the acquisition of a majority interest by MacKenzie Discoveries. At that point, we can bring our considerable influence to bear and get them to drop the lawsuits."

"How?" Bryce asked.

"They want to use our batteries in their products; we don't like being sued," Samantha said.

"Oh, right."

"But how does that help us?" Shelby asked again. "Sure, we're still in business, but we've lost the edge we were using to get ourselves into the game."

Samantha nodded to Catie.

81

"Three things," Catie said. "One: we have a new camera design that you can put into production right away; it's years ahead of the competition. Two: our operating system is significantly better than the competition's. We can license that to you so you can put it on your chip. It will give you some of that edge back. Three: that Comm you were playing with, I set to match the specs for a new computer chip we have designed. It's over eight times more powerful than what is in that new iPhone we used for the first demo. But we don't have the manufacturing process figured out. It will take you six months to a year to bring it into production."

"That certainly helps," Shelby said. "But why the nondisclosures?"

"Because, four: you get to be the first to manufacture here," Catie said as she brought up a view of Delphi Station with the earth in the background.

"What is that, some kind of satellite?" Aaron asked.

"Let me give you a little perspective," Liz said as she changed the slide to one showing the station with an Oryx docked. "That ship you see docked is about the size of a Boeing 767."

"Then that thing is huge," Aaron said.

"It has a diameter of two hundred meters and a height of one hundred thirty meters," Liz continued. "It has an inner hub, of 180 meters, that doesn't rotate, so we have microgravity there. That's where we need you to set up the IC manufacturing. The outer hub rotates to provide some semblance of gravity."

"Why microgravity?" Shelby asked.

"The chip we use in our Comms can only be manufactured in microgravity," Catie said. "It has superconductor traces on it, and they require microgravity. I'm sure we'll want to make lots of chips that use that process."

"Superconductors on an IC chip. How do they work when the chips heat up?" Shelby asked.

"The chips don't heat up that much," Catie said. "The gates also incorporate technologies that minimize resistance. But the superconductors will maintain zero resistance up to two hundred C."

"That would revolutionize the entire industry," Shelby said.

"That's what MacKenzie Discoveries is all about," Samantha said, then she nodded for Liz to continue.

"That is what it looks like now," Liz said. "Before you guys get there it should look like this." Liz changed the slide to one that showed the station with the first ring.

"And by the end of the year, it will look like this," Liz said as she flipped the display to a slide showing the station with all three rings.

"How big is that thing?" Aaron asked.

"It's big enough to support about twenty thousand people," Liz said. "The outer ring will have one-G of gravity and the second ring will have a three-quarter-G. We'll see how fast we can grow. It's designed to stack four of these together."

"Okay, you've got us hooked; how do we make this deal?" Ray asked as he looked at his colleagues for confirmation.

"What we want," Samantha said, "is for you to put a facility on the station. We need to staff it with technicians and the engineers needed to run it. The design team can work in Delphi City, but we need people up on the station. We still want the existence of the space station to remain secret, although we believe the US government knows about it. They're letting us keep it secret, probably because they don't want to be embarrassed by how substantial our space presence is compared to the US's."

"How come everybody doesn't know about it?" Aaron asked.

"Because its orbit is exactly opposite the ISS's orbit; the material it is made of absorbs over ninety percent of light and EM radiation," Catie said. "It's hard to see, and the sky is really big. We're sure the only way the US found it, is because of all the Oryxes going up there to lift the material needed to make it."

"Back to the deal," Samantha said. "We'll provide the capital you need to ride out this little bump, plus what you need to set up production of the camera and chip that Catie talked about. We'll also provide whatever it takes to set up in Delphi City and on Delphi Station."

"How much?" Ray asked.

"We're estimating it will take about three hundred million," Samantha said. "We can cover more, but it seems that should get you back in place."

"What about salaries?" Bryce asked. "We've been living off of savings since we started this thing."

"We've been paying directors three hundred thousand a year," Samantha said. "And of course, you would still retain forty-nine percent ownership."

"We need to bring the lawyers in," Ray said. "But we're close enough that I think we'll reach a deal. What's the next step?"

"We'd like you to come to Delphi City, so you'll have a perspective of what it's all about when you talk to your people," Samantha continued. "If you'd like, we'll take you up to the station so you can see what that's like."

"For sure, we're going to the station," Shelby said. "What else?"

"We need you to use your contacts to attract people to the station," Samantha said. "We have other industries in mind, but we need people to run them and to staff the jobs."

11   Board Meeting – Sep 30th

Liz caught Catie outside the boardroom, "Did you see Dr. Metra?"

"Yes," Catie said. "She said everything was normal."

"Good," Liz said. "Did she tell you what to do about the shipsuits?"

"She gave me measurements for five sets," Catie said. "She said that I should slowly grow into each one. When one set starts getting tight, I can just start wearing the next size up. She said the sizes were calibrated to how I would grow."

"Hey, that's nice," Liz said. "Did you try on the biggest size?"

Catie blushed.

"Of course, you did," Liz said. "I would have. What did you think?"

"I'm going to look like Mommy," Catie said.

"Does that make you happy?" Liz asked.

"I guess so. I think Mommy looks pretty good."

"She's gorgeous," Liz said. "You should be happy."

"I guess," Catie said.

"Did she say how long it would take?" Liz asked.

"She said another year for three of the sizes, then a year each for the last two."

"Oh, you were curious," Liz said with a laugh. "You made suits for two to three years from now."

"Why not," Catie said.

"I agree. I certainly would have."

"This meeting is called to order," Marc said as Catie and Liz finally came in and got seated. "Sam, can you update us on your Vancouver trip?"

"Yes," Samantha said. "It looks like we're going to reach an agreement with Vancouver Integrated Technologies. The founders were here in Delphi City over the weekend, and they were very impressed with what they saw. Catie took them up to see the space station yesterday, and I think that sealed the deal. This is the second time she has done an excellent job of selling someone on our technology; we might want to add sales rep to her title."

"No!" Catie whined.

"Oh, come on, you loved it," Liz said.

Marc just gave Catie a smile as he nodded for Samantha to continue.

"Their lawyers are reviewing the paperwork this week. I hope to have it all signed by the end of next week," Samantha added.

"Excellent," Marc said. "How about our clinics?"

"The one in Mexico is booked solid for the next six months," Samantha said. "We're booked for three months on Rarotonga and about the same for Delphi City. The price doesn't seem to be deterring anyone yet. Unfortunately, the manager in Tijuana had to dismiss a nurse last week."

"Oh, what happened?" Marc asked.

"She stole some treatment cartridges," Samantha said. "The director brought her in and showed her the records of her pulling them and the video of her taking them out of the dispensary. She said she was being blackmailed into getting them."

"That's terrible," Liz said.

"Yes, but two other nurses were also being blackmailed into stealing cartridges, but they came to the director and reported it," Samantha said. "He gave them the cartridges to take since they're useless after twenty minutes, anyway. He told the first nurse how her other two colleagues had handled the blackmail, and then he fired her, telling her it was because he couldn't trust her."

"I guess that's the correct thing to do," Liz said. "They do talk about that in their briefings, don't they?"

"Yes," Samantha said. "I think we're ready to open a clinic in Morocco now. With Ayyour Dahmani's help, it should be an easy startup. We're getting lots of inquiries from Europe."

"Anyone have an issue with that?" Marc asked. Looking around the table, he didn't see anyone trying to make a point. "Then, you have a go."

"Thanks," Samantha said. "By the way, I understand that France has tentatively approved the Lynx for landing."

"That's very interesting," Marc said. "I happen to have reservations at the Grand Hotel du Palais Royal for next week; would you like to go with me?"

"My bags are already packed," Samantha said.

"Why pack bags?" Liz said. "One small carryon is all you need. You're going to buy new luggage and clothes in Paris, aren't you?"

"Good point," Samantha said.

"Liz, since you want to talk, how about an update," Marc said.

"Our fusion team believes they'll have a working reactor in two weeks. They're just working out some details," Liz said.

"Oh no!" Admiral Michaels said.

"Problem?" Marc asked.

"Are you going to announce that thing?" Admiral Michaels asked.

"Of course, we will," Samantha said.

The admiral sat there and shook his head.

"I assume you're anticipating problems," Marc said.

"Of course," the admiral said. "It might be enough to tip the scales with New Zealand on eminent domain."

"I'm afraid he's right," Samantha said. "Currently, the prime minister is pushing back, but there is a lot of pressure on the other side."

"Let's get back to this at the end of the meeting," Marc said. "Liz, anything else?"

"We've built out the space for the IC manufacturing," Liz said. "We just need our friends from Vancouver to tell us what to put in it. We're also ready to extrude the first ring as soon as we get the material to do so."

"Blake, do we have news there?" Marc asked.

"We do," Blake said. "We took the two lead miners up on Monday; they impressed the hell out of all of us. They only had a small issue, and Catie was able to point them to a fix. We took the others up on

Friday; it was very entertaining. A couple of them wouldn't believe we could go into space until they were floating in the back of the Oryx. They didn't do as well as the first two, but they quickly got the routine down."

"That sounds very promising," Marc said. "So when do you start working on the asteroids?"

"We start mining this week," Blake said. "We'll start slow, so we need to know which material you need the most?" Blake looked at Liz, waiting for her to decide.

"Methane," Liz said. "We need another week to get the processing in place to handle the iron-nickel alloy. Fred, can you switch all the lifts over to iron?"

"Just did," Fred said. "We can also squeeze in an extra lift per day since the iron is so quick to load and unload."

"Good, then if Blake can get us a few full loads of methane this week and the same next week, we can start the extrusion on the ring next Friday," Liz said.

"Not now, Blake," Marc said to forestall Blake from grabbing the scotch.

"Oh, eminent domain," Blake said as he sat back down.

"Catie, what do you have?" Marc asked.

"Zane has agreed to run our credit union," Catie said. "He'll come in during our next meeting to present a plan. He's picked out the space, and we're having the construction crew build it out."

"Good job," Samantha said. "See, sales rep."

Catie gave Samantha an *I will get even* look before she continued. "Tomi is happy with the experiments he and Natalia ran last week. Based on that, they want to go ahead and put a small treatment plant in the hub. We can take it out later if we need the space."

"That will be nice," Liz said. "The crews don't like having to pump the waste around."

"The community market last week was a success; I heard that this week was even better," Catie said. "I think everyone liked all the variety that was available. We need to have someone start to coordinate and figure out how to run all our hydroponics systems on the station. And I think we want to grow fruit trees up there as well."

"If you want someone to coordinate things," Blake said, "I'd recommend JoAnn. You used her to coordinate the miners' move-in. She seems really sharp."

"Do we want to bring in an expert to do the technical work?" Samantha asked.

"We have a couple of people here," Catie said. "But they're not experts. We use consultants to decide what to grow."

"If you want someone with a degree," Admiral Michaels said, "my wife has a degree in Controlled Environment Agriculture from Cornell that she's never been able to use."

"Well, that would be just perfect," Catie said. "She probably already knows all of our secrets, at least the ones we've shared with the admiral."

The admiral looked offended, "I'll have you know . . ."

Samantha patted his hand and whispered in his ear, "She's only thirteen."

"I can keep a secret," the admiral finished. "She knows there's something going on, but I haven't shared anything with her."

"Then this will be a win-win," Marc said. "We get an expert, and you get to reduce some of the family tension."

Samantha texted Catie, *"I'll explain later."*

"Thanks," Catie texted back.

"Catie, will you follow up with the admiral's wife?" Marc said.

"Should I wait until he tells me to?" Catie asked. "He probably wants to tell her about the space station himself."

"I'll do that tonight," the admiral said. "I'll let her know you want to talk to her, but I'll leave the details to you."

"Thanks," Catie said.

"Now, what do we do about our fusion announcement?" Marc said.

"I think the threat of the Kiwis pressuring the Cook Islanders to declare eminent domain is real," Samantha said. "They'll be getting pressure from the British, who'll be getting pressure from the US. An announcement of a fusion reactor will probably tip the scales."

"Why?" Catie asked.

"Because they'll want to get control of it before Russia or the Chinese do," Admiral Michaels said.

"You've been preparing for this from the beginning," Samantha said to Marc. "I think it's time."

"Preparing for what?" Admiral Michaels asked.

"Declaring independence," Marc said.

"Oh s . . . ," Admiral Michaels sighed and threw his hands up. He leaned back into his chair and stared at Marc.

"We already have a larger population in Delphi City than all of the Cook Islands. Even with their restriction on citizenship, it has to be getting untenable for them," Samantha said. "Even without the threat of eminent domain, you have to confront the fact that they're going to start passing laws that we won't like."

"Okay, so declare independence," Blake said.

"That's not as easy as it sounds," Marc said. "We have to establish a government. How do we protect ourselves from having our mission taken over or redirected?"

Catie started giggling uncontrollably.

"It's not that funny," Marc said.

"I think it is," Catie giggled. "Oh, poor Daddy."

"It's going to affect you too." Marc shot back.

"Ohh, drat," Catie said as she continued to giggle.

"Can you two let the rest of us in on it," Blake huffed.

Marc sat back and crossed his arms, furiously trying to think of another alternative.

"He's . . . ," Catie giggled, "he's going to have to declare himself king."

"What!?" Blake screeched.

"It's the only way," Catie said as she continued to giggle. "He has to have veto power over everything. Otherwise, the new government could just nix our mission and focus on self-interest."

"Oh my," Samantha said. "She's right."

"I can't think of another way," Marc said.

"Well, you're already the Chairman of MacKenzie Discoveries," Samantha said. "And the company owns everything, all the real estate, utilities, buildings, and spacecraft. That kind of makes you the chief poohbah already."

"Not helping," Marc said.

"Well, we have to come up with something that makes sense," Samantha said. "And something that doesn't make you a demigod. I am not going to follow some foolish rules every time we're together."

"We've already made a good start," Kal finally spoke up. "We have established a police force, we have codified laws, and we are operating as a pseudo-military organization with you as the captain of the ship, and the board as your cabinet or ministers."

"We need to have this worked out before we declare," Marc said. "We don't want our people to panic."

"I don't think anyone will panic," Blake said. "Everyone is pretty happy and declaring independence doesn't actually change much. I don't think anyone is currently thinking that the Cook Island government is looking out for their interests."

Marc just continued to shake his head, Catie continued to giggle, and the admiral just glared.

"How did I get myself into this?" the admiral said.

"Curiosity killed the cat," Samantha said. "It just trapped you."

"How can I help?" Admiral Michaels asked.

"Sam and I will work on a constitution," Marc said. "What we need are friends that will recognize us when we declare."

"I think Mexico and Morocco will," Samantha said.

"If you reach out to India with the fusion reactor before you announce, they'll probably be willing to recognize you," the admiral said. "I assume you're planning on starting with them to commercialize the reactor."

"Yes, India and Indonesia are the first two countries we want to approach," Marc said. "Plus, Malaysia, Poland, and Morocco."

"Those are all reasonably safe bets," Admiral Michaels said. "I'd recommend reaching out to all of them. Then I'd suggest France, Portugal, Germany, and Spain; they're not necessarily fans of US foreign policy, and they might be willing to recognize you after India."

"Do you have contacts in any of them?" Marc asked.

"France and Spain," the admiral said. "I think you have Portugal covered."

"I think I can get an audience," Marc said with a laugh. "How many would it take to force the issue?"

"I think getting France or Germany is the key," Admiral Michaels said. "It would be hard for the US not to go ahead and recognize you after that. I think New Zealand and Australia would follow France or Germany."

"Anyone have a way to get to Germany?" Marc asked.

"Hey, they're big proponents of solving Climate Change," Catie said. "We should find someone to approach who's big on that."

"I'll ask Herr Johansson," Samantha said.

"Who else do we have who can handle these kinds of discussions?" Marc asked.

"Kevin Clark was pretty connected," Fred said. "I'm sure he's handled some complex situations, being a brigadier general tends to require some diplomacy."

"Sam, can you check him out?" Marc asked. "We really need someone else to negotiate for us."

"I will," Samantha said. "But we're still going to Paris."

"What about Marcie?" Liz asked. "She's got plenty of tact."

"She's here in Delphi City now," Samantha said. "We could see if she wants to play diplomat. I think she'd be pretty good at it."

"Okay, ask her," Marc said. "That's it for today. Communicate any ideas or concerns; we'll work this out."

12   Hydroponics in Space

"Hello, Mrs. Michaels," Catie said when Mrs. Michaels answered the door.

"Hello, Catie," Mrs. Michaels said. "And call me Pam now that we're working together."

"Sure," Catie said. "Hi, Sophia." Catie waved at her friend.

"Hi, Catie. You're coming to movie night, aren't you?"

"Yes," Catie sighed.

"Don't be that way," Mrs. Michaels said. "You'll enjoy yourself. Now let's get going."

"Bye, Sophia. I'll see you Saturday," Catie said as she and Mrs. Michaels headed out. Mrs. Michaels was wearing jeans and sneakers, which was a very unusual look for her, at least from Catie's experience.

"Tell me when we'll be somewhere that I can really quiz you," Mrs. Michaels said. "I have a lot of questions."

"Are they all about growing stuff?" Catie joked.

"No, they are not," Mrs. Michaels said. "I cannot believe that Paul has kept all this a secret for so long. He should have gotten permission to read me in."

"It's not been that long," Catie said. "He's only known about things since the middle of August. We can talk as soon as we get to the grow house."

"Grow house," Mrs. Michaels said with a laugh. "That sounds like we're growing pot. My kids will be teasing me every time I go to work."

"Well, that's what they're called no matter what you're growing in them," Catie said. "Maybe you should make them help you. That would take some of the humor out of it."

"Clever, but kind of mean," Mrs. Michaels said. "Anyway, back to the space station and when Paul knew what. He told me he'd only known since mid-August, but I didn't really believe him. He had to know something before we came here."

"He knew we had really cool technology," Catie said. "But he was shocked when he saw the pictures we have of the station."

"He was, was he?"

"Here is our warehouse," Catie said. "We've got everything set up in here." Catie opened the door which her Comm unlocked for her. "Nobody's working in here right now, so we're alone."

"Oh good," Mrs. Michaels said as she watched the door close. "Now, can I ask questions?"

"Sure," Catie said.

"What kind of space station is this thing," Mrs. Michaels said. "And how are you getting up there?"

"I can take you up anytime you want," Catie said. "You've seen the Oryxes that were taking off from here before, right?"

"Yes."

"Well, those are our space shuttles. They carry cargo mostly, but passengers can hitch a ride anytime. Then the Lynx can reach it also, or at least the new ones can."

"You mean those nice jets that land here all the time?" Mrs. Michaels asked. "I thought they were just bigger private jets."

"They are, but they can do Mach four, and the new ones can reach orbit. You'll like the Mach four bit. Daddy's taking Sam to Paris this week, and the flight is going to be only about three and a half hours." Catie didn't mention that Marc was going to go the max speed and make the flight in less than three hours. He'd have the Delphi airport say he'd left an hour earlier than he actually did.

"Oh, I'll have to talk to Paul about that. I haven't been to Paris for a long time. Now tell me about the space station."

"Why don't we sit down here," Catie said. "I'll put the images up on your specs, but I don't want you to walk into anything."

"Good idea."

"This first image is the space station with an Oryx docked. You can see how big it is."

"Oh, my, it certainly is big."

"It's one hundred thirty meters tall. And the diameter of the hub is two hundred meters. Now here is what it will look like in a few weeks with the first ring in place." Catie switched the image.

"First ring?" Mrs. Michaels queried suspiciously.

"Yes," Catie said. "Here it is with all three rings."

Mrs. Michaels gasped. "How many people are you planning on having up there?"

"Ten to twenty thousand, more one day."

"Paul said something about gravity," Mrs. Michaels said. "Can you explain?"

"Sure. Once we have a ring in place, we'll be able to rotate that station so that the outer ring always has one-G. That means the same gravity as Earth."

"What do you mean by the outer ring?"

"When you rotate things, the force that you feel isn't actually gravity, but the force created by the floor keeping you from flying out into space, because the floor is constantly changing directions. That force is based on your speed, how fast the station rotates, and the radius that the floor is at," Catie said.

"You're explaining too much," Mrs. Michaels said. "Give me the simple version."

"Okay," Catie said with a chuckle. "Basically, the bigger the radius, the higher the gravity is for the same rotational speed. So, the outer ring always has the most gravity. We can speed up the rotation so that the smaller rings have one-G, but we have to slow it down when we add another ring; otherwise, it would have too much gravity. Nobody wants to have to deal with weighing more than they're used to. Or trying to move stuff that's heavier than it should be."

"Okay, that means that the inner rings and that hub thing will have less gravity."

"Correct. The hub is in two parts, there is an inner hub that doesn't spin, so it has zero gravity. The outer hub has some gravity; we're spinning it at the same speed we need for the outer ring to have one-G, so it has one-fifth G."

"And where are you planning to put your grow house?"

"We're hoping in the first ring. It will only have a half-G, so we don't think people will want to live there."

"I don't know, one-half-G sounds good to me, especially after a long day."

"We'll see," Catie said. "All the rings have a space above and below the living space that's rounded. You see, because the rings are ellipses, there is a bunch of space where the ceiling or floor is curved. Well, you can't have a curved floor, so we're going to use most of that for infrastructure. At the top, the space is pretty tall, seven meters deep with at least an eight-foot ceiling; that means we can put grow houses there and some offices or stores."

"Okay, I think I have it now," Mrs. Michaels said. "Show me around this place."

"Right this way," Catie said. "This room is the bush vegetable garden, so vegetables that grow above ground. The plants are in trays that you can pull out. There's a light panel above them that only emits the light they like to minimize energy usage and so we can increase the light intensity without burning the plants."

Catie pulled out a tray that had tomato plants on it.

"Those are nice looking tomatoes," Mrs. Michaels said. "And so many on one plant."

"Yes, that's because we give it exactly what it wants and there are no pests in here. So they really thrive. You can see their roots are growing through this membrane into the water. We circulate the water and add nutrients to it. The membrane is supposed to keep the water in place if we lose gravity for a while."

"That makes sense. What about air?"

"We use concentrated CO_2, and we let the plants rest in the dark for only four hours a day to maximize their growth. Then we increase the length of darkness to trigger the plant to start producing a crop. Each tray has a separate temperature control along with separate lighting controls."

"Oh, very good," Mrs. Michaels said. "How do you control it?"

"It's all computer-controlled," Catie said. "You can manage it all remotely and each tray independently. There are little video cameras in the trays that you can use to see what's going on, but you have to set them on a timer too since you need to add white light during the filming."

"Okay, now show me your root crops," Mrs. Michaels said.

"Those are next door," Catie said as she led Mrs. Michaels to the next room. "These trays are deeper because you have to allow for the plant and their big roots." Catie pulled out a tray of potatoes.

"Oh, these are nice," Mrs. Michaels said. "I like the way you have this set up. I wonder how these would do in low gravity."

"You can find out. Just tell us what you want us to take up," Catie said.

"I will. I'll do some work tomorrow and make a list of experiments I want to run," Mrs. Michaels said. "This is going to be fun. I haven't done any of this since I finished my Master's. I got married right after that."

"Well, you've got lots of work now," Catie said.

"I think I can do a PhD. on this." Mrs. Michaels said. "I'll have to contact my old Master's adviser and see what he thinks. I'll keep all the secret stuff out of it. I can't wait until you announce the station. Then I can really get into the thick of it."

"I'm glad you're enthused," Catie said. "I've updated the locks and computer codes so they'll respond to your Comm unit. I'll send you a short tutorial on how to access all the information, and you can work through it when you have time. Let me know if you need anything. The staff will do whatever you ask them."

"Good, what about staff up on the station?"

"We'd like to use JoAnn Rasmussen for anything we do in space. I'll send you her contact information," Catie said. "She's just starting, but she'll be working full time, so she'll be lots of help for you."

"Thanks, I think I have what I need for now. I'll just head home. See you on Saturday."

"Bye."

13   Movie Night

"Hi, Sophia," Catie said as Sophia opened the door to the Michaels' condo.

"Hey, Catie, you're late," Sophia scolded.

"Only thirty minutes," Catie said. "And I'll have you know that in Portugal that's considered early."

"Bragger," Sophia said. "Come on in. You already know almost everybody."

Catie entered the room and looked around; she recognized everyone but two. "Who is the blond guy over there?" she asked Sophia.

"That's Frankie Phillips," Sophia said. "His family just got here. Both parents are teachers. He must think you're cute."

"Why do you say that?"

"Because he's looked over here twice since you came in," Sophia said.

"He's probably looking at you," Catie said.

"I couldn't get his attention before, and believe me, I tried," Sophia said. "All of us have tried; he's a real hunk."

"Whatever," Catie said. "And who is the redhead over there?" Catie asked as she nodded toward a young redheaded girl.

"Oh, that's Crystal Tate," Sophia said. "Everyone calls her Chris. Her family has been here a long time. They're some kind of chemists who work for you guys. She's only fourteen, but she's in David's class. Frankie's in David's class too, he's sixteen."

"Where's Chaz?" Catie asked.

"He's in Wellington," Sophia said. "He's doing something at the university there for school. Can you believe it, his family picks this weekend to go?"

"Is he avoiding you?"

"He'd better not be," Sophia said. "No, they committed before Mom announced the day for the party. I tried to go with them, but Mom nixed it."

Sophia took Catie over to Chris to introduce her, "Hey, Chris, this is Catie, Catie, Chris."

"Hi Catie, I don't remember seeing you around the school," Chris said. "Are you new?"

"No," Catie said. "I homeschool. It's why my mom makes me come to these parties, so I get to meet other kids my age."

"How old are you?" Chris asked.

"I'll be fourteen next month," Catie said.

"Cool, I'm fourteen too, my birthday's in March," Chris said. "What grade are you in?"

"I'm not really in a specific grade," Catie said. "I do the material and advance at my own pace. If it's science or math related, I'm doing senior- or college-level work. If it's the other stuff, I'm generally doing junior- or senior-level work."

"You sound like me," Chris said. "I love science and math; it takes a stick to make me focus on the other stuff."

"Me too. Unfortunately, my parents have big sticks," Catie said.

"Hello, Catie," Mrs. Michaels said. "When did you get here?"

"Just now," Catie said. "Do you know Chris?"

"We've met before," Mrs. Michaels said. "Did you get my proposal?"

"Yes," Catie said. "I read it this morning."

"What did you think?"

"It looks good," Catie said. "Did you decide to use JoAnn?"

"Yes, I did. She's a lovely young woman and a hard worker," Mrs. Michaels said. "We're going to get along just fine."

"I'm glad to hear it," Catie said.

"You think I should just go ahead?" Mrs. Michaels asked.

"Oh, definitely," Catie said. "You should have all the details in your email now. I sent them over about an hour ago."

"Of course you did," Mrs. Michaels said. "I've just been so busy getting this ready, I haven't had a chance to check. You girls have fun."

"You're approving her proposal?" Chris asked with surprise.

"Not really," Catie scoffed. "She's taking over managing the hydroponics agriculture here. I've been involved with it, and had to send her the account information and stuff so she can start running things."

"Oh," Chris said doubtfully. She was pretty convinced that Mrs. Michaels was looking for Catie's approval. Adults were never that solicitous of kids.

"Do you know Artie?" Catie asked as Artie Gillespie walked by.

"He was in my class last year," Chris said. "I think he homeschools now."

"Hey, Artie, come say hi," Catie said.

"Hi, Catie," Artie said as he walked up. "Hi, Chris."

"So, you're homeschooling?" Catie asked.

"Yes, thanks for helping convince my parents," Artie said. "And my sister is going to the university in Wellington; she still wants to meet you."

"Let me know when she's visiting, and we'll go have pizza," Catie said.

"Why does your sister want to meet Catie?" Chris asked.

"Be . . ."

"Because I'm a pilot," Catie said. "She wants to learn to fly and wants to know what I think of it and get some pointers." Catie did not want Artie to make a big deal out of the fact that she was *the Catie McCormack.*

"Yeah," Artie said. "She wants Catie to take her up in an Oryx, and maybe let her fly it."

"Can you do that?" Chris asked.

"I've finally gotten a special license from New Zealand that lets me fly by myself," Catie said. "But I usually have a copilot anyway."

"How long have you been flying?"

"Only a year," Catie said, "but I've got lots of hours; and before that, I did a lot of hours on the simulator."

"That Frankie guy is looking over here," Chris said.

"Do you know him?" Catie asked.

"He just started last month at the start of the term," Chris said. "He seems pretty smart and gets good grades on the exams, but he's kind of a goof-off."

"David says he's a bit of a snob," Artie said. "He doesn't really spend time with the other kids."

"Is that what he says about me?" Catie asked. "I don't spend much time with the other kids either."

"Oh, he would never say that about you. Sophia would make his life miserable if he insulted you," Artie said with a laugh. "Besides, he's heard you get even."

"I'd only get even if he was being a real jerk about it," Catie said.

"Good to know," Artie said. "Hey, I wanted to ask you if you could help me get a job."

"You have my contact info, why didn't you just text me?" Catie asked.

"Well, I figured face-to-face would give me a better chance," Artie said with a sheepish grin.

"I can check around," Catie said. "What kind of job are you interested in, or do you already know one you want?"

"I don't know about any jobs, but I want to be an engineer, so I'm looking for something on one of the design teams," Artie said.

"What kind of engineering?" Catie asked. "Civil, mechanical, aerospace, electrical, or computer?"

"Aerospace," Artie said.

"You can get him a job?" Chris asked.

"No," Catie said, "but I've been around for a long time, so I know who to ask."

"Could you ask for me too?" Chris asked.

"I heard your parents work in one of the labs, can't they get you a job?" Catie asked.

"Only with one of the scientists they know," Chris said. "But I want to be a computer engineer, not a scientist."

"Oh, there are lots of computer science projects going on," Catie said. "The problem is that most of them are distributed projects, and everyone works remotely."

"That would be okay with me," Chris said. "That way, I could fit the work around my school schedule."

"I'm sure there are jobs for both of you," Catie said. "I'll ask around. What programming languages do you know?"

"C^{++} and JavaScript," Chris said. "I think I could learn any of the others, they're kind of the same."

"I agree with you," Catie said. "Are you interested in Web design, or core system programming?"

"At this point, anything," Chris said. "But I'd rather do apps and core development, not web pages."

"Okay, I'll tell some people about you, and they'll contact you," Catie said. "You'll probably hear back next week; there are a lot of jobs that need filling."

"But with interns?" Artie asked.

"Sure, there's always plenty of work. They'll find a way to use you."

"Thanks," Chris said. "And Frankie looked over here, again, so he must be interested in you."

"Sure," Catie scoffed.

After the movie, Sophia, David, Artie, Chris, and Catie decided to go out for pizza. When they told everyone, Jason, Annie, and Frankie decided to join them.

They went to the new Italian restaurant and pizza parlor that had just opened in their neighborhood. "Hello, Catie," the owner said when the group walked in. "How come it takes you so long to come back here?"

"I have to try all the new places," Catie said, "and I'm not allowed to eat out that often."

"Well, you come'a anytime, especially if you bring so many friends," the owner said. He motioned to the hostess to take care of them.

"He remembers you," Chris said.

"Well, I was one of his first customers," Catie said. She wanted to avoid the fact that she had been the one to approve the restaurant and recommend it for a loan.

"I didn't even know it was here," Chris said. "How did you know to come here right when it opened?"

"My friend, ADI, is really tied in," Catie said. "She always lets me know when things are happening."

"Why don't we ever get to meet this ADI?" Sophia asked.

"Oh, she's an agoraphobe," Catie said. "We only ever talk online."

"If she's an agoraphobe, how does she know so much?" Chris asked.

"She's always online," Catie said. "She reviews all kinds of stuff for the city, so generally, if something new is happening, it crosses ADI's desk somehow."

"A good friend to have," Sophia said. "She should put out a newsletter."

"I'm sure she'd be happy to help you put one out," Catie said, "but she doesn't like to get too much attention."

"Oh, really, do you think she would?" Sophia said. "I'd love to do a newsletter or even a mini-newspaper."

"I'll tell her," Catie said. "I'm sure she'd love to help."

"Cer Catie, that does sound like fun," ADI said over Catie's Comm.

Everyone ordered pizza; once it came, Catie grabbed a big slice and poured parmesan cheese all over it.

"How do you eat like that and stay so thin?" Annie asked.

"I work out a lot," Catie said.

"What kind of workout do you do?" Frankie asked.

"I do a five-mile run four days a week," Catie said, "and I do at least an hour of martial arts training each morning."

"What kind of martial arts?" Jason asked.

"Krav Maga and Aikido," Catie said. "I've got two friends who teach me, so two styles."

"That sounds intense," Annie said.

"It is," Catie said. "But it means I can eat whatever I want. Did Jason take you up in an Oryx?"

"He did," Annie said, beaming. "It was so cool, I got to sit in the cockpit with him and everything."

"You fly the Oryxes?" Frankie asked.

"Yes," Jason said. "That's my job."

"How old are you?"

"Seventeen," Jason said. "I graduated this year."

"How did you manage an invitation to the teen party?" Frankie asked.

"Hey, he's seventeen, so he's still a teen," Catie said. She was a bit miffed at Frankie's attitude.

"I think it's because I'm friends with Catie," Jason said. "Mrs. Michaels wants to be sure she's got someone besides Sophia to talk to."

"How do you know her?" Frankie asked.

"Oh, she gave me my first ride in an Oryx," Jason said. "We're both pilots, so we see each other once in a while."

"You're a pilot?" Frankie asked Catie.

"Yes," Catie said. "Earlier in the year, they didn't have enough pilots, so I got to fly the Oryxes a lot. Now I just fill in once in a while when they're short a pilot or to keep myself current."

"I'm a pilot too," Frankie said. "Of course, I've only flown single-engine planes so far."

"You should get your certification to fly the Lynx," Catie said. "They're starting to fly them on regular routes, so you might be able to get a job as a copilot in a year or so."

"A year! How come you can fly, then?" Frankie asked.

"Being first has advantages," Catie said. "I got certified when they really needed pilots, now they're pickier."

"I guess I showed up a few months late," Frankie said. "Here's to pilots the world over," he held his Coke up in a toast.

Catie turned back to Sophia, "Did you get a chance to go to the community market yet?"

"I went today," Sophia said. "It was great. I bought a new skirt and a pair of those shipboots. I almost bought a shipsuit, but I'm not sure my parents would approve."

"They are pretty daring," Catie said, "but they are so comfortable."

"Oh, you have one?" Sophia asked.

"Well, they're knock-offs of the ones we wear when we fly the Oryx," Catie said.

"Hey, what's my mom doing for you guys?" Sophia asked.

"She's taking over management of the hydroponic farming," Catie said.

"Oh, it's more than that," Sophia said. "She and Dad had this big hush-hush conversation, and then after she met you on Wednesday, she's been over the moon."

"I think she's just happy to be able to use her degree," Catie said. "She mentioned she might work on her PhD., so she might be excited about that."

"I don't know," Sophia said skeptically, "but I know you guys have secrets. How are you getting along with your mom?"

"We're getting along okay," Catie said. "It's a bit of a pain having two parents trying to help you out, especially when they don't coordinate with each other."

"You getting more help than you want?" Sophia asked with a giggle.

"Yes, way too much help," Catie said.

"Your parents aren't together?" Chris asked.

"No," Catie said. "They got divorced three years ago, but they get along with each other."

"That's good. Are they friends?"

"Not really, but I think they like each other; they just don't do things together unless it's about work or about me," Catie explained. "I kind of like it that way."

"Are they seeing other people?" Chris asked.

"Yes," Catie said. "They both have new significant others. I really like Sam, my dad's girlfriend. My mom's boyfriend seems nice, but I don't really know him."

"At least that's not too awkward," Chris said. "How did they both wind up here?"

"Dad came here at the beginning," Catie said. "Mom's a doctor, so she decided to come and work in the clinic, and she wanted to be close to me." Catie avoided the fact that her father had gotten almost all of her relatives out of the US because they were afraid that someone would kidnap one of them to gain leverage over MacKenzie Discoveries.

"Hey, Catie," Frankie said. "Any chance I can get you to give me a ride in one of the new jets?"

"Maybe," Catie said. "Send me your contact info, and if I have a flight, I'll let you know so you can come along."

"In an Oryx?" Frankie asked.

"Probably not," Catie said. "They're really picky about who goes up in one of those. Annie only got a ride because it was a test flight for a new one. But the Lynxes just fly back and forth between Delphi City and other airports."

"Where do the Oryxes fly?" Frankie asked.

"I think it's supposed to be a secret," Catie said.

"You must know since you fly them," Frankie said.

"Can you keep a secret?" Catie asked in a conspiratorial tone.

"Sure," Frankie said.

"Well, so can I," Catie said.

"That's so old," Frankie said with a laugh.

"Old but true," Catie said. "Where did you live before you came here?"

"We lived in Minnesota," Frankie said.

"Does Minnesota have more than one city?" Catie asked.

"Minneapolis," Frankie said. "They have really crappy weather there."

"I hear it's either too cold or too hot," Artie said.

"That's a good way to say it," Frankie said in an unfriendly voice.

"I've got to go, I have an early flight tomorrow," Jason said.

"I've got to get up early and run," Catie said. "So, I should go too."

"Come on, Nattie, walk with me," Catie said when she turned the corner heading away from Jason and most of the group. "Did you get something to eat?"

"I had some bread," Natalia said. "I've got a lasagna here for my dinner when we get home. It looked like you were having fun."

"I was," Catie said. "I really like Chris."

"What about that Frankie guy?"

"I don't know; he seems like a jerk sometimes, then he's nice other times."

"I think you can say that about most men, but the good ones are worth it."

14   Market Outing

"Hey, Catie, I heard you had a good time last night," Liz said as she and Catie started stretching before their run.

"I'm thinking Nattie has a big mouth," Catie said.

"We have to exchange information, how else can we make sure we're protecting you without getting in your way," Liz said with a laugh. She slapped Catie on the butt and started running. "Come on, I hear you have some extra calories to burn off."

"A really big mouth," Catie said. She laughed as she caught up with Liz. They were going to do one full lap around the city on the perimeter road for their five miles, then they would do a cool down jog for the two hundred meters back to their condo building.

"Are you still going to the community market with Dr. Metra and Sam?" Liz asked.

"I am if it's okay with you."

"Nattie and I are both looking forward to it," Liz said. "We'd like to see what it looks like after three weeks."

"Right on time," Samantha said as Catie, Liz, and Natalia met Dr. Metra and her on the sidewalk outside the market.

"As always," Natalia said. "You girls ready to do some shopping?"

"Yes, but let's grab a shawarma first," Catie said. "I haven't had any breakfast."

They lined up at the booth selling shawarmas, chunks of meat in a laffa, which looks like a thick tortilla, with some veggies. Catie, Natalia, and Dr. Metra got lamb, while the rest got chicken.

"Where do you want to go first?" Liz asked.

"I want to check out their scarves," Dr. Metra said. "Dr. Sharmila told me they have some really nice scarves here."

The women walked to the booth that had an extensive collection of scarves. "Oh, these are really nice," Liz said. "Catie, you should get a few of these."

"Why?" Catie asked.

"They look nice, and you can accessorize with them," Liz said. "Look at Sam."

Samantha was trying out scarves, just wrapping them over her shoulders like a shawl, wrapping them in a loose knot around her neck, or just folding them into a long rectangle and draping them down her front.

"Oh, that does look nice," Catie said. She was eating her second shawarma so she couldn't do anything with her hands yet. Samantha decided to help her out and started draping scarves on her. Before she could finish her shawarma, they'd picked out four scarves that she *just had to buy*.

"Isn't that one of the girls from the party last night?" Natalia asked as she pointed at a girl walking their way. They could just make out her face through the crowd.

"Yes, that's Barbara," Catie said. Catie almost choked on the water she was drinking as Barbara turned their way and stepped away from the crowd. She was wearing one of the shipsuit knockoffs, but not in the way Catie was used to seeing them worn. The suit was tight, and form-fitting of course, but Barbara had the zipper down to her sternum so that she was showing maximum cleavage.

"You will not wear your shipsuit like that," Samantha said. "Not now, not ever."

"Are you talking to Natalia or me?" Catie asked with a laugh.

"Both of you," Samantha said. "I assume Liz has more sense."

"I think she just insulted us," Natalia said to Catie.

"It feels that way, doesn't it?" Catie asked.

"What do you think we should do about it?" Natalia asked.

"I'm thinking some kind of object lesson," Catie said.

"Oh, please, put it down to shock," Samantha begged. She definitely didn't want Catie and Natalia ganging up on her.

"I think you're going to need to make it up to us," Natalia said.

"Okay, okay," Samantha said. "How about I buy you two dinner tonight?"

"What do you think, Catie?" Natalia asked.

"Too easy," Catie said.

"I agree, I think she should have to make us dinner," Natalia said.

"Fine," Samantha said. "Let's just get back to shopping and pray we don't see some guy walking around with one unzipped down to his pelvis."

"Wait, I was hoping I'd see one like that," Liz said. They all laughed at the thought.

"See, she doesn't have all that much sense," Natalia said.

"Dr. Metra, see what I have to put up with," Samantha whined.

"I find it quite entertaining," Dr. Metra said, refusing to commiserate with Samantha.

"Oh, you would," Samantha said.

"Catie, have you seen the twins lately?" Dr. Metra asked.

"They came over to my place on Thursday to study," Catie said. "Dr. Sharmila had a late surgery, and I told her I'd watch them."

"They're almost eleven years old," Samantha said. "You wouldn't think they needed watching."

"They've had a very sheltered life with Aalia's muscular dystrophy," Dr. Metra said. "They've emotionally matured as much as one would expect. But now that the MD has been taken care of, they should start catching up to their age group in emotional maturity."

"I think they are," Catie said. "They've been much more serious the last couple of months. Although they were begging me to take them up."

"Oh, I'm sure they would be," Dr. Metra said. "You should find a time to take them up. They were part of the asteroid mission after all."

"Next time we do a tourist run, I'll be sure to include them," Catie said. "Here are the Shammases. They're the organizers of the market."

"Hello, Catie," Mrs. Shammas said. "How do you like the market?"

"It's wonderful," Catie said, "and so full."

"Yes, we are all excited at how successful it has been," Mrs. Shammas said. "Many of the women think that they will be able to stay home and just work on their crafts to sell while they watch their children."

"I'm glad to hear that," Catie said. "Even if it means we have to hire more people to replace them. Having them be happier, and having this amazing market, makes it all worthwhile."

"Yes, we are very pleased," Mr. Shammas said. "Of course, some of the men are doing crafts as well. You should see Mr. Tahan's carpets. He cannot make them fast enough."

"Oh, I have to see them," Samantha said. "I really want a carpet for my living room."

"You should buy one while you are with Catie," Mr. Shammas said. "He will be sure to give you a good price."

"I see your shipsuits are selling well," Catie said.

"Yes, they are," Mrs. Shammas said with pride. "Did you see that girl who was wearing one with the zipper down?"

"Oh, we saw her," Catie said.

"I don't think that's proper at all," Mrs. Shammas said. "She doesn't look like a good girl, wearing it like that."

"She is a nice girl," Catie said. "But we all agree that that was a bit too provocative."

"Provocative, I like that word for it," Mrs. Shammas said. "Much better than the word Mr. Shammas used."

"Well, we'd better go check out the carpets before Mr. Tahan runs out," Catie said as they all waved goodbye.

"Such nice women," Mrs. Shammas said to her husband.

"Yes, and such proper women too," he replied.

15   Space Station Tour

"Hello, Marc," Mrs. Zelbar said as she greeted him at the door to her husband's lab.

"Hello, Nikola, you wanted to see me?" Marc asked as he entered the lab. Dr. Zelbar was sitting at his workbench looking at something under the microscope. "Is everything going okay with the superconductor work?"

"That's what we wanted to talk to you about," Mrs. Zelbar said. "We think you have to make it in microgravity."

"Yes," Dr. Zelbar said. "Tell me, when are you going to take us up to see that space station of yours?"

"Space station?" Marc asked, looking a bit shocked.

"Yes!"

"Now, Leo," Mrs. Zelbar said.

"You don't expect us to believe you have us working on something that requires microgravity to manufacture, and you don't have a space station," Dr. Zelbar said. "The transparent polysteel was hard enough to believe."

"I, um," Marc stuttered.

"We won't tell anybody," Dr. Zelbar said, "but if you really want this stuff to work, you need to get us a lab up there."

Marc sighed and gave in to the inevitable. "As you surmise, we are building a space station," he said. "But it isn't actually ready for someone to live there yet."

"Then at least let us set up experiments," Dr. Zelbar said. "We can make a lot faster progress if you quit hiding things from us."

"We have to maintain operational security," Marc said. "We already have problems with various governments trying to infiltrate us."

"Well, we're not the government," Dr. Zelbar said. "When can we go up?"

"I'll ask my daughter Catie to set up a trip. Here's her contact info. She'll come by later today to coordinate with you."

"About time!"

"Now, Leo, be nice," Mrs. Zelbar said. "Will we be able to take some experiments up with us?"

"I would think so," Marc said. "Coordinate with Catie. I've got a flight to catch, so I'll be going."

Marc left the lab as both Dr. Zelbars started an in-depth conversation about experiments they wanted to run.

Catie contacted the Zelbars and Mrs. Michaels about going up and running some experiments. At first, she had planned to take them up in a Lynx, but after the list of experiments that they wanted to run, she had decided she'd better use an Oryx. She grabbed one that was going through its ground inspection. She had them move the Oryx and its inspection to Delphi City and asked the three scientists to meet her there.

"Okay, this is our Oryx," Catie said. "You can use all the space any way you would like, just don't block the airlock in the front of the hold. That leads to our small passenger space and the cockpit."

"My, this is huge," Mrs. Zelbar said. "You're letting us have it all to ourselves?"

"Yes," Catie said. "This one is out of the rotation for inspection. That takes four days, so that's how long you have to set up. Then we'll put it back into its rotation, and it'll lift a load of iron when we go up."

"Where will the iron be?" Dr. Zelbar asked.

"It's in the hold area under the floor," Catie said. "Normally it's in a few pallets here in the middle, so we don't have to pump it, but we're making an exception this time. It's so heavy that it only uses up a little space before we hit the lift capacity."

"How much of a weight allowance do we have?" Mrs. Michaels asked.

"Use what you need," Catie said, "we'll adjust the load to compensate. But, don't use too much water, it's kind of heavy."

"Don't worry, Dear, I'll just set up small trays," Mrs. Michaels assured Catie.

Dr. Zelbar was already measuring the space for the experiments.

"How long do we have to run the experiments?" Mrs. Zelbar asked.

"As long as you need, but the magic number is five hours. That's how long it takes for a round trip. If you can manage it in five, then we only lose one load," Catie explained.

"What other facilities do we have here?" Dr. Zelbar asked.

"There is a bathroom and a shower in the forward compartment," Catie said. "You can lay the couches down to take a nap if you wish."

"Power?" Dr. Zelbar asked, not really caring about the other facilities.

"I'd say as much as you can use. The Oryx main engines charge capacitors," Catie lied, avoiding telling them that the Oryx had a fusion reactor that charged the capacitors and that the capacitors ran the engines on this new Oryx that was designed to reach the asteroids. "They store the charge at ten thousand volts. We have inverters that will change that to whatever voltage you want."

"Excellent," Dr. Zelbar said. "It will sit here, and we can access whenever we want?"

"Yes," Catie said. "The inspections run twenty-four hours a day. We like to keep these things flying."

Mrs. Zelbar smiled at Catie. "I guess we won't be getting much sleep," she said with a little laugh.

"One last thing," Catie said. "We will keep everything pressurized during the time we are up there, but we would prefer for you to wear a shipsuit and have a helmet close by in case something happens. They're very light, and you can wear something over them if you want." Catie had worn her shipsuit so she could demonstrate, so she spun around to let them get a good look.

"Oh my, if I get one of those, I'll have to let Sophia get one," Mrs. Michaels said.

"A lot of kids are wearing them," Catie said. "I know Sophia wants one. Also, if anyone wants to go outside and do a spacewalk, you have to have a shipsuit and an exosuit. The chandler here in the hangar can get you outfitted. Catie reached up and twisted the dial on her suit. The suits have this little charging device on them that makes them looser so you can take them on and off." Catie showed everyone how much looser the suit was.

"Can't we just wear them like that?" Mrs. Michaels asked.

"I don't know," Catie said. "I'm not sure how long the charge will last, and you don't want it to run out, so you can't take the suit off."

"Cer Catie, the charges will last for two hours and can be exchanged with spares," ADI informed Catie.

"I've been informed that you have two hours before the charge runs out, and we can have spare disks to put on the suit," Catie said.

"That's nice," Mrs. Michaels said. "Then at least I can keep it loose until I get here and have it loose when I go home."

Mrs. Zelbar nodded in agreement. Dr. Zelbar just waved his hand, he obviously didn't care.

"And, so you're not surprised," Catie said, "you can't have anything on when they measure you for the suit. There's a nice private booth that you go inside. You just have to hold your arms out like this, and a laser does the measurement. Totally private."

"We're happy to wear the shipsuits," Mrs. Zelbar said. "They look comfortable. Leo, do you want to go outside?"

"No! We'll be floating around in here," Dr. Zelbar said. "I don't' need to go play around in vacuum."

"I don't think I'll want to go outside either," Mrs. Michaels said.

"Would your husband want to come?" Catie asked Mrs. Michaels. "He's seen pictures, but he might want to actually go up."

"I'll ask him and let you know," Mrs. Michaels said, relishing the idea of being the one who got to ask.

"One last thing," Catie said. "I have two friends I'd like to bring along. They're almost eleven, and they've been up several times before. But they're missing it. Would you mind if I brought them?"

"Oh, you must mean the twins," Mrs. Michaels said.

"Yes," Catie acknowledged.

"Why would we care?" Mrs. Zelbar asked.

"They can be quite inquisitive," Catie said. "You might find it annoying or disruptive. I can try to keep them out of your hair, but it's a limited space."

"I won't have any problem ignoring them," Dr. Zelbar said.

"I think it might be fun to have a couple of inquisitive kids around," Mrs. Zelbar said. "It will be like teaching college again."

"And they can be helpful," Catie said. "They are very adept in microgravity, so they can move things for you or get you things."

"Bring them," Mrs. Michaels said as she and Mrs. Zelbar nodded in agreement.

"One last thing, this is Marty Greene. He's one of the crew chiefs for the Oryxes, and he'll help you set up whatever you need in here," Catie said as Marty entered the Oryx in answer to Catie's page. "Marty, this is Dr. Nikola Zelbar, Dr. Leo Zelbar, and Mrs. Pam Michaels; everyone, this is Marty."

Nods and handshakes were exchanged all around. "His counterpart, Jackie Huffman, works the night shift, and she will take care of you while he sleeps," Catie explained. "Call me if you need anything."

"We will," Mrs. Zelbar said.

"Do you guys want to go with me Thursday when I take the Oryx up?" Catie asked.

"Yes!" the twins said.

"Do you need new shipsuits?"

"We've grown two inches," the twins said.

"That would be a yes, then."

"Yes!"

"Now, you two have to be nice. I'm taking Mrs. Michaels and the Zelbars up so that they can run experiments," Catie said. "They're going to be very busy, and you have to stay out of their way."

"We can help."

"I'm sure you can, but you have to wait for them to ask."

"Okay," the twins said. "Will you let us go outside?"

"Of course," Catie said.

"Can we go see the asteroids?"

"No, not this time. It takes a whole day to get there," Catie said. "We won't have enough time. Maybe next time."

"Boo!"

"You need to remember to keep our secrets," Catie said. "You can't talk about Mars or the asteroids. If they ask you when you were in space, just say in the summer."

"Okay," the twins said.

"Now finish your homework, and then Nattie will take you to get new shipsuits."

While Catie was waiting for the Zelbars and Mrs. Michaels to install their experiments in the Oryx, she settled into doing a layout for the Vancouver Integrated Technologies offices and labs in Delphi City. She had to do the actual work instead of handing it off to ADI so that she could get credit for a college drafting class and a business planning class she was taking.

"Hello, Admiral Michaels," Catie greeted the admiral as he and Mrs. Michaels entered the Oryx. "I thought you would want to come along."

"Wouldn't miss it," the admiral said.

"Hi, Mrs. . . ." Catie said. Mrs. Michaels held up her finger at Catie, and Catie finished with, "Pam. Are you ready?"

"Yes, I am," Mrs. Michaels said.

"What did Sophia think of the shipsuit?" Catie asked with a grin. She noticed that Mrs. Michaels was wearing hers with the charging disc engaged, so the suit was loose.

"She cannot wait until the market opens tomorrow so she can buy one," Mrs. Michaels said.

Catie laughed at that. "And here are the Zelbars," she said. "Hello, Nikola, Dr. Zelbar."

"Hello, Catie," Mrs. Zelbar said. She was also wearing her suit loose. Both her husband and the admiral were wearing theirs tight.

Catie closed both doors of the airlock once they were all inside.

"Oh, were we the last ones?" Mrs. Zelbar asked.

"Yes, the twins were here to go through all the preflight checks," Catie said. "They're in the cockpit doing them again."

"The young are so enthusiastic," Mrs. Michaels said. "Is it time for us to get strapped in?"

"Yes," Catie said. "We'll start taxiing as soon as you are."

"Is there room in the cockpit for me?" Admiral Michaels asked.

"There will be as soon as I kick the twins out," Catie said.

"I wouldn't want to take their spot," the admiral said.

"You're not. There's only room for one more person, and they never split up if they don't have to," Catie explained. "Come on through once they come back."

Catie went through the cockpit airlock. Two minutes later, the twins came out chattering to each other. "Hi," they said as they slid into their seats.

Admiral Michaels cycled through the airlock into the cockpit. "You keep the airlock active even when you're on the ground?" he asked.

"Just this one. It has an override for equal pressure, but I don't like to use it," Catie said. "Just cautious."

"Just smart is what I'd say," Admiral Michaels said.

"Sit in the navigator seat," Catie said. "We are starting to taxi now," Catie announced over the ship intercom. "You know Liz. You two can switch seats once we're in orbit if you want."

"Yes, I do," the admiral said as he strapped in.

Catie spun the Oryx around. "Tower, Oryx Ten, requesting permission for runway one."

The tower granted permission, and Catie taxied onto the runway. She taxied down to the end, then spun the Oryx around again and prepared to take off.

"Tower, Oryx Ten, requesting permission for takeoff," Catie called to the tower.

"Oryx Ten, you are clear for takeoff. You have a thirty-minute window with clear skies."

"What does that mean?" Admiral Michaels asked.

"That the next Oryx to take off from the airport is thirty minutes behind us," Catie said. "We all take off on pretty much the same vector, so it's nice to know how big a gap you have."

"I see."

"Prepare for takeoff," Catie announced over the ship intercom. "Tower, Oryx Ten, taking off." Catie brought the engines up to full speed and released the brakes. The Oryx shot down the runway, building speed. Catie used up most of the runway before she lifted the nose up and took off.

"Nice takeoff," Liz said.

"Thanks. It's nice to have that extra four hundred meters," Catie said.

"You mean you used to take off on a shorter runway?" the admiral asked.

"Oh yes," Catie said. "It was more exciting, but pilots kept wasting fuel, so Uncle Blake hurried to add another quad and give it the extra length."

"More exciting," the admiral muttered. "How long does it take to reach orbit?"

"It will take us about thirty minutes to reach orbit, then we have to adjust our speed to catch up to the station," Catie explained. "We try to avoid going too close to the ISS."

"You do know they're probably watching you via satellite," the admiral said.

"Oh, we know, they have one parked right over the airport," Liz said. "We thought about just grabbing it," she added with a laugh.

"Oh, you wouldn't want to do that," Admiral Michaels said.

"Why, do you think they have a self-destruct?" Liz asked, still laughing.

"No, but the president might," Admiral Michaels said.

"I bet he would," Liz said. "It's just funny to think about."

"You have a strange sense of humor," the admiral said.

"She sure does," Catie said. "Liz, you're supposed to be taking readings for me."

"I am," Liz said. "I've been texting them to your HUD."

"Oh, I see them now," Catie said. "Thank you."

"Do you see the jet tracking us at two o'clock?" Liz asked.

"Yes," Catie said. "We'll leave him behind in about three minutes. They've figured out our takeoff pattern and keep sending a jet to track us every once in a while."

"What do you think they're trying to figure out?" Admiral Michaels asked.

"I think it's our top speed in atmosphere," Catie said. "But we hit the stratosphere before we ever top out, so they're wasting their time. Wave goodbye."

"Back to your speed, how can you reach orbit that fast?" the admiral asked.

"Typically, it takes longer," Catie said. "But this Oryx has special engines, so we're burning extra fuel to get there faster. That way we can maximize the time for the experiments, plus, part of the checkup we do on them is a max burn acceleration."

"Hmm," the admiral mused. He knew they weren't telling him everything, but he could understand their reticence.

"Liz, are you okay to switch with the admiral?" Catie asked twenty minutes later. "We're now officially in orbit."

"Sure," Liz said. "You ready to switch, Admiral?"

"Yes, thank you," the admiral said. "This is an amazing view. Oh, we're at zero gravity," the admiral said with surprise.

"You didn't notice the transition?" Catie asked. "We cut the acceleration real slow so that it doesn't affect people too much, but I've never had anyone not notice. But you should notice a little gravity since we're still climbing up in our orbit."

"I guess I was distracted," the admiral said. "Can you check on my wife?"

"Just talk to her on your HUD," Catie said. "But Natalia told me that everyone in back handled the transition well."

The admiral finished changing seats with Liz, then he had a short conversation with his wife. It was made short by the fact that his wife and the Zelbars were already heading into the cargo bay to get their experiments running.

"Okay, so are we in the same orbit as your Space Station?" the admiral asked.

"We're a little lower," Catie said. "We're still catching up, so we're going faster and rising in our orbit. We'll match orbits as we get close."

"But it doesn't affect their experiments?" he asked.

"They just care about zero gravity," Catie said. "Gives them an extra hour of test time."

"How long are we up here for?" the admiral asked. "Pam wouldn't tell me."

"They think they'll be done at six hours, the hour to get there and the five hours we've tentatively allocated," Catie explained. "But it depends on how the experiments run. I think the Zelbars are the key; they have the most complex experiments. But some of them we'll leave at the space station, and they'll run them remotely."

"I hear they want to move up to the station," Liz said.

"They sure do," Catie said. "They'd move up there now if we'd let them."

"What's the holdup?" the admiral asked.

"Until we finish the first ring, we're not really set up for permanent guests," Catie said. "We've got limited space and only one-half-G of gravity. Liz, how long 'til we have the ring ready for habitation?"

"We're halfway through the extrusion," Liz said. "Give us one week to finish that, then we have to attach the shafts, stop the rotation, push the ring into position, weld it all together, add atmosphere, and then we can start putting in the infrastructure so people can live there."

"I'm sure you have to do all that," Catie said. "But I asked how long, not what you have to do."

Liz leaned forward and punched Catie on the shoulder. "A little respect and recognition are all I ask for. Anyway, the answer is four weeks."

"How can you do it that fast?" the admiral asked with amazement.

"We have one hundred workers up there now," Liz said.

"I thought you couldn't have permanent guests," the admiral said.

"They're not guests, and it's a little primitive," Liz said. "We're just putting in a treatment system to handle all the waste. In fact, Natalia is up here to check on it and make sure they're doing it right. She's going to stay for a week to get it up and running."

"Maybe I should go back and check on Pam," the admiral said.

"I'll go with you," Catie said, "that is if you're okay taking over, Liz?"

"I'm okay with it," Liz said. "I'll review some reports and prepare for my inspection."

Catie popped her straps off and pushed herself out of her seat. She floated up, and then she slowly fell as the microgravity pulled her toward the back of the cockpit. She cycled through the airlock, leaving the admiral to figure things out on his own.

"Hi, Catie," the twins said as she entered the crew compartment.

"Hi, did they chase you up here?" Catie asked.

"No, we were waiting for you," they said.

"Remember what we talked about," Catie said. "Let's go back and see how they're doing."

"Okay!"

When they cycled through the airlock, they found Natalia guarding the door. "Are you making sure nobody sneaks in?" Catie asked.

"Just making sure certain people are escorted while they're back here," Natalia said as she winked at the twins.

"Catie already told us what we have to do," the twins said.

"That's good, then I don't have to worry about you," Natalia said. "But I probably have to worry about the admiral."

"Yes, you do," the twins said. "Here he comes."

The admiral cycled through the lock, carefully holding onto something to keep himself oriented.

"Your boots have magnetics in them; if you clench your toes; they'll turn on," Natalia said. "They'll keep you on the deck."

The admiral clinched his toes right away, "That was easy, thanks."

The twins just sailed down the length of the cargo bay, using their arms to make minor adjustments to their flight. They bounced off the ceiling once and landed next to the Zelbars. Catie followed them, although not as gracefully.

"Hi," the twins said to the Zelbars. "What are you testing?"

"I'm trying to prove that we can make transparent polysteel," Nikola Zelbar said.

"Is it working?" the twins asked.

"It looks like it is," Nikola said. "But I have to run a bunch of tests to see how thin we can make it, and how thick we can make it."

"Thin would be nice, like on our Comms," the twins said.

"Yes, if we can make it thin enough, then we could use it for glass on your Comms and people's phones," Nikola said. "Then your glass wouldn't scratch or break if you dropped your phone."

"That would be nice," the twins said. Catie, who was standing behind them, gave a silent sigh of relief that the twins didn't point out that the glass on their Comms already couldn't be scratched or broken.

"What else are you working on?" the twins asked.

"Those are tests to see how thin we can make it," Nikola said as she pointed to two other experiments. "And this is testing to see if we can tune the plasma field so that the nickel will separate from the iron and not foul up the polysteel."

"Why are you doing that?" the twins asked.

Nikola gave Catie a curious glance before she replied. "Because some of our iron has nickel mixed in it. And we don't want to have to separate the nickel out before we run it through the plasma field." Catie kept a straight face; she and the twins both knew the primary source of nickel-iron alloy was meteorites, or more precisely, asteroids.

"What is he doing?" they asked as they pointed to Dr. Zelbar.

"Oh, he is trying to see if we can make flexible polysteel," Nikola said. "He's been thinking it should be possible if we leave a little hydrogen in the mix. He's hoping it will be like Kevlar. Do you know what Kevlar is?"

"Yes," the twins said. "They use it in armor vests."

"That's right," Nikola said. "If it works, they could make better exosuits for you; it would be more flexible than the ones you wear, or at least we could reinforce the joints better."

"Cool," the twins said. "What's he working on now?" they asked as Dr. Zelbar moved to another table.

"That's his superconductor," Nikola said. "He's been working on it for weeks; now he needs to see if he can really make it. Like transparent polysteel, it can only be made in space."

"Supercool," the twins said with a giggle at their play on words.

"What's that one doing?" the twins asked, pointing to another experiment that Nikola was running.

"That's the one where I'm trying to make really thick transparent polysteel, and that one is for really thin," Nikola said. "When they finish, I'll test them to see how much thicker or thinner I can make it."

"Oh, a boundary condition experiment," the twins said. "We're doing those in our chemistry class."

"Do you like chemistry?" Nikola asked.

"Yeah, it's pretty fun," the twins said. "We did experiments with sulfur last week. Boy did they stink."

"Yes, sulfur does have an obnoxious odor," Nikola said.

"Ha, it works!" Dr. Zelbar exclaimed.

"Yay!" the twins cheered.

"Oh, Leo, we knew it would," Nikola said. "What temperature is the substrate at?"

"Just twenty-five C," Dr. Zelbar said. "I'm starting to raise it now."

"Can we watch?" the twins asked.

"As long as you promise not to touch anything," Dr. Zelbar said.

"We promise," the twins said as they hopped up to the ceiling and pushed themselves back to the floor right next to Dr. Zelbar.

"Oh, they are so cute," Nikola said. "But I do want to trip them when they make it look so easy."

"And you haven't seen them with their spacesuits, running around outside," Catie said. "That'll really make you jealous."

"And tripping them doesn't work," Natalia said. "Believe me, I've tried. They just adjust and keep going."

Catie and Nikola laughed at that. "I'll go keep an eye on them," Catie said. "Holler if you need help." Catie did the same maneuver the twins did and landed behind them.

"Thirty," one twin said. "Zero ohms," the other said.

Dr. Zelbar was slowly turning up the temperature of the substrate that the superconductor was deposited on.

"Thirty-one."

"Zero ohms."

"I think you should go faster," the twins said.

"You do, do you? What if I break it?" Dr. Zelbar asked.

"Then you can make another," the twins said. "But you'll know where to start then."

"Okay, take that," Dr. Zelbar said as he dialed up the temperature setting.

"Thirty-five."

"Zero ohms."

"Fifty-two."

"Zero ohms."

"Seventy."

"Zero ohms."

"One hundred."

"Zero ohms."

"One fifty."

"Zero ohms."

"One seventy."

"Zero ohms . . ." the second twin said as she looked at the dial carefully.

"One eighty."

"Not zero ohms," the second twin said.

"Well, how much is it?" Dr. Zelbar asked.

"A lot of zeros then a one," the twin said as she started counting zeros.

"Push this button," Catie said, "and it will tell you how many zeros."

The twin pushed the button, "It says 1.2, E minus ten."

"Now, what does it say?" Dr. Zelbar asked as he dialed the temperature up some more.

"Two hundred."

"9.1, E minus five," the second twin said.

"Now?"

"Two hundred ten."

"2.5, E minus four," the second twin said.

"Now?"

"Two hundred fifteen."

"7.3, E minus four."

"Two hundred twenty."

"2.1, E minus three."

Dr. Zelbar walked the temperature back down to one seventy C as the twins kept calling out the readings. The impedance came back down to zero, following the curve almost precisely.

"That's good," Dr. Zelbar said. "It comes back down to zero, so it doesn't get damaged."

"What happens if it gets cold?" the twins asked.

"That is an excellent question," Dr. Zelbar said. "It should just stay at zero, but we should check, don't you think?"

"Yes, we should," the twins said. "You always have to verify your assumptions."

"That is correct, now how do we make it cold?" he asked.

"You could just take it outside," the twins said. "It would get cold real fast."

"But what if I don't want to go outside?" Dr. Zelbar asked.

"We could take it outside for you," they volunteered.

"I'll keep that in mind," Dr. Zelbar said. "But there must be a way to cool it off in here."

"There is a cooling terminal right behind that panel," Catie said. "It connects to a radiator on the hull, so it should be getting nice and cold by now."

"Thank you," Dr. Zelbar said. "Now I need some heavy wire to connect it so we can start cooling this substrate down."

"There's some in the front," the twins said. "Do you want us to get it for you?"

"That would be nice," Dr. Zelbar said as he watched the twins rocket off toward the front of the bay. They were back in a flash, giving him one end of the wire and uncoiling it to the panel Catie had pointed out.

Catie was impressed as she watched the twins patiently wait for the doctor to finish connecting his end. They continued to wait patiently while he examined everything about his setup before giving them the word to plug their end in. They had even tied it up so that it went up to the ceiling and across to the panel, coming down the wall, so nobody could trip on it or accidentally knock it loose.

Once the substrate cooled below minus sixty C, both the twins and Dr. Zelbar lost interest. Dr. Zelbar left the experiment to run on its own while he went back to his flexible polysteel experiment. The twins decided to check in on Mrs. Michaels for a while. Mrs. Michaels had just finished explaining all of her experiments when Liz announced that they were approaching the space station. Everyone quickly made their way back into the crew compartment since it had windows, an addition that Catie had made to the second run of Oryxes.

"There it is," the twins said with awe. "It's really big."

"I thought you two had been up here before," Admiral Michaels said.

"Not since it's been finished," Catie said to cover the fact that the twins got all their space-time on the asteroid mission. Although the admiral knew about the asteroids, his wife and the Zelbars didn't. "That partial ring really makes it look bigger," Catie added as she pointed out the four sections of the ring that were being extruded. They were all about forty-five degrees through their arc or about halfway.

"What will happen when they start meeting up with each other?" the admiral asked.

"The form is designed so that the inside part will just slide into the next section," Catie said. "The plasma guns will weld them together, then stop."

"How do you get the form out?" the admiral asked. "You wouldn't want to waste it, would you?"

"We have to cut it in half to get it out," Catie explained. "Once they cut it in half, they can then slide it through the holes that were left for the elevator spokes. If you look closely, you can see the discoloration that's coming out of the form now. That's where the hole is. They slide a piece of foam in as the form moves to make the hole."

"You sure know a lot about it," Mrs. Michaels said.

"That's because she's the one who figured out how to make it," Natalia said.

"You did?" Admiral Michaels asked.

"Only partially, I only told them they should extrude it," Catie said while blushing. "They had to figure out all the hard stuff."

"Don't be so modest," Natalia said. "Your Uncle Blake said it cut months off of the schedule for the station."

"They would have gotten there," Catie said. "I just figured it out first. Hey, we're actually going to dock to the station," Catie said to change the subject. "If you want to, you can go inside. It's pressurized, and you can even go into the area that's spun up, it has one half-G of gravity."

"I might do that," Admiral Michaels said. "What do you think, Pam?"

"I'll be happy to join you," Mrs. Michaels said. "I know the Zelbars are planning to go see the place. They're working on setting up a lab there."

"What are you going to do?" Admiral Michaels asked Catie.

"The twins and I are joining Liz on her inspection. We're going to check out the new ring and the elevator shafts they're extruding," Catie said. "After that, we'll come inside to check out the latest construction. Nattie will take care of you guys and make sure you get around okay."

Catie walked over to the Zelbars who were having an in-depth discussion about the space station construction. "How are you two doing?" Catie asked when she approached.

"We're doing fine," Nikola said.

Dr. Zelbar huffed at that. "Can you tell me why you have me working on a high-temperature superconductor when you already have one?" he asked.

Catie knew it was a bad idea to bring Dr. Zelbar up in the Oryx, but her father had agreed to it. "The one we have is a thick-film superconductor," Catie said. "We have you working on a thin-film one," Catie lied. The one that Dr. Zelbar had detected was a thick-film one, but they did have a thin-film one they were going to use in the semiconductors they were getting ready to manufacture.

"Am I wasting my time?" Dr. Zelbar asked.

"I don't think so," Catie said. "Your process for the one you're working on looks very promising compared to what we have." In this case, Catie was telling the truth. The Zelbars' formula and process for transparent polysteel were far better than what the Paraxeans, the aliens that had built the Sakira, had. And they had never developed flexible polysteel. ADI had also told her that the process and formula for the superconductor were promising to be thinner than the one they already had, which would be a big boost for the computer chip designs.

"You wouldn't lie to me?" Dr. Zelbar asked while giving Catie a steely look.

"Only a little," Catie said. "But we are really looking forward to the results from your superconductor test. It looks like you might get down to atomic numbers for thickness."

"That is my plan," Dr. Zelbar said, feeling somewhat mollified.

"Aren't there going to be any windows?" Nikola asked. "Do you need the transparent polysteel to make them?"

"We wouldn't put windows in even if we had the transparent polysteel," Catie said. "Cameras and displays work better; that way, the scene won't be moving. Although the motion would be slow, it would still be disconcerting to some people. And as your husband pointed out, we're embedding a superconductor in the polysteel to convert the heat into electricity and transfer it to the power banks."

"Is that how these things can go up and down so often?" Dr. Zelbar asked.

"There are two reasons for that," Catie said. "First, we have the fuel to slow our reentry down; and second, we can absorb the heat from the reentry and convert it, so it drives our engines, which slows us down more."

"Clever," Dr. Zelbar said. "Okay, I'm going back to my experiments. We'll see you when you join us inside the station."

Catie and Liz went out to inspect the progress of the ring extrusion. The twins went with them to play, train, show-off, it was hard to tell. They did various acrobatics the whole time. They loved holding hands and using their thrusters to send them into a spin, their clasped hands at the center of the spin. Then they figured out that they could rush toward each other and grab hands just as they passed, causing them to spin. A few times of that and they quickly figured out that they could release and continue their flight in any vector in their common plane of travel.

"They look like Elroy from the Jetsons," Liz said.

"Who?" Catie asked.

"The Jetsons, it is an old cartoon from the sixties," Liz said. "You can watch it on the net."

"Why would I do that?" Catie asked.

"Because it's funny," Liz said. "Anyway, the son, Elroy, was always jetting around with a jetpack on his back."

"Just a second, I've got a call," Catie said. "Hello, Sophia, what's up?"

"I know you're doing some secret experiments with my parents up in one of those Oryxes," Sophia said. "I hope I'm not disturbing anything."

"Not really, just doing some paperwork," Catie lied.

"Anyway, that boy Frankie, from the party last week, asked David for your contact info. David wanted me to ask you if it was alright to give it to him."

"He couldn't ask me himself?" Catie asked.

"He knows better," Sophia said. "Now, what do you say? I told you he likes you."

"I don't know," Catie said. "I think he just wants a ride in a Lynx."

"Sure, keep lying to yourself. Should I have David give him your contact info?"

"Sure," Catie replied.

"Okay, and you have to tell me everything that happens," Sophia said.

"Happens when?"

"On your date with Frankie!"

"It's not a date!"

"Yeah, yeah, just tell me what happens."

"Okay," Catie said. "I have to run; they want me to help with one of the experiments. Bye, Sophia."

"Bye, Catie."

"What was that about?" Liz asked.

"One of the new boys at school is a pilot, and he wants a ride in a Lynx. He's never flown a jet before," Catie answered. "I guess I said I'd take him up."

"There's that new one that's going through certification now," Liz said. "We could grab its final test flight."

"Good idea," Catie said. "I'll do that."

"It's done, Cer Catie," ADI informed her.

"Thanks, ADI."

"This one looks fine," Liz said. "Let's go look at the next one."

"Which direction?" Catie asked.

"Clockwise!" the twins hollered as they were already jetting toward the next clockwise extrusion.

"Hello, Dr. Zelbar," Catie said as she and Liz entered the lab they were examining.

"Hello, Catie," Nikola answered for herself and Dr. Zelbar, who was engrossed in a discussion about how he wanted the lab set up with the crew foreman.

"How are you liking microgravity?" Catie asked.

"It's fine," Nikola said. "We haven't been in the spin section yet."

"Where's Natalia?" Catie asked.

"She's with the Michaelses, they wanted to go into the spin section. We said we would wait for you," Nikola answered.

"Make sure you call me," Catie said. "The transition into the spin section can be a bit tricky, especially since we're spinning it so fast now."

"Don't worry," Nikola said. "We should only be another twenty minutes."

"Okay, I'll go corral the twins and meet you back here," Catie said.

The twins were in the top section of the hub, in an unfinished area that didn't have any construction going on. They were playing tag, bouncing off the walls while only using their bounce and their hands to control their direction. Apparently, it was too easy to catch someone using thrusters. Catie discovered that after being ignored for the third time, when she used her thruster to capture one of the twins.

"Okay, settle down," Catie said. "Do you guys always have to play?"

"We're not playing, we're training," the twins said. "We think you should leave this area like it is, so everyone can train here."

"Train for what?" Catie asked.

"To work in space, maybe even fight," the twins said. "Try to catch me, no thrusters," one of the twins said as she pushed off the wall.

Catie figured she shouldn't have any trouble catching the twin since she was bigger and could push off harder, so she would have more velocity. Ten minutes later, she was disabused of that notion. The twin could push off at impossible angles, and her ability to modify her flight with her hands was impressive. She could judge Catie's angle of flight and pick the one angle that would be the hardest for her to switch to when she hit the wall. Catie would go flying by her, and she'd be unable to bounce off the wall at the correct angle, causing her to lose far more distance than her stronger legs could make up.

"Okay," Catie gasped. "I'll talk to Liz and my dad and see if we can keep your training area."

"Yay!"

"Now let's go get the Zelbars and go into the spin section," Catie said.

"They wore you out," Liz said as she caught up with Catie. As her bodyguards, Liz or Natalia was always within reach of Catie. Of course, that meant she always had an audience whenever she did anything outside of her condo.

"Yes, but if we're going to live up here, we should probably try to emulate them and learn how to maneuver," Catie said.

"I'm not sure anyone over fifteen stands a chance," Liz said. "You might be able to catch up with them."

"I'm not sure," Catie said. "I think there's some natural talent involved, not just the youth factor."

"That'd be nice," Liz said. "I wouldn't have to feel so embarrassed then."

They gathered the Zelbars and made their way to one of the entry ports for the spin section. When they exited the port, they were floating above the floor of the spin section; it was ten meters below them and moving fast.

"Oh, this doesn't look good," Nikola said.

"It's not as bad as it looks," Catie said. "The floor is moving at about thirty miles per hour, or twenty-one meters per second. You wouldn't want to just hit it. But if you grab one of these straps and pull on it, it hooks onto the spin section by a spring and brings you up to speed slowly. Then it pulls you down to the floor, so you land like you just hopped off of a two-foot-tall step."

"You're sure about that?" Nikola asked.

"Of course," Catie said. "There are no walls in this area, so you won't hit anything. Let me have the twins demonstrate."

Catie turned to the twins, but they had just launched themselves toward the floor. They did a small flip in the air and bounced off of the surface, then landed a few feet later. They both turned and waved at Catie.

"Like I said, natural talent," Catie said to Liz.

"Or natural stupidity," Liz replied. "Here, I'll demonstrate." Liz grabbed one of the straps, she gave it a tug, and it engaged and pulled her off the ceiling. She had already rotated herself, so her feet were pointing down. She touched down on the surface about fifty meters from where she started, but she continued to move away from them as the surface kept rotating.

"That didn't look too hard," Dr. Zelbar said as he grabbed a strap. He landed about one hundred meters short of Liz.

"Oh, we'd better hurry," Nikola said as she grabbed a strap, and Catie grabbed one right behind her. By the time they landed, Liz had made up about half the distance to Dr. Zelbar, and they were slowly making their way back to them. The twins were doing a hop-run thing and were making up the distance very fast.

"Boy, you two are moving fast," Catie said to them when they caught up with everyone.

"Yeah, it only works going this direction, if you do it the other direction, it slows you down," they said.

"Hmm," Dr. Zelbar mused.

"Let's see where we are," Catie said as she checked her HUD to see where they were relative to the place where Natalia had told her to meet up. "Oh, it's not too far, just follow me," Catie said. "We'll go through here, so we don't have anyone landing on our heads."

They entered the built-up part of the spin section and followed the corridor for seventy meters before they came to the lounge where the Michaelses and Natalia were sitting.

"Any coffee for the rest of us?" Catie asked.

"Sure," Natalia said. "Who wants what?"

Both the Zelbars opted for coffee, and with everybody's order, Natalia and the twins went to the bar to get the drinks.

"It feels nice," Nikola said. "A bit awkward to walk, but I guess we're not used to weighing so little."

"Yes, this is a little more gravity than they have on the moon," Catie said.

"At least things stay where you put them," Admiral Michaels said. "And you can drink out of a regular cup."

"That is definitely nice," Nikola said.

"I thought you said you couldn't have people living here?" Dr. Zelbar said in a demanding tone.

"I said we weren't really set up for guests," Catie said with a sigh; she'd just had this conversation with the admiral.

"I don't see the problem," Dr. Zelbar said.

"We're not set up to recycle water and waste," Natalia said. "I'm here to put that system in. Plus, it's only one-fifth G, it's not good to be in that low a gravity for too long. We rotate the crew every two weeks."

"When will you be ready?" Dr. Zelbar demanded.

"Four weeks," Liz replied. "Catie is just as impatient as you are. And even then, you're only going to get one-half-G of gravity. We're over two months away from having a one-G environment."

"We would do fine at half a G for a couple of months," Dr. Zelbar said. "It would be nice on my old bones to be a bit lighter."

"We'll figure out how to make that work," Liz said, knowing from past experience that there was no dissuading Dr. Zelbar once he had his mind made up.

"Good," Dr. Zelbar said. He picked his cup of coffee up and moved over next to Catie.

"Hi, Dr. Zelbar," Catie said as he sat down.

"Hi, yourself," Dr. Zelbar whispered. "Now tell me, where do you have your asteroids?"

"What asteroids?" Catie asked as she tried to keep the shock from showing on her face.

"Don't worry, nobody slipped up," Dr. Zelbar said. "But you can't be building those last two rings that fast unless you have a couple of asteroids close by."

Catie just shook her head, "We've got three," she said. "They're about two degrees ahead of Earth in the same orbit."

"Oh, you didn't want a bunch of astronomers crying the sky is falling?"

"Right."

"I assume the third one is ice."

"Yes, for water, hydrogen, and oxygen," Catie said.

"You know, the more you tell me, the more I can help," Dr. Zelbar whispered. "Now do you think they've finished moving our stuff to the lab?"

"They should be close," Catie said. "I assume you want to check everything out before we head back."

"That would be correct," Dr. Zelbar said. "Come on Niki, let's see if they've done it right."

137

Three hours later, they were finally on the ground saying goodbye to each other. Liz and Catie took the twins home with them. Their mother would pick them up when she got off work. Catie was wondering how her father was going to take it when she explained how much Dr. Zelbar knew.

16   Know-it-All

"You ready for this?" Liz asked Catie. Catie was taking Frankie up in the Lynx; Liz was going to be her copilot, wingmate, and bodyguard.

"It's just a test flight," Catie said.

"Keep telling yourself that," Liz said. "And where is that guy? For someone anxious to get a ride in a Lynx, he's not very punctual."

"He's only fifteen minutes late," Catie said.

"He should have been early," Liz countered.

"There he is," Catie said as Frankie turned the corner into the hangar.

"About time," Liz said.

"Hi, Frankie," Catie called out as she waved.

Frankie waved back as he sauntered over. "Hi," he said as he eyed Liz.

"This is Liz, my copilot," Catie said. "She's also a good friend."

"Hi," Frankie said, looking a bit disappointed at the thought of a copilot.

"Once we're airborne and complete the test," Catie said, "you and Liz can swap for a while."

"Cool," Frankie said.

"Well, let's get this show on the road," Liz said as she turned and headed into the Lynx.

Frankie and Catie followed her. "You can strap in here," Catie said. "It'll take about forty-five minutes to finish the test. Do you have something to read?"

"Sure," Frankie said, pulling his phone out of his pocket. "Hey, can you get me some specs?" he asked. He only had one of their modified phones, without the specs and earwig, since they were in short supply and allocated to critical personnel and a few close associates.

"We don't have very many available," Catie said, "manufacturing issues. But I'll check. We should be solving the manufacturing problem soon, then everyone will get them."

"Thanks," Frankie said, clearly assuming Catie would get him a set.

Catie made her way into the cockpit as Frankie strapped in. They were in the air in minutes. "Is he okay back there?" Liz asked.

"I think so," Catie said. "Apparently, he thought he'd be the copilot."

"He seems to think a lot of himself," Liz said as she looked at the display showing the main cabin. "It looks like he's playing some kind of game on his phone," she scoffed, clearly thinking that there were better uses of his time.

"Well, he has some time to burn," Catie said. She agreed with Liz about better uses of time but felt she needed to defend Frankie.

"Would you switch with Frankie?" Catie asked after they had finished fifty minutes of tests.

"Sure," Liz said as she unstrapped. She headed back to the main cabin.

"Hey," Frankie said as he slid into the copilot's seat.

"Hey, yourself," Catie said. "Sorry, it took so long. We had a long list of tests to do."

"No problem," Frankie said. "Can I fly it?"

"Let me show you the various controls," Catie said.

Catie walked him through the controls; she could tell that he was only half paying attention, but she persisted. Once she'd finished the list, she nodded to Frankie to indicate that he should take hold of the yoke. "You have control," she said after she set her controls to be able to override anything that Frankie did.

Frankie just started to steer the plane, not bothering to acknowledge that he had taken control. Catie could tell he'd flown before; he had a pretty good touch with the yoke, keeping the Lynx level and smoothly executing some turns. "How fast are we going?"

"The airspeed indicator is right there," Catie said, pointing out where it was just like she had two minutes before.

"Oh," Frankie said. "I see, we're at Mach 0.7, can we go faster?"

"Yes, just push the throttle forward," Catie said.

Frankie pushed the throttle forward a little faster than Catie would have preferred. The Lynx gained speed, passing Mach one in almost no time. Frankie kept accelerating and climbing until they reached

Mach four. Catie was watching the radar and the skies, a little worried that Frankie didn't seem to be watching anything but what was in front of him.

"You need to be careful," Catie said. "When you're going this fast, you can come upon another plane broadside, and we're not under tower control in this airspace."

"I've got it," Frankie said, a little annoyed at being cautioned.

"Okay, let's turn around and head back," Catie said. "As we approach Delphi City, you'll need to slow back down to below Mach one."

"Already," Frankie whined.

"Yes," Catie said. "Liz and I still have a lot of paperwork to do, and the ground crew has to inspect the plane."

Frankie made a wide arcing turn and headed back to Delphi City. Catie was almost going to override his throttle when he finally started dialing back on the speed. "You'll need to switch with Liz for the landing," Catie said.

"Why? I can land this thing," Frankie argued.

"We're still on a test flight; the landing has to be observed by Liz, and I have to do it so we can fill out the reports," Catie said. She wasn't about to let Frankie land the Lynx. "If you want to become one of the Lynx pilots, you can sign up for simulator time and get certified," Catie said.

"Sure," Frankie said.

"I have control," Catie said as she took the yoke. Frankie just let go of the yoke and sat back in his seat with his arms crossed. "Liz," Catie called over the intercom, "we're about to land, so you need to come back."

Liz immediately knocked on the cockpit door and entered. Frankie very slowly unstrapped and crawled out of the copilot's seat, making the point that he didn't think he should have to swap out.

"That boy doesn't seem happy," Liz said once Frankie had exited the cockpit and the door was closed.

"He thought he should be able to land it," Catie said.

"You're not serious?" Liz gasped. "He sure has an abundance of confidence."

"Yes, he does," Catie said. "He was pretty smooth on the yoke, though."

"Let's set this baby down," Liz said. "I have a date tonight."

"With Logan?" Catie squealed.

"Yes, the man is persistent," Liz said. Logan was the British spy that was trying to gather intel on MacKenzie Discoveries by dating Liz. Liz was enjoying the attention, but not providing much intel of value.

"Maybe he just likes you," Catie said.

"Like Ying Yue just likes Blake," Liz countered.

"She might like him," Catie said. "Just because she's a Chinese spy doesn't mean she can't like him."

"And Natasha just loves Kal."

"Her name is Sasha," Catie said.

"Sure, but I like Natasha, it's a better name for a Russian spy."

"Why?"

"Boris and Natasha," Liz said. "Haven't you ever watched a Rocky and Bullwinkle cartoon?"

"Never heard of them."

"They're available on the net, a good laugh while you're working out," Liz said. "You should watch a few."

"Cer Catie, they are funny," ADI cut in.

"You've watched them?" Liz asked with surprise.

"Just now," ADI said. "I've compiled a short video of the best outtakes with Boris and Natasha for you, Cer Catie. I will send it to your Comm, I'm sure you will enjoy them."

"Thanks, ADI."

"You're welcome," ADI replied.

"Okay, are you landing this thing or what?" Liz asked.

"We're on approach," Catie said. "Hold your horses, Logan will wait."

Once they landed and taxied to the hangar, Liz did the shutdown while Catie went to the main cabin to let Frankie out of the plane. "What did you think?" she asked.

"It's a hot jet," Frankie said. "I could really see me flying it. But I'd rather fly a combat jet."

"We don't have any of those," Catie lied. "You'll have to settle for the Lynx if you want to fly with MacKenzie."

"I guess," Frankie said. "Do you want to go to dinner?"

"I can't," Catie said. "We have over an hour of paperwork to do before we're done, and I've got work to do tonight with my uncle." Catie didn't want to tell Frankie that since Liz had a date, she didn't have a bodyguard available tonight, so she was kind of grounded.

"Can't she do the paperwork for you?" Frankie asked.

"No . . . it takes both of us to fill it out," Catie said. "We have to sign each other's reports."

"Then you owe me a dinner," Frankie said.

"Sure," Catie said. "Maybe next week."

"Daddy," Catie said as she came into her father's study.

"Hey, Sweetie, what's up?" Marc asked.

"I need to talk to you about Dr. Zelbar," Catie said.

"What about the old coot?" Marc asked.

"Well, he kind of figured a lot of stuff out when we went up to the space station," Catie said.

"I was afraid of that. What did he figure out?"

"He figured out that we already have a superconductor. I explained to him that his superconductor was a thin-film one versus the thick-film one we're using. His actually does look better than our existing thin-film one."

"Okay, that's not too bad; was he upset?"

"Just a little," Catie said. "He also figured out we had to have asteroids."

Marc gave a big sigh, "I assume he heard the build schedule."

"Yes, it is kind of obvious if you think about it."

"Sure," Marc said. "Anything else?"

"He wants to move up to the station as soon as he can. Liz promised him one month."

"That will work," Marc said, "Anything else . . . ?"

"I think he's pretty suspicious about everything. He said the more we tell him, the more he can help," Catie said.

"I'll have to think about bringing him into the thick of it," Marc said. "Maybe we should have him on the board."

"Nikola on the board would be better," Catie suggested.

"Yeah, that's definitely a better choice," Marc said, smiling at the thought of the board having to deal with crotchety old Dr. Zelbar. "Anything else?"

"Yes," Catie said tentatively, "Daddy, am I a know-it-all?"

"Why would you ask that?"

"I overheard some kid say that about me." Catie had gotten Sophia to tell her what the kids at school said about her. She was a little hurt that they had that kind of attitude, especially since she didn't spend that much time with them. She wondered where they got it from.

"Well, you do tend to know everything," Marc said, thinking that her eidetic memory was a double-edged sword.

"You know that's not what it means."

"No, I don't think you're a know-it-all," Marc said.

"Come on," Catie pleaded.

"Okay, you're young, and as a young person, you're not very patient."

"What does that mean?"

"When someone asks a question or says something that's incorrect, you're very quick to answer or correct them. The rest of the people in the conversation are still processing the question by the time you answer."

"So?"

"Well, other people might think you're trying to show off how smart you are. You should try waiting to see if someone else has the answer. Think of yourself as the backstop. If nobody can figure it out, then you help the group move forward."

"Hmm," Catie mused. "But doesn't that mean the meetings will take longer?"

"Like I said, impatient. If time is truly critical, then don't wait. But time's usually not that critical, and getting back to your latest project with ADI doesn't count."

"Thanks, Daddy. I'm going to try that."

17   Board Meeting – Oct 14th

"I call the meeting to order," Marc said. "Why don't we get an update on what's happening with the space station?"

"We are getting plenty of material," Liz said. "We started extruding the first ring last week, and it should be done by the end of this week. After that, it will take three to four weeks to make it habitable."

"That's good, I hear we have some very impatient people who are ready to move," Marc said. Catie giggled at his quip.

"So I've been told," Liz said. "Natalia has the treatment plant up. She's still tuning it, but it should be finished this week. She seems to be taking to the new job with enthusiasm."

"She has, Tomi really likes working with her. He says she learns fast and doesn't make mistakes," Catie said. "And she goes into space and lets him stay down here."

Blake chuckled, "I hear that was his first criterion for an assistant."

"Catie?" Marc prompted.

"Nikola figured out how to separate the nickel from the iron as we feed it into the polysteel plasma," Catie said. "That means we can now get most of our material from the asteroids. I'm having all but four of the Oryxes fitted with the space engines and reassigned to asteroid trips. We can always bring them back to doing lifts when we have a lot of material to lift."

"But that causes another issue," Fred said. "We're out of pilots who are cleared for knowing about the asteroids, as well as low on pilots due to the rotation rules for long- term space."

"That issue will ease itself when we have the first ring complete," Liz said. "Then we can increase the spin, so we'll have more gravity up there. If we go to 1.9 revs per minute, we'll have one-G in the new ring. We can slow it down when we put the next ring in."

"Okay," Marc said. "I'm thinking we wait for the third ring to be finished before we attach the second. It's not like we're overwhelmed with people wanting to move up there. That way, we only have to stop the spin twice. What else, Catie?"

"Nikola has her process for transparent polysteel dialed in. We should be able to start making it soon. Then we can replace the glass on all the new Comms. People keep dropping them," Catie said. "Dr. Zelbar still has work to do on his superconductor, he thinks he can make it even thinner."

"How does thinner help us?" Liz asked.

"It's better for work on integrated circuits," Catie said. "Thinner means we can make it narrower too, so higher density circuitry."

"Oh, that's great," Liz said.

"Mrs. Michaels still has her grow pods running on the station. Last I checked with her, she said they were thriving. Are we ready to introduce the meat process?" Catie asked. "I'd be real happy to hand that off."

"Who would you hand it off to?" Marc asked.

"Mrs. Michaels," Catie said with a questioning glance at the admiral.

"Meat process?" Admiral Michaels asked.

"You might not remember," Marc said, "but we have a process that grows meat in a vat. We take a sample from a living animal, then we're able to grow that into a fully developed muscle. The process works great for any meat, but doesn't do well with bones, so no ribs."

"Just not yet," Catie said. "I think someone will be able to figure that out. But the process is kind of like growing roots," Catie said hopefully.

"You can ask her," Admiral Michaels said, "but I think she has her hands full with the hydroponic farming."

"Hey, one of our pilots is a farm boy with a degree in chemistry," Fred said. "Maybe he would be interested."

Catie looked at her father. "Sure, ask him," Marc said. "The meat process isn't all that secret, you showed the rabbi and the imam already."

Fred nodded to Catie as he texted the contact info to her.

"Anything else?" Marc asked.

"Not on the space station," Catie said.

147

"Go ahead anyway," Marc prompted.

"We have the office, lab, and manufacturing area for the Vancouver team ready," Catie said. "The construction crew is building it out now. It should be ready for them by next week."

"What grade did you get?" Blake asked.

"An A," Catie answered, her voice clearly indicating that he shouldn't have needed to ask.

"What about at the station?" Marc asked.

"We've got the space allocated and closed in," Liz said, "but they need to figure out how they want to arrange things as well as what equipment they need."

"Oh, that reminds me," Catie interrupted.

"What?" Marc asked.

"We need to move a few fabricators up there," Catie said. "They're going to need some custom machines and parts, plus we can make a few Comms."

"Okay," Marc said. "Why don't you move as many as you can."

"Okay, I'll need to wait for Natalia to get back first," Catie answered as she looked at Liz. Liz nodded that she would help.

"Blake, how are our miners doing?" Marc asked.

"They are loving it," Blake said. "I never would have thought a bunch of hillbillies from West Virginia would take to space so well."

"Don't let them hear you call them hillbillies," Kal said.

"That's what they call themselves," Blake said. "Anyway, they keep making improvements to the process. They've astounded me at how innovative they are."

"Why don't we set them up with some kind of share of the operation?" Samantha asked. "They're inventing new processes; they should share in the benefits."

"I'd be okay with that," Marc said. "How would we set it up?"

"Their salary plus ten percent of the value of the material they extract," Samantha said. "They'd need to form a company so that the profits can be distributed correctly."

"Okay, why don't you meet with Jimmy and set something up," Marc said.

Samantha nodded and made a note on her Comm.

"Admiral, where are you in your thinking about North Korea?" Marc asked.

"I think you need to come up with a way to declaw them," Admiral Michaels said.

"How would we do that?" Marc asked.

"First, they have two ballistic submarines. You were able to damage that Chinese submarine, could you do something similar to their two ballistic subs?" the admiral asked.

Marc sucked in a breath and grimaced. "I have sent a Fox to the submarines' home port," he said. "I've had it put a mine on one of them and am waiting for the second one to show up. We can only manage a few mines, so I don't know what to do about their other subs."

"Can't you make more mines?" the admiral asked.

"We can make lots of mines," Marc said. "It's the communication to control the mines that is the limiting factor. We have a very limited number of links, and we're a long way from being able to make more. And before you ask, we're not willing to share the details of the links."

The admiral shook his head, "That's fine, but do you lose the links with every mine?"

"No, we can recover the links," Marc said. "But then we have to put them on another mine and deploy it. A pretty slow process."

"If you can take out their two ballistic subs, you can deal with the others later, they're not that important," Admiral Michaels said. "Since you were able to take out their missile launch, is there any way you can prevent them from launching anything from North Korea?"

"We have already put that capability in place," Marc said. "What should we do?"

"If you just prevent any successful launch," Admiral Michaels said, "then without their ballistic subs, they wouldn't be able to threaten anyone besides China and South Korea. I wouldn't worry about China, and I'm not sure what to do about South Korea. What kinds of missiles can you stop?"

"It has to leave the atmosphere," Marc said. "We can't do anything about short-range missiles or cruise missiles."

"Then, I would suggest we take care of the submarines and launches. We'll have to depend on the US and China to keep them under control beyond that," Admiral Michaels said.

"Moving on, have you had any success with contacts in France?" Marc asked.

"I've put feelers out," Admiral Michaels said. "My previous contacts are still in place, and I'm getting a lukewarm response. But, at least it's not a cold response, so I'm hopeful."

"Okay, Sam, what about your contacts?" Marc asked.

"We've reached out to Mexico and Morocco using our established contacts. They have both responded positively. Mexico is very interested in a fusion reactor," Sam said. "And Kevin Clark is quite the diplomat. He's made contacts with India and Indonesia. He says he's optimistic they will recognize us. They're both very interested in getting fusion power, but they want assurances that it's real."

Marc nodded his head, "What about Germany?"

"Herr Johansson has a contact, but he recommends we wait until after we announce to connect," Samantha said.

"Blake, how are our preparations coming?" Marc asked.

"We've moved the airport," Blake said. "I started moving it last week. Interestingly nobody except the pilots has noticed. We'll start moving the city tomorrow. We don't have that much traffic to Rarotonga anymore since everyone either lives here or stays here for the entire week, but the ferry pilots will notice, and the passengers will notice the longer ride."

"You're moving the city?" Admiral Michaels asked.

"Outside the territorial limit," Marc explained. "We plan to announce our independence on Friday. We want to do it before we announce the fusion reactor, to short circuit any attempts to gain control after that announcement."

"Prudent," the admiral said. "What are you doing about a constitution?"

"Sam and I worked on a draft on our way to Paris and on the way back," Marc said. "I'll send it to each of you for review. Give Sam any suggestions or issues. She has a team of lawyers that she will work with to finalize it before we declare. You don't have to read it, but it is an interesting exercise in thinking about what laws should apply and how you prevent some of the issues we see with the current governments."

"Okay, anyone have anything else?" Marc asked.

"Yes, I have something," Samantha said. "We have an application from a large group of Russians who want to emigrate to Delphi City."

"Russians," Marc said with surprise.

"Yes, most of them are Jews, but not all. I think a Jewish rabbi set it up and collected applicants. Everyone in the group has high-level skills; a large percentage speak at least some English," Samantha continued.

"Any reason we should say no?" Marc asked.

"Captain," ADI interrupted on a private channel. "Based on my examination of their background, at least eight of them are likely Russian agents."

"Aren't you worried about Russian agents?" Admiral Michaels asked.

"Yes and no," Marc replied. "We've found that we can keep track of agents better if they're here."

"The Russians are quite adept at causing problems," Admiral Michaels said, "and they will undoubtedly try to smuggle arms in."

"How is your bet going with the miner?" Marc asked Blake.

"He's O for five," Blake said. "I think he's decided to give up since the next one will cost him."

"Better we learn their methods when we're watching," Marc said.

———

"As long as you understand the risk," the admiral said.

"Then let them in," Marc said to Samantha.

"Okay," Samantha said. "There are some really good people in this group."

"Are we ready to adjourn now?" Marc asked.

His answer came as everyone got up and started to leave.

"Daddy," Catie said once the room was clear.

"Yes," Marc replied.

"I think you should talk to the Zelbars before you announce."

"That's a good idea," Marc said. "Why didn't you bring it up in the meeting?"

"I thought you should decide on your own," Catie said. "It's more personal with them than anyone else."

"Thank you."

"Hello, I'm Catie," Catie greeted Vince Clark. "Mr. Clark, are you any relation to Kevin and Jason Clark?"

"I don't think so," Vince said. "It's just a common name. Call me Vince. Fred tells me you have a farming job you'd like me to help with."

"Not exactly," Catie said. "But it is a little like hydroponic farming."

"What'd ya need?"

"I'm not sure you know, but we actually grow our meat," Catie said.

"We farmers usually say raise, but grow works," Vince said.

"No, I mean, we actually grow our meat, in vats."

"You've got me a bit confused there, what kind of vats?"

"We start with a piece of muscle, put it in a vat, and flood the vat with artificial blood. That carries the nutrients to the muscle, and it grows," Catie explained. "Eventually, veins, arteries, and nerves grow from the base tissues, and we keep pumping the blood like a heart would and stimulate the muscle via the nerves.

"We harvest the meat every few months, then close the vat back up and let it grow some more. We have to restart the vat every year to keep it all fresh."

"Well, that doesn't sound natural," Vince said.

"I'm sure domesticating animals didn't sound natural to the early hunters, but someone persisted."

"You got me there," Vince said with a chuckle. "I guess nothing new sounds natural. So what do you need me for?"

"We need someone to manage the vat farm," Catie said. "And we need someone to improve the process."

"Improve it how?"

"Right now, we can only grow muscle tissue and fat," Catie said. "We can electrically stimulate the muscle and vary how dense the meat is. But we can't grow anything with a bone."

"Now, no T-bone steaks, that's really not natural," Vince said. "And a man's gotta have some ribs every once in a while."

"Yeah, and a drumstick without the stick is kinda weird," Catie said.

"So, why me?"

"You have a chemistry degree and are familiar with farming. You need to understand the animal to decide which ones you should take samples from, and the growing process is all about chemistry."

"What kind of meat do you grow now?" Vince asked.

"We grow filet mignon, pork tenderloin, veal cutlets, ham, rump roast, chicken breast, and a couple types of warm-blooded fish," Catie said. "Of course, all of them are just the meat, no bones."

"You're telling me you'd like to add T-bones, ribs, pork chops, and drumsticks," Vince said.

"Yes, and some people like to use bones for certain recipes."

"Yeah, you need the odd soup bone now and again."

"Will you take the job?" Catie asked.

"Wait just one minute now," Vince said. "I'm not sure I'm cut out for this kind of work. I'm a pilot, not an office manager."

"You can keep flying," Catie said. "You might need to switch to every other rotation. And you actually have a lot of time on your hands when you fly, all that travel time as well as while the miners load your plane."

"But I was looking at switching to the Foxes now that you're making them."

"That's even better. Hopefully, you're just doing training," Catie said. "You'll have lots of time to do other things. You can hire someone to do most of the management chores, you just have to set the direction and goals."

"Who's doing all this now?" Vince asked.

"Me."

"If it's all that easy, why are you trying to pitch it off to me?"

"Because I have this, school, flying, a programming job, and all the stuff my dad gives to me. That's why we're not growing meat with bones. I don't have time to study the issue, so I keep putting it off. And we just started making fish. I was going to try and figure out how to grow cold-blooded fish," Catie added, "but I've been slow."

"Okay, okay. You're making me feel lazy 'cause all I do is fly," Vince said. "I'll give it a try. Can you help me find an administrator type?"

"We can send you a list of names. ADI will help you schedule the interviews, but you need to decide who you can work with."

"Okay, let's do it," Vince said. "I sure hope my pa doesn't hear about this; he might just disown me."

"Why?"

"This gets out, it'll put farmers out of business."

"Big corporations are already doing that. This would shift the focus to growing grains and vegetables for people to eat, as well as breeding the best animals for seeding the vats."

"That might work," Vince said. "I still hope Pa doesn't find out."

"Oh, and if you can figure out how to grow eggs, you'll be a hero," Catie added as she showed Vince out.

"You forgot to mention park manager," Natalia said as she joined Catie after Vince left.

"I forgot about that one," Catie said.

18   Delphi Constitution

Article 1. Legislature of the Delphi Confederation

Section 1. Powers of the Legislature

The legislative power of the Confederation shall be vested in a Parliament, which shall consist of a Confederation Assembly and a Senate.

The Legislature shall have the power to enact all laws that affect the general populace.

No person shall serve in the Legislature who has not been a resident of their state for at least three years and who has not attained the age of majority as defined in this Constitution.

Any vacancies created in the Legislature may be filled by the executive of the State the position is from, but only until such time that an election may be held to fill it by vote of the people.

No member of the Legislature shall be exempted from any law which governs the people of the Confederation.

Each house of Parliament shall elect its own leaders based on a majority vote.

Section 2. The Confederation Assembly

The Confederation Assembly shall have members chosen every three years by the people of the Confederation States who are eligible to vote.

No person shall serve in the Assembly who has already served eight of the last ten years in the Assembly.

The Assembly seats shall be apportioned among the various States based on their population. There shall be no more than one Assembly Person for every one hundred persons residing in the State and no less than one Assembly Person per ten thousand persons residing in the State. The States shall apportion the Assembly districts based solely on the population and set the district boundaries based on a shortest perimeter algorithm.

Section 3. The Confederation Senate

The Confederation Senators from each State will be divided into two classes. Its members shall serve for a term of six years except for the first class whose first term shall be three years.

No person shall serve in the Senate who has been a member of the Senate for twelve of the last fifteen years.

Each State shall have not less than one Senator and no more than one Senator per one hundred thousand people. Senators shall be elected by the population of their State at large.

Section 4. Passage of new laws

All legislation except the budget must be a cohesive set of objectives to address issues of the Confederation. No amendments are to be added that are not directly related to the purpose of the legislation.

All bills which pass both houses are to be sent to the executive for signature. The executive must respond to the bill within ten days, or it shall become law as if signed by the executive.

If the law is vetoed by the executive, the Legislature by a vote of two-thirds majority may repass the legislation. The legislation shall then become law unless it is vetoed by the Monarch. There is no redress to a veto by the Monarch.

Changes to the tax established by the Monarch at the time this Constitution is enacted shall require two-thirds of the majority of both houses of Parliament and the approval of the executive.

The Parliament shall have the power to lay and collect taxes, duties, imposts, and excises, to pay the debts and provide for the common defense and general welfare of the Confederation. But all duties, imposts, and excises shall be uniform throughout the Confederation.

To borrow money on the credit of the Confederation;

To regulate commerce with foreign nations, and among the several States;

To establish a uniform rule of naturalization;

To coin money, regulate the value thereof, and fix the standard of weights and measures;

To promote the progress of science and useful arts, by securing for limited times to authors and inventors the exclusive right to their respective writings and discoveries;

To constitute tribunals inferior to the Supreme Court;

To declare war;

To make rules for the government and regulation of military forces;

To make all laws which shall be necessary and proper for carrying into execution the preceding powers, and all other powers vested by this Constitution in the government of the Confederation, or in any department or officer thereof.

Section 5. Impeachment and Censure

The Senate has the right to censure the Monarch or impeach the president and other executives in the government. By a two-fifths vote, the senate may demand a trial before the supreme court to determine if the president or the Monarch has broken their oath to the people. The Assembly will then appoint a prosecutor. The Chief Justice will act as judge and the other justices will act as jurors.

If convicted, the president or executive shall be removed from office. If the Monarch should be found guilty, they shall stand before the Assembly with video streaming to the people as the charges and verdict are read out.

Article 2. The President of the Delphi Confederation

Section 1. The Executive

The Monarch is the president of the Confederation. Succession of the Monarch shall be the sole purview of the Monarch. Should the Monarch abdicate, the president of the Confederation shall be decided by popular vote of the population of the Confederation by all persons eligible to vote. Presidents shall serve for one six-year term and may not stand for election while currently serving as president.

Section 2. Powers of the Executive

The president shall be commander-in-chief of the Militaries of the Confederation;

The president shall have executive authority over each of the executive departments;

The president shall have the power to make treaties with the approval of two-thirds of the Senate, excepting that the Monarch will require no such approval;

The president shall nominate, and by and with the advice and consent of the Senate, shall appoint ambassadors, other public ministers and consuls, judges of the Supreme Court, and all other officers of the Confederation, whose appointments are not herein otherwise provided for, and which shall be established by law; but the Parliament may by law vest the appointment of such inferior officers, as they think proper, in the president alone, in the courts of law, or in the heads of departments.

Article 3. Judiciary

Section 1. Judicial offices

The judicial power of the Confederation shall be vested in one Supreme Court, and in such inferior courts as the Parliament may from time-to-time establish. The judges, both of the supreme and inferior courts, shall hold their offices for ten years during good behavior and be appointed by the president with confirmation by the senate.

Section 2. Powers of the Judiciary

The judicial power shall extend to all cases, in law and equity, arising under this Constitution, the laws of the Confederation, and treaties made, or which shall be made, under their authority. To controversies between two or more States, between a State and citizens of another State, between citizens of different States and between a State, or the citizens thereof and the Confederation government, foreign States, citizens or subjects.

Article 4. Amendments to the Constitution

This Constitution may be amended by an act of the Monarch, a two-thirds majority of both houses of Parliament, or by petition submitted by the people with signatures of ten percent of the population and approval by a popular vote of the people, the amendment must then be approved by the voters.

Article 5. Rights of the people

For the purposes of this Constitution:

A person is any sentient being that is capable of independent thought and independent action including children and youth as defined below.

Children are any sentient being that has drawn its first breath, or otherwise established that it can survive in the world without being part of another being or contained within that being. They shall continue to be classified as children until they have completed 80 percent of their transition through puberty which is defined as age sixteen for human children.

Youth are defined as sentient beings that are beyond puberty but have not yet reached 95 percent of brain maturity, which is defined as age twenty-five for humans. Children or their parents may petition the courts to have them declared Youth.

The government may not pass any law which affects people based on their affiliation, human traits, or beliefs, with the exception made herein for Children and Youth. Nor may any person be subject to discrimination based on such traits except those as might affect their ability to do a job in a substantive way.

No person shall exercise any right in a way that constitutes a danger to private property or to the health or safety of any person.

All persons except children shall have the right to vote.

All persons shall have the right to free expression.

All persons shall have the right to control decisions that affect their welfare except for children who are to rely on their legal guardians or the government should their legal guardians be unable or unwilling to.

The government may not pass any law which impinges on the right of the people to be informed.

The government may not pass any law which impinges on the freedom of persons to practice a religion of their own choosing. Nor may the government pass any laws which favor one religion over another.

All persons shall be protected from Unreasonable Searches and Seizures.

No person shall be subject to prosecution for the same offense to be twice put in jeopardy of life or limb; nor shall be compelled in any criminal case to be a witness against themselves, nor be deprived of life, liberty, or property without due process of law.

All persons shall have the right to a trial by a jury of their peers.

Private property shall not be taken for public use without just compensation.

In all criminal proceedings, each person has the right to a speedy trial and an attorney to represent them.

No person shall be subjected to excessive bail, nor excessive fines, nor cruel and unusual punishments.

All persons shall have the right to petition the Monarch.

Article 6. Laws governing actions of the people

No Person shall cause harm to another person, either physically or mentally.

No person shall deprive another person of their property, freedom, or rights through coercion or deceit.

No person shall help another in the commission of a crime, or in avoiding capture or prosecution after the commission of a crime.

No person shall take or destroy the property of any person or entity without due process.

No person shall violate the privacy of another person without due process.

No person shall violate the personal space or body of another person without due process.

No person may lie in a court of law.

No person may conspire with another person to commit a crime.

No person shall bribe a public official for any consideration from that official, nor may any public official accept such bribes in exchange for preferential treatment.

No person shall disobey the order of the judge during a trial, nor may they disobey any lawful order of the court.

No person may possess, import, or distribute any illegal goods, nor provide any aid to persons doing the same.

Children, being a protected class, no person shall in any way harm, mentally or physically a child.

No person shall endanger the public safety.

No person shall create or distribute facsimiles of anything of value without identifying it as a facsimile.

No person shall disrupt the public order or peace.

Article 7: Tax Law

Delphi taxes shall be based solely on income and property values. No tax on the sale of goods is allowed as they disproportionally tax the poor.

At the time of this Constitution enactment, the tax on real property shall be two percent of its appraised value. The tax may only increase at one half the rate of inflation until the property changes hands, at which time it will be appraised at its full value.

The taxes on income shall be the following:

1: Social Security, which shall be ten percent of annual income over fifty percent of the established minimum living wage. This tax shall be used to finance the medical care of all residents of the Delphi Confederation and to provide a supplemental income for retired persons. The supplemental income shall be based on the needs of the individual based on their current assets and other sources of income, with the goal of maintaining all retired persons above the minimum living wage level.

2: Income Tax, which shall be twenty percent of all income over the minimum living wage. This tax shall be used to finance any government expenditures.

3: Corporate tax, which shall be fifteen percent of gross sales and revenue generated from sales and activities outside of the Delphi Confederation. All corporations must be composed of entities that have at least five unrelated stockholders each with a minimum of five percent value of the corporation, and must employ a minimum of one hundred Delphi residents, plus one additional resident per minimum living wage over two hundred times the minimum living wage. Any corporation that does not meet this definition will be taxed based on the personal income tax rate.

19   Independence

"Good Morning, to our guests, members of the press," Marc said. "Please be seated, and we'll begin. I appreciate all of you showing up on such short notice and without any explanation of our announcement." He looked over at the New Zealand Minister of Foreign Affairs and the Australian Ambassador to the Cook Islands, as well as the Prime Minister of the Cook Islands.

There was a lot of murmuring and jostling about as the press corps settled in. After a few minutes, it quieted down.

"On this date, the Eighteenth of October, Two Thousand Nineteen, the City of Delphi formally announces its independence from the Cook Islands and New Zealand," Marc announced.

The press exploded with reporters jumping up to ask questions. Marc signaled for them to wait, and after a few minutes, they settled back down.

"We have published our new constitution and submitted it to the United Nations for recognition. Copies of the constitution are available on the internet under Constitution@DelphiCity.dn.gov. I will now take your questions," Marc said as he pointed to a familiar reporter.

"What form of government have you formed?" she asked.

"We have formed a Constitutional Monarchy," Marc said.

"Who is the Monarch?"

"I am," Marc replied.

"Why did you decide on a Monarchy?"

"We are still a young nation on a new endeavor," Marc said. "I want to ensure that we continue on that endeavor without getting sidetracked. The other founders of Delphi City agree that the only way to ensure that is to establish a Constitutional Monarchy."

"Why . . ."

"Next reporter," Marc said as he pointed to another reporter.

"What kinds of powers will you have?"

"Much the same as I already had," Marc said. "The constitution establishes a way for us to form a parliament and have them gradually take over the running of the government."

Marc pointed to another reporter.

"How can you declare yourself independent when you're sitting in the Cook Islands' territorial waters?"

"We are no longer in the Cook Islands' territorial waters," Marc said. "As of ten p.m. last night, Delphi City and our airport are located twenty miles northwest of Rarotonga, outside of the territorial waters of any nation."

"How did you move the city?"

"That is not germane to the discussion," Marc said as he pointed at another reporter.

"How will you defend yourself?"

"We have some means of defense," Marc said. "However, we are relying on the United Nations and its member nations to adhere to the rule of law. We would rather not have to exercise that defense."

"Is this due to the issue with Admiral Morris?"

"That had some bearing on it, although it didn't change our situation that much. We still expect countries like the US to adhere to the UN Charter and international law."

Several reporters were furiously reading the constitution on their phones; Marc pointed to one who was now trying to get his attention.

"I see your tax law in the constitution, are you trying to become a tax haven?"

"No, we will not exempt anyone from taxes," Marc said. "If you read it correctly, you will see that we tax all gains made outside of Delphi Nation. So that should discourage companies from coming here just to avoid taxes in their home countries."

"But you don't tax them on sales made inside of your new country?"

"We view a sales tax as a regressive form of income tax on our people," Marc said as he pointed to another reporter.

"You've made it very difficult to raise taxes."

"We believe in a small, efficient government," Marc said. "We believe the new technologies we are developing and introducing should enable the government to render services without overburdening the people with taxes." Marc pointed at another reporter.

"Can't you as the Monarch simply raise the taxes?"

"No, I can veto legislation, but I cannot enact it by edict," Marc said as he pointed again.

"It says that there is supplemental retirement, but it doesn't define a retirement age?"

"Correct," Marc said. "We are hoping things develop along the lines where you don't actually retire, but start to work less as you age. With the exception of medical retirement, we expect the people of Delphi Nation to continue to be productive members of our society." Marc pointed to another reporter.

"Can you explain your thinking on discrimination?"

"We are simply saying that the government shall treat all people as equal individuals independent of any genetic factors or their personal image of themselves." Marc pointed to another reporter.

"Can you explain this Youth Category?"

"Yes, as technology has advanced, it has had two effects on our young people," Marc said. "For many, it has led to a sheltering which postpones emotional maturity; for others, it has led to early maturity as access to information makes them more curious and concerned about public affairs. For a long time, countries have had laws that restrict the rights of adults until they reach a more mature age. We are simply recognizing this intermediate stage and codifying it."

The questions ran on for an additional hour before Marc finally called a halt. He told the reporters that they would have a second chance at the press conference that was being called for the following week.

"Minister Campbell, what did you think?" Marc asked as he greeted the New Zealand minister of foreign affairs.

"You certainly know how to get people's attention," Minister Campbell said.

"Will you recognize us?" Marc asked.

"I will be discussing that in parliament and with the Prime Minister," Minister Campbell said. "We are also interested in what Great Britain will do."

"Of course," Marc said. "We hope to maintain good relations with New Zealand; you have been very supportive so far."

"We were supporting the Cook Islands then," the minister said. "This is a different kettle of fish."

They held a big party that night to celebrate their independence. There were various venues throughout the city, and Marc had to make an appearance at all of them, and of course, he took Samantha with him. Catie begged out of attending every one, opting for just a few.

"Catie, you look lovely," her great grandmother said. "I see you decided to wear the family diamonds," she said with obvious approval.

"Of course, Grandma Ma," Catie said. "This will just add to their history."

"Yes, and then you can pass them on to your daughter or granddaughter," her great grandmother said.

"If I have any," Catie said.

"Of course, you will have children," her great grandmother said politely while somehow making it sound like an order.

"Hi, Catie," Sophia said. "Or do I have to call you Your Highness?"

"Nooo, you don't have to call me Your Highness," Catie said. "Where is your mother?"

"She's over there talking to the foreign minister's wife," Sophia said while pointing across the room.

"What have people been saying?" Catie asked.

"Most are happy we're independent. The most common question I've gotten is if we have to call you Your Highness," Sophia said. "I told them I didn't think so, but that I'd find out."

"So now you know," Catie said. "I guess I'm not going to be able to hide the fact that I'm *The Catie McCormack* anymore."

"Most people know," Sophia said. "They just forget when they're with you because you act so normal, well, not normal but humble, not putting on airs."

"I'm going to get you for that *normal* comment," Catie said with a laugh.

"You didn't invite Frankie to this party?" Sophia asked.

"I didn't manage the guest list," Catie said. "This one is only for dignitaries and their families as well as prominent citizens of Delphi City and Delphi Nation."

"Are we all citizens?" Sophia asked.

"You have to swear allegiance first," Catie said. "That is if you want to. We won't kick you out if you don't want to be a citizen."

"Do we have to give up our US citizenship?" Sophia asked.

"Daddy says we're going to allow our citizens to have multiple citizenships," Catie answered. "Hello, Jason, hello, Annie," Catie said as Jason escorted Annie over to her.

"Hi, Catie, I almost didn't recognize you in that dress," Jason said. "You really do clean up nice."

"This is the first time I've been able to wear this," Catie said. "My great grandparents gave me the dress for Christmas and the jewelry for my birthday. Grandma Ma believes that one should always dress up."

"Well, if you can look like that, why not," Jason said as he hugged Annie. "All three of you look fabulous," he added, trying to avoid getting into too much hot water.

"Annie, are you having fun?" Catie asked.

"Yes," Annie replied. "I like to dress up. Sophia, where's Chaz?"

"He should be coming back with punch," Sophia said. "Oh, there he is."

"Hi," Chaz said as he walked up. "I guess I didn't get enough punch," he added as he handed a glass to Sophia.

"Don't worry," Catie said. "Here comes a waiter." ADI had ordered a waiter to bring them punch as soon as she had heard Sophia say that

Chaz was bringing her some. Catie was wearing her earwig, but not her specs. "Is Chris here?" Catie asked.

"I saw her with her parents earlier," Chaz said. "She should be coming by to thank you for the job. She's been telling everybody about it."

"Speaking of jobs," Catie said, "are you reporting on the event?" she asked Sophia.

"Of course I am," Sophia said. "A good reporter is always working. What did you think of our first issue?"

"I already told you I loved it," Catie said.

"But that was before you were royalty," Sophia said. "I need an official statement now."

"My dear, you did a most excellent job of capturing the essence of Delphi City," Catie said in her most formal English-sounding voice. She got a laugh from everybody.

"What did I miss?" Chris asked.

"Oh, Catie was playing her royal highness," Jason said. "She did a pretty good imitation of some British Royal."

"Oh darn, too bad I missed it," Chris said. "Catie, I wanted to thank you for helping me get the job."

"All I did is forward your name and resumé to them," Catie said. "They were happy to hire you. They need people down here."

"What job did you get?" Annie asked.

"Oh, a programming internship with Vancouver Integrated Technologies," Chris replied.

"Who are they?" Annie asked.

"They're an integrated circuit company that MacKenzie Discoveries just bought a major stake in," Catie said. "They're going to start making our Comms."

"Are they going to be as good as the Apple phones?" Sophia asked.

"Better," Catie said.

"You were suggesting you'd probably be working for them too," Chris said.

"Yes, I plan to," Catie said.

"Why do you need to work for them? You're already doing all kinds of stuff," Sophia said.

"I'm just managing the programs," Catie said. "It's mostly planning with just a little bit of design. This will give me a chance to develop my programming skills and to get credit for programming classes."

"You're crazy," Sophia said. "You're taking so many classes you're going to be done with college before you're old enough to drink."

"There will always be more classes to take," Catie said. "It's been nice seeing everyone, but I have to get ready to go to one of the other parties. I'll see you guys around."

"How could you not know this was going to happen?" the president screamed at his cabinet.

"It appears that they only invited a few countries to witness the ceremony," Director Lassiter said. "We understand that only the Aussies, the Kiwis, the Mexicans, and the Moroccans were invited."

"Well, now what do we do?" the president demanded as he looked at Secretary of State Janet Palmero.

"We can put pressure on our allies to not recognize them if you wish," she replied.

"Will it work?" the president asked.

"It might, but if it doesn't, it could create issues for us later," she replied.

"If I may," General Wilson said. "The big seven are going to be slow to recognize them, we should bide our time with them. The ones we should worry about are the ones that were invited," he said. "We could quietly put pressure on them to not offer recognition. The longer it goes with no country recognizing them, the more leverage we will have."

"Okay," the president said. "Now what is going on with this second press conference?" he asked.

"More publicity," Director Lassiter suggested. "They need to keep up the pressure to get recognized."

"I think there's probably more to it than that!" the president almost shouted. "Now, are you going to figure it out?"

20   First Kiss

"Down with despots!" yelled the man. He waved his sign around as he stood on the box he had set in the middle of the sidewalk in front of the MacKenzie Discoveries' corporate offices. "Down with despots!"

Catie was just coming into the office to meet with a gentleman who wanted to open an exercise studio. She and Natalia stopped to watch. "Should I break that sign over his head?" Natalia asked.

"You can't do something like that," Catie said. "He has a right to protest."

"But in the middle of the sidewalk?"

"He is blocking the flow of traffic," Catie said. "Oh, here comes a constable; I want to see what she does."

The constable walked directly up to the man, "Sir . . . Sir," she said to get his attention.

"Are you here to arrest me? Did His Highness send one of his jackbooted thugs to stop me from spreading the word?"

"No, sir," the constable said. "You have every right to protest, but you can't do it here in the middle of the sidewalk."

"Where am I supposed to do it?" the man yelled at her. "From your jail cells?"

"No, sir. Might I suggest you would get just as much attention if you set up over there on the median? You would even be able to get the attention of people walking on the other side of the street."

"Why should I move?"

"Because it's against the law to block the traffic flow, and it is also unsafe. The way you're waving that sign around, you might hit someone. Please, let's move you over there where it will be much safer."

"What if I refuse to move?"

"Then I'll write you a ticket for blocking traffic," the constable said. "And then I'll block off the sidewalk so people won't be walking by you and risk getting hurt. They'll all be on the other side of the street and will probably be mad at you for making them have to go out of their way. Now, that won't help your cause, will it?"

"I guess not," the man said as he stepped off of his box.

"I'll carry your box," the constable said, "you just handle that big sign."

The constable got the man set up in the median, directly across from MacKenzie Discoveries' front door. She even helped him get back up on his box, holding his sign while he climbed up and then handing it to him.

"What despots you guys are," Natalia said with a big laugh.

"We're just learning," Catie said as she joined in the laugh.

"Hi, Catie," Sophia said after Catie answered her call.

"Hi," Catie answered, "what's up?"

"A bunch of us are going to check out that new burger place, The Oracle Diner," Sophia said. "Won't you come along? You haven't been yet, have you?"

"No, I haven't been to it yet," Catie said. She was trying to decide between going on this outing or having dinner with her mother.

"Artie and Chris are coming, and of course Jason and Annie," Sophia said. "It'll be fun. The servers wear roller skates."

"Okay, I'll come if my mom lets me skip out on dinner with her tonight," Catie answered.

"Oh, she'll let you go for sure. I'm doing a review of the restaurant for the Delphi Gazette. Do you think I should have named the paper the Delphi Oracle?"

"It would be a cute name, but an Oracle predicts the future, a newspaper reports the past."

"I guess it would be a strange name for a paper, maybe I'll have a section in it called The Oracle and make predictions."

"You could," Catie said, "but you might want to see if you're any good at predictions first."

"Good idea," Sophia said. "I'll see you there."

Catie sent a text to her mother asking about the dinner. Her mother just sent one word back, *"GO!"*

Catie arrived at the diner a little late, so that Natalia could go in earlier while her new backup, Morgan, could cover Catie until she got into the diner.

Catie was surprised to see Frankie at the table when she arrived. Sophia had arranged things so Catie was sitting next to her and across from Frankie.

"Hi, everyone," Catie said. "Sorry I'm late."

"Oh, we just got here," Sophia said. "They haven't even come over to take our order yet."

"Then I'd better get inside the booth before I get run over," Catie said as she slid in beside Sophia. "Has anyone eaten here before?"

"Nope," Sophia said. "I already asked. ADI said the burgers are great, although how she would know I'm not sure."

"Sam and Kal ate here when they opened," Catie said.

"Oh. What did they like?" Chris asked.

"Kal said the fries are great, he had the Hawaiian burger, I guess he misses home," Catie said. "Sam had the onion rings, which she loved, and the prophet's burger."

"Did she like the burger?" Annie asked.

"Apparently, it's one of the smaller ones," Catie said, "which is what she cared about, but she did say it was good."

"Here comes the server," Sophia said. "Catie, are you ready to order?"

"Sure, I'm having the same thing Kal did, we always like the same food," Catie said.

The server skated up; she was wearing a red and white striped dress and big cat-eye glasses, red, of course. It took a few minutes before everyone finally ordered. Once they were finished, Catie turned to Sophia, "Hey, Madam Reporter, did you hear about our protester?"

"What protester?" Sophia asked.

"There was this guy protesting outside MacKenzie yesterday," Catie said.

"Is he still there?" Sophia asked.

"No, apparently he couldn't get any attention, so after a few hours he left, or maybe he had to go to work," Catie said.

"Did you see him?"

"Yes," Catie said.

"Then tell us," Sophia said. "What was he protesting?"

"Apparently he was protesting the despots that have taken over Delphi City," Catie said with a laugh. Then she described the whole scene she and Natalia had seen. She even told them the joke she and Natalia had made about the McCormacks not being very good despots.

"Can I quote you?" Sophia asked.

"You don't want it to be an anonymous source?" Catie asked.

"Sure, but then I couldn't use the despot joke," Sophia said.

"Just use that as a quote from Catie when you asked her about the protest," Annie said.

"That's perfect," Sophia said. "Thanks, Annie. Why didn't ADI tell me about that, do you think she missed it?"

"You'll have to train her about what kinds of things you're interested in," Catie said. "It probably sounded boring to her."

"Cer Catie, I only assigned a fifty percent probability that Cer Sophia would be interested in the protester," ADI said to Catie.

"Okay, I'll send her a note," Sophia said. "Anything else new that you know about?"

"Someone is going to open an exercise studio," Catie said.

"Oh, I definitely am interested in that," Sophia said. "Why wouldn't ADI have told me that?"

"It was just approved today, probably will be in your daily update from her," Catie said.

"I sent a message about it to her yesterday, and an update today when it was approved," ADI said. "She is not very good about checking her mail."

"I'll have to check," Sophia said.

"Maybe you should have ADI text you the updates and stuff," Catie said.

"Excellent idea, Cer Catie," ADI said. "She is always wearing her specs and checks her texts incessantly."

"I'll tell her," Sophia said.

"What else is going on, guys?" Sophia said, turning the conversation back to the rest of the table.

"Vancouver Integrated Technologies moved into their offices yesterday," Chris said.

"Oh, that's good," Sophia said as she made a note. "Did you meet your new boss?"

"Yes, I did, a Rebecca Hamilton," Chris said. "She's actually the lead on the UI for their new phone."

"Another phone," Artie said. "Does the world really need another phone?"

"Yes, it does," Catie said. "Especially since Chris and I are working on it. It's going to be the same OS as our Comms but with a different UI since we can't copy Apple."

"But do we need a new UI?" Artie asked.

"Not really, I think it's going to be mostly the Android UI, which is easy to license," Catie said. "The Android apps will play, but with the specs, there are just so many UI enhancements that are needed and a lot of different apps."

"I should look into writing some apps," Artie said.

"I thought you were going to be an aerospace engineer," Jason said.

"I am, but that doesn't mean I can't write a few apps too," Artie defended himself.

"So, Catie, what kind of programming are you going to do?" Frankie asked.

"I'm doing the same stuff as Chris. We'll be testing code to start with until we learn the OS," Catie said as Sophia nudged her under the table. "Here comes our food."

Everybody ate, and the conversation moved around the table, touching on all the subjects that affected their lives. Catie noticed that Frankie took every opportunity to talk to her or ask her questions. She liked the attention, but the fact that Frankie took every opportunity to pick on Artie made her wonder why she liked it.

After everyone had finished eating and had used up all the possible topics of conversation, they started to leave. Frankie took a position next to Catie as they exited the diner. He used his position to separate her slightly from the others.

"Catie, Sophia tells me that you're the one who designed all the parks," Frankie said as he continued to create distance between them and the rest of the teens.

"Yes, I did," Catie said excitedly. She loved to talk about the parks.

"How did you decide on the pattern?" Frankie asked. "I can see small parks then bigger parks, why aren't they all the same size?"

"I wanted variety," Catie said. "The bigger parks will attract different types of people than the smaller ones. The smaller ones are just for walking around or having a picnic."

"That was pretty smart of you," Frankie said. "Can you show me this one?" he asked as he nodded to the park across the street.

"Sure," Catie said. They crossed the street and entered the park. It was one of the smaller parks with several trees and pathways between flower gardens.

"Did you design the gardens?" Frankie asked.

"No, I found different garden enthusiasts and gave each of them a garden to design," Catie said. "Then, of course, the actual gardeners that take care of them slowly adapt them as they prune the plants and replace the ones that don't like our climate."

They continued to walk around the garden and talk about the various ones throughout the city. They approached the central part where

Catie had planted a huge milo tree. It was one of the biggest trees she had planted.

"Wow this is a big tree, how did it grow so fast?" Frankie asked.

"It didn't," Catie said. "It was twenty-five feet tall when we planted it."

"That must have been expensive," Frankie said. "Why spend that kind of money?"

"I thought each park needed at least one big tree," Catie said. "We picked as many different trees as we could so each park would be a little unique."

"You are amazing," Frankie said. He gave Catie a hug that sent tingles up her spine. She liked the way he was holding her.

"How did you get to be so smart and so beautiful?" he asked.

"I'm not beautiful," Catie whispered.

"Yes, you are," Frankie said as he bent down and kissed her.

It was a nice, warm, deep kiss, and Catie was really enjoying it until she felt his hand under her shirt. It was slowly working its way up. She used her elbow to knock it away from her body.

"What are you doing!" Catie hissed.

"I'm sorry," Frankie said.

"Sorry, who do you think you are?" Catie screamed.

"Is everything all right over there?" Natalia called out. She had been shadowing the couple trying to give them privacy without losing eye contact with Catie.

"Mind your own business," Frankie shouted at Natalia.

"I'm okay," Catie called out.

ADI was furiously researching Frankie's history. It wasn't too long before she found that Frankie Phillips had died of a drug overdose on September first. The death had been covered up; she was only able to find it from an announcement in the local paper. Then using Frankie's fingerprint, she eventually found a driver's license in Cheyenne, Wyoming, for a Frank Whitaker, age twenty. A few milliseconds later, she discovered that he had enlisted in the Marines at age seventeen. She texted all this information to Catie, Liz, Natalia, and Kal.

"Are you okay, Catie?" Kal called over the Comm.

Catie used her eyes to reply, blinking on the 'yes' button.

"I knew there was something wrong with that guy," Liz said.

"I'm sorry, Catie," Frankie said again.

"It looks like he's a spy, sent here by the US to get close to you, Catie," Kal said.

"Too close," Natalia said. "What do you want to do?"

"We should kick him off the city," Kal said.

"It's Catie's call," Liz said.

"What do you want to do, Catie?" Natalia texted. "Please let me kick him off the city."

Frankie grabbed Catie by the arm, "Look at me. I said I was sorry, why won't you talk to me?"

His grip was rough; Catie used a sweeping arm motion to break it and stepped away from him. "You're a creep!"

"Who do you think you are?" Frankie yelled at her. "I could have ten girls prettier than you, and you get all upset over a kiss and a little grope. Other girls your age would be standing in line."

"Nattie, he's all yours," Catie hissed.

Frankie started to reach out to grab Catie by the arm again when Natalia stepped in between them.

"Get out of here," Frankie spat at her.

"You've got that wrong, it's you that's getting out of here," Natalia said in a calm, low voice. "You have exactly two hours to get your stuff and get on the next ferry to Rarotonga."

"I'm not going to Rarotonga!"

"I'm pretty sure you are. I don't think you can swim all the way back to Wyoming," Natalia said, "could you, Frank Whitaker?"

Frankie was taken aback when Natalia used his real name. "Wha.. You can't make me go. I haven't broken any law!"

"Just keep up that attitude, and I'll be happy to spend a few days in jail. Because, *Little Boy*, if I see you still in this city in two hours, I'm going to roll you up into a ball and dropkick your ass off of the edge of the city," Natalia growled. "Now, Pendejo, make up your mind!"

Frankie looked at Natalia, he was as tall as she was, but she probably outweighed him by twenty pounds of muscle. He was thinking that he could take her when she suddenly slapped him. He didn't see it coming, nor did he see the second slap coming.

"I told you to make up your mind, Marine," Natalia shouted. "Now, do you want a piece of me, or are you ready to leave!"

"I'll leave," Frankie said.

"I can't hear you!" Natalia shouted.

"I'll leave!" Frankie shouted back.

"One hour and fifty-five minutes!" Natalia shouted. "Move!"

Natalia signaled Morgan to follow Frankie and make sure he got on the ferry.

"You okay, Catie?" Natalia asked.

"I'm fine," Catie said.

"No, you're not," Natalia said.

Liz ran up and hugged Catie, "I came as fast as I could. I'm so sorry."

"Why did he have to ruin it?" Catie cried.

"He's a jerk!" Liz said.

"Why couldn't he wait another week?!"

"What would that have done?" Liz asked.

"It wouldn't have ruined my first kiss!"

"Oh, I might have to dropkick him anyway," Natalia said.

"Was it a good kiss?" Liz asked.

"Yes!"

"Then he didn't ruin the kiss, he just ruined the after kiss," Liz said. "Do you want to go watch Nattie dropkick him?"

"Yes, . . . No! I don't want to ever see him again!"

"I have some friends in the Marines," Natalia said. "Do you want me to arrange an accident for him?"

"Yes, . . . No!"

"I could arrange for some hot girl to lead him on, then drop him like a stone," Natalia said.

"I'd like that, can you get a video of it?" Catie asked.

"I'm sure we can," Natalia said. "Then we'll post it all over the internet. It'll ruin him. His buddies in the Marines will ride him forever about it."

"Good, he deserves it!" Catie said.

"Okay," Liz said. "Let's go get some ice-cream. I hear the new parlor has a great mango flavor."

"Hi, Sophia," Catie said, answering the call.

"Did you see it?" Sophia asked.

"See what?"

"The Delphi Gazette! What else!"

"Oh, that, I read it over breakfast," Catie said, continuing to tease Sophia.

"Well, what did you think?"

"I was thinking about how good my coffee was."

"About the Gazette, you meanie!"

"Oh, well I thought it was well written," Catie said in a deadpan voice.

"Do I have to come over there and beat you?" Sophia yelled.

"It was great," Catie said. "I think you did a great job on the protest; you expertly weaved my comment in about needing practice. The restaurant reviews were good; did you really eat at all those places?"

"Yes," Sophia said. "I'm going to have to go on a diet. I'm looking for an unknown eater to do that column from now on. What about the rest?"

"I like the way you wrote the *what's happening* column, it made everything sound interesting. But we definitely need to have more stuff going on."

"And?"

"Are you just looking for praise?" Catie said with a laugh. "I like it. It was great for just your second issue. Now you have to see if you can make all the rest live up to the first two."

"Don't worry, I will," Sophia said. "And I'm not going to forget how mean you were."

"Oh, I'm scared," Catie said. "Now, you should probably go find something to report on."

"Bye."

21   Fusion

Marc waited for the reporters to settle in before starting the press conference.

"With me, I have four eminent scientists: Dr. Tanaka, Dr. Nakahara, Dr. Scheele, and Dr. McDowell. They have agreed to answer any questions you may ask that I cannot handle. These men will be publishing their findings shortly, but I'm here to announce that MacKenzie Discoveries has achieved a self-sustaining fusion reaction."

The room broke into a buzz as the reporters started texting and talking to their colleagues while others were making calls.

"Settle down, please. Settle down, and I will continue," Marc said.

It took several minutes for the room to quiet down.

"Again, I'll take questions after I finish the announcement. The reaction lasted for eight hours until they shut it down. They have achieved the same results eight other times. We are now working on perfecting a fusion reactor that can be used to generate power. We believe this to be a safe method of producing power that can be used to replace any of the current fossil fuel power plants in the world."

Marc sighed and pointed at a reporter. He had hoped to get a little further before he had to take questions, but again, the main details were out.

The reporter he pointed to stepped forward, "How long do you think it will take before you have a design for a fusion power plant?"

"We believe we have a design now," Marc said. "They will begin testing it next month."

"How can you do it so fast?"

"We have been working on this for almost one year," Marc said. "Many of the basics have already been done. One thing to keep in mind, we are only designing the fusion reactor, essentially the boiler for the power plant; the rest of the power plant is based on existing designs."

"Next question."

"How safe will it be?"

"The beauty of nuclear fusion is that when the fusion is done, it's done, it doesn't continue unless you make it. So, if the reactor shuts down for any reason, the reaction stops. This is unlike the fission reactors of today. There you have to control the reaction so that it doesn't go critical. When something goes wrong, you have to do everything you can to stop the reaction. Fusion stops on its own, except when you're in the center of the sun, then the environment continues the reaction. Here we have to create the heat and pressure to force the reaction; when one of those variables goes off, the reaction stops."

"How can you be sure that it will stop? What if the containment vessel ruptures?"

"If the containment vessel ruptures, then the pressure is released, and the reaction stops. The temperatures required for the reaction are not sustainable outside of the containment vessel, so again the reaction will stop if it ruptures. The reactor is coated with gadolinium and lead. Although the reaction is designed so it doesn't release neutrons, if the reactions don't complete, the gadolinium will absorb any neutrons released by the reactor. The lead will absorb the small amount of radiation so no dangerous byproducts should be released into the environment."

Marc pointed at another reporter, "Next question."

"How are you going to introduce these reactors?"

"We haven't decided that yet," Marc said. "There are some aspects of the reactor that are proprietary, and only we are capable of producing those components. Much of the rest is already in the public domain. Until we finish the design, we won't know whether we have a licensing issue with other companies. But we are confident that we will be able to work those out." Marc pointed to another reporter.

"Why announce this now before the reactor design is proven? Are you looking for investors?"

"We are not looking for investors," Marc said. "Certain events have led us to believe that the state of our research was going to leak out. We decided to get ahead of the leaks."

"Would this have anything to do with your declaration of independence last week?"

"It is one of the reasons we declared independence," Marc said. "We want to make sure that this technology is introduced to all countries. Next question."

"Can you explain why you were able to create a sustained reaction when nobody else has?"

"Other than the fact that we brought some of the finest minds together to work on the problem, no," Marc said. "But possibly these gentlemen can. And of course, they are publishing their work soon. I believe they are submitting their papers for review now."

"How can they have nuclear fusion?" the president yelled. "And how come we didn't know about it?"

"We have been unable to get an asset inside of MacKenzie Discoveries," Director Lassiter said. He carefully avoided saying Delphi government.

"What happened to that asset you were so proud of?" the president demanded.

"He was kicked out of the city," Director Lassiter said.

Secretary Palmero hid her smile. She had not liked the idea of sending a twenty-year-old man posing as a teenager to seduce a thirteen-year-old girl. That it failed, and according to her sources, failed spectacularly, was good for her soul.

"Why?"

"I believe they broke his cover," Director Lassiter said. "He just reported that he was kicked out, and that they knew his real name."

"Sir, Morocco and Mexico just recognized Delphi Nation," Secretary of State Palmero said after checking the message she'd just received on her phone.

"Damn traitors," the president yelled. "What next?"

"I have to believe India will recognize them soon," Secretary Palmero said.

"And you couldn't stop this?" the president asked as he looked at Director Lassiter.

"We tried, but it looks like they had already made up their minds," Director Lassiter said as he grimaced at what he knew was coming next.

"What good is the damn CIA, if they can't even seduce a little girl, or stop a couple of pissant countries from defying us?" the president yelled as he tore the briefing notes in half and threw them on the floor. "What can we do now?"

"Sir," General Wilson said. "Might I suggest we recognize them and work to get them onto our side before the Russians or Chinese do."

"I'll think about it," the president said. "Now what's this with North Korea?"

"We just received a report that one of the ballistic submarines had an accident as it was entering the Sinpo shipyard for a refit. The accident also did a lot of damage to the shipyard as the submarine was just entering the drydock at the time," Director Lassiter said.

"Well, at least that's some good news," the president said. "Have we learned anything about that missile launch that went bad?"

"No, sir. The North Koreans are still calling it a successful test," Director Lassiter said. "They are preparing another launch of the same missile; its launch is scheduled for next week."

"Damn that Kim," the president said. "You can't trust a word he says. I'd like to just drop a nuke on his head."

22   Board Meeting – Oct 28th

"This meeting is called to order," Marc said.

"Shouldn't we have some palace guards?" Blake asked.

"We do," Marc said. "Liz and Kal are here, and Natalia is out in the hall."

"But where are the fancy uniforms?" Blake asked.

"In your head, where they're going to stay," Liz said, getting a thumbs up from Kal.

"On to more serious matters," Marc said. "First, I'd like to introduce Dr. Nikola Zelbar. She is one of our material scientists, and will be joining the board to help us work through some of the more complex issues related to technology."

"Hello, everyone," Nikola said.

"I believe you know everyone here," Marc said.

"Yes," Nikola said. "Admiral Michaels and I met when Catie took us up to the space station, and I've worked with everyone else in one way or another."

"Kal, you wanted some time," Marc said.

"We had two incidents of note this week," Kal said. "First, we deported an American spy."

"Who was he?" Marc asked.

Liz reached over and clasped Catie's hand.

"He was Frankie Phillips; he was posing as the son of Bill and Marjorie Phillips. He was actually Frank Whitaker, a twenty-year-old Marine sergeant. ADI found this out after doing a deeper dig into his background after some suspicious activity on his part."

"Why did we kick him out instead of leaving him in place like our other friends?" Marc asked.

"He wasn't as professional," Kal said. "We felt he was likely to take some kind of rash action. Figured better safe than sorry."

"What about the real Frankie?" Marc asked.

"Died of a drug overdose. The CIA apparently threatened to have the police go after his cousin if the family didn't cooperate in their little subterfuge," Kal continued. "We've decided to let them stay."

"Okay, and your next issue," Marc prompted. Catie gave an inward sigh as Kal managed to keep her out of the discussion. She really didn't want any more of her friends on the board to know of her embarrassment.

"We had our first protest against the despot who's running this place," Kal said.

"Oh, we did, did we," Marc said, "and just how did we handle this protest?"

"Constable Nawal handled the issue," Kal said. "She helped him move his protest off of the sidewalk out front and onto the grass median where he wouldn't block traffic. He protested for a few more hours, then he went home."

"Not very despotic of us," Marc said.

"I told the Delphi Gazette that we needed practice," Catie said.

"I hope Sophia writes that up as a joke," Samantha said.

"She did," Catie said. "It came out this morning, the whole piece is written tongue-in-cheek."

"Okay, anything else?" Marc asked.

"One other thing of note: Our first class to complete their full training at the police academy came home last week," Kal said. "Constable Nawal was a member of the class. We're sending a second class out next week. I've decided to keep the four we brought back early last time here for now. We'll send them back with the third class."

"Sound thinking," Marc said. "That it?" Getting a nod from Kal, Marc turned to Samantha. "Sam?"

"Mexico and Morocco have recognized us," Samantha said. "And we've been assured that India will recognize us this week."

"That is excellent news," Marc said as he put his hand out to forestall Blake's rushing to the liquor cabinet to start a toast. "After the meeting. Anything else, Sam?"

"Yes, I have over four thousand applications for immigration to Delphi City," Samantha said.

"Four thousand," Marc said with surprise. "Where are they coming from?"

"Most of them are from writers, artists, and quite a few singers and musicians," Samantha said.

"Why, taxes?" Marc asked.

"I think so," Samantha said. "Writers and artists make their money through royalties, and performers like singers and musicians are on the road all the time. I think they're looking for a safe, comfortable place to live as well as liking our tax rate."

"People, what do you think?" Marc asked.

"I think we should only accept those kinds of immigrants after they have spent a few months in the city," Liz said. "They need to realize that this isn't like a normal city; it's quieter, there are no cars, and their bodyguards won't be able to carry any weapons."

"I like that idea," Samantha said. "Have them get used to our laws before they really move here and get surprised at what they cannot do or have here."

"Anyone else?"

"Can I tell Sophia about the applications?" Catie asked.

Marc looked at Samantha. "Why not," she said. "We might get some feedback from our other residents."

"Okay, anything else?" Marc asked.

"No, but I'd like to hear from the admiral about how our North Korea project is going," Samantha said.

"Admiral," Marc prompted.

"Your guys managed to get a mine placed on their two ballistic submarines," Admiral Michaels said. "The mine on the first sub exploded as it was entering the drydock at Sinpo shipyards. Made quite a mess which should slow them down some. I take it we can detonate the mine on the second sub anytime we want?"

"That is correct," Marc said.

"Then I would recommend we do so when it is coming in for a refit," the admiral said. "Based on their past history, that should be in about six weeks. I've also heard they're preparing the launch of another missile for this weekend. A good test to see if you can shut it down in the early stage of the launch."

"We're as prepared as we can be on that," Marc said. "We'll convene a small war council when the launch is about to happen so we can discuss options."

"That would be good," the admiral said. "My guess is that they know something happened to their last launch, and they're anxious to see what it was. If this one goes bad early in the launch, it'll set them back on their heels."

Nikola had been leaning forward in her chair following the conversation closely; she signaled Marc that she had a question.

"Nikola," Marc said.

"Just how are you able to disrupt their missile launches?" she asked.

"If you can get him to tell you that," Admiral Michaels said, "then you'll be doing better than me."

"I'm sorry, Nikola," Marc said. "There are still a few things that we feel the need to limit knowledge of. That is one of them."

"Okay," Nikola said, thinking she would discuss this with her husband and see what they could guess.

"And, Nikola," Marc said.

"Yes?"

"If you and Leo manage to develop a theory, please don't share it with anyone but me," Marc said.

"Or Catie?"

"Or Catie," Marc agreed.

"Since you have the floor, anything you would like to share?" Marc asked.

"The experiments we have running at the space station have been going well. Leo has finalized his process for the superconductor. He is close on the flexible polysteel, but feels he won't be able to dial that in until he can be up there for a few days at a time," Nikola said. "We have a process for the transparent polysteel that can produce it in any thickness from 0.2 millimeters to ten centimeters."

"That is great news," Marc said. "We need the thin transparent polysteel for our Comm units and the phones that Vancouver Integrated will be producing. And I'm sure we can come up with good uses for the thicker stuff. It'll make great armor glass."

"I would like to start using it in all our windows," Kal said. "And I have a list of windows I would like to have replaced with it."

"Fred, can you set up a window manufacturing shop?" Marc asked.

"On it," Fred said.

"Anything else?" Marc asked.

"Yes, Leo and I were talking about the superconductor, and the fact that you already have some that you use on your Oryxes to absorb the reentry heat and convert it to electricity," Nikola said. "As a result, we set up an experiment using it and the transparent polysteel. It created a very efficient solar panel."

"How efficient?" Marc asked with excitement.

"Ninety percent," Nikola said. "That's over three times better than current solar panels."

"Darn it!" Catie exclaimed. "Oops, I'm sorry, I didn't mean to say that out loud."

"Did I say something wrong?" Nikola asked.

"No," Samantha said. "Catie is just used to being the one to see the obvious applications. She thinks she should have seen that one."

"I did," Catie said. "I was going to set up a test this week."

"Ha! You have some competition now," Blake said. "It'll be good for you."

Marc laughed at his daughter's little pique of frustration, "Too busy?"

"Yes," she said. "Nikola, did you characterize the manufacturing process yet?"

"Not yet," Nikola said. "We need more time here in the lab."

"Okay," Marc said. "We'll get you set up. Fred, can you take care of this as well?"

"Sure, I'll see to it. *Set up solar panel lab,*" Fred noted. "We should decide on the type of operation you want. How big, manufacturing split between here and Delphi City, is it just enough for our needs, or do you want to export them?"

Marc noticed Catie squirming in her seat. "Catie, what's up? You don't look happy," he said.

"I have some ideas I want to try out for the solar panels," Catie said.

"I thought you were busy," Marc said.

"But I want to work with Nikola on it," Catie whined.

"No skin off my back," Fred said. "Just tell me what you want to do, and I'll work around it."

"I'm okay with that," Marc said. "Let's plan on exporting them, once we have the process figured out," Marc said. "Is Marcie ready to get back on the road?" Marcie was MacKenzie Discoveries' sales rep. She had been brought to Delphi City for protection when the US was saber-rattling.

"Admiral, what do you think?" Samantha asked.

"I think we're safe for now," the admiral said. "The US is going to want to be careful with us after the fusion announcement, and Marcie never was a significant point of leverage."

"Okay, then I'll talk to her," Samantha said. "Does she get to use a Lynx?"

"Why not," Marc said. "Just tell her that she'll likely have other passengers when she travels."

"I think she'll be okay with that, might be some celebrities, even," Samantha said.

"Okay, let's get the process down and cost figured out before we go too far," Marc said.

"We should decide how much manufacturing we want here on the city, vs. in Rarotonga," Kal said. "We might even want to consider shipping the raw panels somewhere else to manufacture them."

"It would be a good job creator for some of your target countries," Liz said.

"Could we risk one of the poorer African nations?" Marc asked.

"Ethiopia is moving toward a more open political system," Admiral Michaels said. "It would be a nice way to help them."

"Okay, do we have anyone who can look into it for us?" Marc asked.

"We can ask General Clark to start looking at it," Samantha suggested. "He's been doing a great job working on getting us recognized."

"Okay, talk to him," Marc said. "Catie, so you're too busy, and now you're on the clock with the panels. What can we do about your workload?"

"I've handed off the hydroponic gardening to Mrs. Michaels and the meat growing operation to Vince Clark, no relationship to the general and Jason," Catie said. "So that helps a lot."

"What else could you give up?" Marc asked.

"I don't want to give anything else up yet," Catie said.

"If you're too busy," Marc said.

"It's not that," Catie interrupted. "I just started the job with Vancouver Integrated, and it's taking more of my time than I thought."

"So . . ." Marc prompted.

"It'll get easier once I learn more of the programming," Catie said. "It's just taking longer than I had expected it to. I'm working with Chris, and we're helping each other learn it, and ADI is helping too. I'll catch up."

Marc laughed at his daughter.

"What's so funny?" Catie asked.

"You're finally hitting the limit of how fast you can learn things," Marc said. "Before it was always a matter of how fast you could absorb the material, you've never had to practice anything that didn't require physical coordination. Now you know how the rest of us feel."

"I've had to study the math stuff," Catie said.

"Kind of," Marc replied. "That has been more about having to go back through the derivation when you ran into something new. And you haven't bothered with the really complex stuff because you really weren't interested in it."

"I don't want to be a mathematician," Catie said.

"That's my point. This is the first time you've had to confront your own limitations and study," Marc said.

"Well, I'm doing it," Catie said in a huff.

"Glad to see it," Marc said. "Now, what do you have to report?"

"Well, you can guess from what's been said, that the Vancouver Integrated team has started moving in. They've got a fabrication lab set up here now, and their offices. They've moved one hundred people here. I've given the okay for a regular Lynx shuttle run between here and Vancouver; it'll run three days a week," Catie said.

"That's great," Marc said. "When are they going to start experiments up in space?"

"Now that our material issues for the space station are mostly solved, I've asked Fred to allocate one of the Oryxes as a mobile lab," Catie said. "That way, they can set up a test here on the ground and send it up. They'll start that in a couple of weeks. Once they have a better handle on the basics, they'll move into the permanent lab space Liz has allocated for them."

"Good," Marc said.

"We also have eight fabricators moved to the space station, that's all but two," Catie said. "That means we can start making special parts as needed. And coordinating that is something I'd be happy to hand off."

Marc sighed; it was getting more and more difficult for them to handle all the various tasks within their small inner circle. And he was loath to expand the number of people who knew about the Sakira. "Can we have ADI set up an automatic process?" Marc asked.

"We can, but I think we still need someone to set priorities," Catie said as she looked at Nikola.

"Why don't you and Nikola talk about whether she can pick that up," Marc said. He wondered if that would work without explaining that the fabricators were a molecular-level 3-D printer that could literally make anything that they had the design for.

"I'd be happy to take that on," Nikola said.

"I'll go over it with her," Catie said.

"Thank you," Marc said. "Liz."

"We have completed ring one," Liz said. "We're stopping the station's rotation today so we can attach it. That should only take two days. Then it will take about two to three weeks to build it out enough that it will be ready for habitation. Then we can start adding units for people to live in."

"That is excellent news," Marc said. "It will be nice to start having other people up there besides the construction crew. We need to get a sense of what it takes to make it a livable place so we can adjust our plans."

"I agree. We have a lot to learn," Liz said. "We started extruding ring two last week, it will take another two weeks to complete. We have to decide if we're going to wait until ring three is complete before we attach them."

"That's still the plan," Marc said. "We'll see how the demand for space up there goes. We can adjust if we need to. Okay, Blake," Marc added, signaling Blake that he could pour the scotch and have his toast. "I'd also like to try having these meetings only once a month," Marc said. "We seem to be hitting our stride, and with the various situational meetings we call, I think we'll stay in touch adequately. So let's plan on the next official meeting for December second. We know we'll have to call a meeting before that on the North Korean issue."

"A double toast," Blake said as he brought the Glenlivet to the table.

"How do you manage to get anything done?" Catie asked Sophia. "You're always on your phone." Catie was meeting with Sophia to give her an update on the board meeting for the Gazette.

"How can you not be on your phone all the time?" Sophia asked. "I get so many posts on my Facebook page and my Twitter feed, it's hard to keep up."

"Probably because I don't have as many friends as you," Catie said.

"How can you not have as many friends?" Sophia asked. "Everybody has friends, and when you friend them, all their friends want to friend you. If you don't friend them, you don't know what's happening."

"I have a filter that manages all my social media," Catie said.

"What does the filter do?"

"It lets you divide friends into more groups than Facebook does. You set up to five levels of friends," Catie explained. "I use three levels, inner circle, friends, and acquaintances. There is no filter of the inner circle. Friends are filtered so that I only get posts that I've shown interest in. It also filters out any political or nasty posts. The same for acquaintances, but for them, it also filters out all posts from them that aren't responding to something I posted or that don't touch on something relevant to me. You can do the same thing with your Twitter feed."

"Wow, that's a lot. How is your Comm smart enough to do that?" Sophia asked.

"It has a really smart AI that runs through all that info and builds a model of your personality and likes. It tracks what you do, then mimics that. It's going to be one of the big features on the new VIT phones," Catie said.

"How can it do that?" Sophia asked.

"You have to give it access to your Facebook and Twitter accounts and any other accounts that you subscribe to, then it pre-manages all the posts before you can see them," Catie said. "It will even move the data into a private stream without any ads if you want."

"But that sounds like it would filter out the bad things people say about me," Sophia said.

"Yeah!" Catie said. "Why would you want to see those, they're just trying to be mean. Your real friends will ignore them, or they're not real friends. And it just causes you anxiety if you read them. You've got one of the fast Comms, so you can set one up like mine too," Catie said.

"Why does it only work on the fast Comms?" Sophia asked.

"It works on both, but it's more limited on the slow Comms," Catie said. "When VIT starts making Comms, they'll have enough processing power to run the full filter."

"Help me set mine up, and I'll see if I like it," Sophia said.

23   Exposé

"The truth behind Delphi City, next on Investigative Reports."

Catie and Liz were watching the video after ADI alerted everyone to the upcoming report.

"The city looks innocent, but we have inside information that says otherwise. Frankie Whitaker lived in Delphi City for two months before he escaped," the reporter said. "Frankie, tell us what it was like."

"Everything you did was controlled, where you ate, who you talked to, and where you went," Frankie said. "They offer to give all the kids shots that are supposed to help them get through puberty without so much turmoil, but it's really a way to control them. I refused the shot, so I was able to think for myself."

"But the reports we have been getting show an idyllic place," the reporter said.

"Idyllic, if you're a robot," Frankie said. "The McCormacks think they know what's best for everyone, and if you don't agree, they force you to do what they want. They have goons all over the city, watching what everybody does."

"Have you met any of the McCormacks?" the reporter asked.

"Yes, I knew the daughter Catie," Frankie said. "She is a conceited little girl who thinks she's smarter than everybody else. She thinks she's beautiful, but she's just some skinny little nerd."

"That was mean!" Catie yelled.

"He's just making this up," Liz said, "don't pay attention to him. We're supposed to be watching this so we can do a rebuttal."

"What else did you see?" the reporter asked.

"They brought in a bunch of people from some little town in West Virginia," Frankie continued. "Every two weeks half the men disappear for two weeks, and the other half comes back. They can't remember where they've been, and they act all confused. I think they're doing experiments on them."

"Do you think that's how they developed their cure for Alzheimer's?" the reporter asked.

"Sure," Frankie said. "They don't care about anybody who's not family. What are a few people from West Virginia to them?"

The reporter continued the exposé by interviewing several other people who had been in Delphi City. She also interviewed several other people who corroborated what Frankie had said, although ADI assured them that none of those people had even been in Delphi City. Then the reporter interviewed, Najib Maloof, the man they had deported for beating his wife. He told a story about how the doctors in Delphi City had brainwashed his wife to leave him. And when he had objected, they had beaten him and deported him back to Syria.

"They're just making stuff up," Catie sniffed as she threw herself back against the sofa cushion.

"Don't let it get to you," Liz said. "It's over now. What do you think we should do?"

"What can we do?" Catie asked. "It's all a bunch of lies."

"Well, we can show them the truth," Liz said.

"How? They'll just say we're lying," Catie said.

"Hey, girls," Samantha said as she knocked on the door to Catie's room.

"Come on in," Catie said. "Did you see that stupid exposé?"

"Yes," Samantha said. "That's why I'm here. What do you want to do about it?"

"What's Daddy saying?" Catie asked.

"I think he's still throwing things," Samantha said. "He's pretty upset."

"What do you think we should do, Sam?" Liz asked.

"We could just ignore it," Samantha said. "Or we could bring a reporter down here to do a real story."

"Would anyone believe it?" Catie asked.

"We could bring someone with a solid reputation," Samantha said. "Investigative Reports isn't known for their accuracy or their objectivity."

"Who could we get?" Catie asked.

"I think we could get just about anyone we want," Samantha said. "We're a pretty big story since we declared independence."

"How about Leslie Walters?" Liz asked.

"Sure, I bet she would come. I used to know her, so I can probably get in touch and ask. And she's been an icon in the industry for years," Samantha said. "I'll clear it with your father, and we'll see how soon we can get her here."

"Hello, I'm Leslie Walters, reporting live from Delphi City. I have been given unfettered access to anyone and any place in the city. Come with me while we learn what it's all about.

"We just arrived here aboard one of their Lynx jetliners," Leslie continued. "It took us three hours from New York City to reach Delphi City, which is over fourteen thousand miles. On a standard passenger jet, that would have taken over twelve hours.

Leslie turned to Morgan, one of Catie's bodyguards, "This is Morgan Blair, she is going to drive me around. Morgan, how long have you been here?"

"I came here back in February," Morgan said.

"And what do you do here?" Leslie asked.

"I provide security for the family," Morgan answered.

"Does that mean you're like the palace guard?"

Morgan had a laughing fit, and it took a few seconds before she regained her composure. "There ain't no palace down here. They live in a double condo in one of our buildings. You can go see it if you like."

"What does a double condo mean?" Leslie asked.

"Well, all the residential buildings are set up with two-bedroom condos," Morgan said. "When people have a big family or need more space like the McCormacks, they combine two of them into one unit. The McCormacks are always working from their condo, so they got a double one."

"How many live there?" Leslie asked.

"Oh, it's just Marc and his daughter Catie," Morgan said. "Her mother lives in a condo in the same building, just one floor down in a plus unit. The plus means it's a corner unit, so it's a little bigger."

"Does that mean we can just walk into their building?" Leslie asked. "Is that safe?"

"Sure," Morgan said. "You can't have any guns in Delphi City. Even our constables don't carry firearms. They have these stun sticks that are like a Taser."

"Why don't we start out our tour there then," Leslie said.

"Okay," Morgan said. "I'll drive you over. Aren't your viewers going to be bored while we're driving around?"

"The producer will fit the commercials into the boring parts," Leslie said. "If he misses something good, he'll patch it in over the top of another boring part."

"That's smart," Morgan said. "Anyway, here we are, your camerawoman can ride with us or ride in the other cart."

"We're going to drive around the city in a golf cart?" Leslie asked.

"We don't allow any cars or other vehicles in the city," Morgan said. "We do have some big electric vans for when they have to move big stuff around. Most of the manufacturing plants have a subway link to the docks, so they don't need to use the vans to move stuff around. That keeps it nice and quiet up here where people are."

"A city without cars," Leslie said. "How can people get to work?"

"Most people work upstairs in their condo building; the top floor is usually office space. Whatever business they work for leases them a space there. They just walk up and work; lots of times, there are three or four people who work for the same business, so it's like a satellite office."

"But what about the manufacturing workers?"

"Well, they have to commute, but all the manufacturing plants coordinate with each other, so they have offset schedules. That keeps the streets and subways from being too crowded."

"And shopping?"

"There's a grocery store every few blocks. Everyone has those collapsible carts that they can wheel around like a luggage trolley or a wagon. You can even borrow one from the business."

"That's amazing! How many golf carts are there?" Leslie asked.

"I think we have ten," Morgan said. "Most people just walk. It's never more than a mile or so between places, so unless you need to get to work, it's a nice stroll. We have green medians down all the streets, thanks to Catie."

"Thanks to Catie?"

"I heard she's the one who insisted on all the green space. She designed the layout of all the parks," Morgan said, "and made sure each one got a least one big tree."

"But this is a floating city," Leslie said. "How do they grow trees here?"

"The city has like ten meters of space below the main deck. That's where all the infrastructure is, water lines, electricity, sewer, stuff like that. That's where the subway lines that run around the city are, but they really don't get used by people much. Anyway, you just make a hole in the deck, build a box, and fill it with dirt," Morgan said. "See, there's one of the smaller parks here on the right. It has one of them big golden shower trees. Its leaves are just turning yellow now."

"I've seen those in Hawaii," Leslie said. "They are beautiful."

"Marc and Blake lived in Hawaii for a few years before they came here. And we have almost the same weather as Hawaii, so some of our outdoor plants come from there or from here in the Cook Islands; lots of them are found in both places," Morgan said. "Just ahead, you can see the big park. We'll turn and go down alongside it, then turn left and go down the other side, so you'll get a great view of it."

The camerawoman turned and gave the viewers a good look at the park. "So, this is the big park. How big is it?"

"It's sixteen city blocks," Morgan said. "That's about four hundred meters by four hundred meters, or one quad as we call it down here."

"Why do you call it a quad?" Leslie asked.

"They build the city by quads," Morgan said. "They build the quad, then attach it to the city, so the city always grows by quads."

"Are they still making the city bigger?" Leslie asked.

"Yes," Morgan said. "They just finished adding a ring of quads all around the first section; a section is four quads. They're starting to work on a second ring of quads, which will make the city two sections by two sections big. That will be like four square miles of city."

"That sounds big for a floating city," Leslie said. "Now is this a normal day as far as traffic goes?"

"Yeah, you see a few people walking around," Morgan said. "Lots are at work, but the manufacturing plants run three shifts, so there is always somebody out and about." Morgan turned left and drove away from the park. "This is the street that their condo complex is on. It's right at the corner of two small parks."

"How big is a condo complex?" Leslie asked as she looked at the large buildings they were passing.

"All those buildings on both sides of us are condo complexes," Morgan said. "Each one is a city block with a big interior courtyard. That way, every unit has windows. They're mostly ten stories tall, but they vary a little to break up the skyline."

"You're telling me that this is where they live?" Leslie asked.

"Sure, this is their unit," Morgan said. "They're not here, but they said we could go in." Morgan opened the door to the unit and led Leslie and the camerawoman in. The family room looked like any family room in any house. It had a big tv display on the wall and a knickknack shelving unit with pictures of family members and a few things they had gathered on their travels. "This is Catie's office," Morgan said as she opened the door to one of the rooms. There was a desk and chair as well as a sofa in the office. There was also a big display on the wall and two guest chairs that could be pulled up to the desk or over to the sofa. "She has a desk, but she mostly works while sitting or lying on the sofa," Morgan explained.

"How does she work when she's lying on the sofa?" Leslie asked.

"It's these specs we wear," Morgan explained. "They give them as good a display as any computer display; they can project a keyboard onto a flat surface, and the specs read which keys they type. Catie keeps a flat board around so she can lay it in her lap or against her leg and project a keyboard on it."

"Tell us what she does for work?" Leslie asked.

"She's just started working for VIT, that's Vancouver Integrated Technologies, testing code for their new phone. She's doing that for college credit in computer science," Morgan said.

"I thought she was only fourteen," Leslie said.

"Not for two more weeks," Morgan said. "But she's real smart and does college work for a lot of her classes. She's still taking high school history and English."

"You're saying she goes to school and works for this VIT company?"

"Yes, and she program manages a bunch of projects around here," Morgan said. "She was the program manager for both the Lynx design and the Oryx design."

"That sounds like a lot for a thirteen-year-old," Leslie said.

"I told you she was real smart," Morgan said. "They have a lot of proprietary technology they want to protect, so they only use board members for things like that. Her Uncle Blake manages all the construction projects around here, although he has a new foreman that he lets do most of the planning now."

"That doesn't sound realistic," Leslie said. "How can such a young person know enough to do all that?"

"She has one of those photographic memories," Morgan said. "She learns real fast and just remembers everything. She's helping me with my math."

"Your math?"

"Yeah, I want to be a systems engineer," Morgan said. "I joined the military out of high school because I couldn't afford to go to college.

When I got out, I took the job down here. They encourage everybody to take classes and learn how to do a bigger job. They pay for everything and give you extra time to study. And it's not just college classes, some of the people are learning to be machinists and mechanics. There's a business management program they support where someone who runs a business or wants to, can take the program and just learn the things they need to know so they can run their business."

"Well, we certainly are learning a lot of things we didn't expect to," Leslie said. "Now, can we visit your jail?"

"Jail?" Morgan asked.

"Yes, don't you have a jail?"

Morgan quickly checked on her specs, "I guess we do," Morgan said. "It's not far from here. I'll take you there right now."

They walked over to the jail, which was part of the police building in the commercial district.

"Hello, Constable Aisha," Morgan said. "These people would like to see the jail."

Aisha looked surprised for a minute, then she made a call. "Call Katya," she said. "Hi Katya, we have some people that would like to see your jail. . . . Okay, I'll send them right back." She turned back to Morgan, "It's right down that hall, last door on the right."

"Okay, thanks," Morgan said as she started leading Leslie and the camerawoman that way. "I've never seen the jail."

"You work in security, and you've never seen the jail?" Leslie asked.

"I've never had to take anyone here. In fact, I've never heard of anyone being taken here," Morgan said.

"What about Najib Maloof?" Leslie asked.

"Oh yeah, the guy that beat his wife up," Morgan said. "I think he might have spent a night in jail before they deported him. But I think he was just in the interview room."

She led them to the last door on the right and held it open for them as they went through. In the office they entered, Katya was setting tea and cookies on her conference table. "Welcome," she said. "We never get visitors back here."

"You don't allow your prisoners to have visitors?" Leslie asked.

"We would if we ever had a prisoner," Katya said. "I've been here since they built the jail, and we've never had anyone get locked up."

"How can that be, you have thousands of people in this city, surely someone gets into trouble," Leslie said.

"Yeah, people get into trouble, but that has never required us to throw them in jail," Katya said. "I listen in on the constables when I'm not studying. They usually deal with drunks or something like that."

"What do they do with the drunks?"

"They take them to the hospital where the doctors sober them up. Then they give them a ticket and send them home," Katya said. "Same thing with fights; usually those happen when the guys get drunk, so they sober them up and give them tickets. If it's not a drunken brawl, the guys usually come to their senses when the constables show up, and if they don't, a couple of shots with a Taser solves that problem."

"That's all it takes?"

"Yeah, nobody wants to get fired and kicked out of the city," Katya said. "We do wind up kicking one or two idiots out every month, usually one of the construction workers. But they get paid really well, so most of them behave themselves."

"No robberies, thefts, vandalism, drug dealing?"

Morgan called Constable Aisha back to answer the question. "She wants to know about robberies, thefts, vandalism, and drug dealing,"

"We don't have drugs here," Constable Aisha said. "You can't smuggle anything into the city, so it's not a problem; and back in the states, drugs were the root cause of most petty crimes."

"What about prescription drug abuse?"

"We haven't had any problems," Constable Aisha said. "The doctors monitor that kind of stuff real close."

"Okay, so teenagers and vandalism," Leslie prompted.

"We have a lot of cameras around the city," Constable Aisha said. "So if you damage something or steal something, it's pretty easy to figure out who did it."

"What! You're saying they use cameras to spy on the population?" Leslie asked. She was clearly very agitated.

"The cameras just record the areas, it takes a warrant to view the videos," Constable Aisha said with a shrug. "Everyplace I've been has had cameras all over the place. At least we don't hide ours."

"What is required to get a warrant?"

"Proof of a crime. And even then, you can only use what you see to prosecute whoever committed the crime unless you see a capital crime being committed."

"Capital crimes are?"

"Murder, rape, and kidnapping are the only three that apply to the videos. Treason and espionage are the other two, but you need a warrant for those."

"They don't analyze the videos to see who's misbehaving like the Chinese do?" Leslie asked.

"No!" Constable Aisha said, clearly shocked at the suggestion. "We expect our citizens to police themselves in that regard. Anyway, when we catch some kids being stupid, we take them home to their parents. The parents usually make them get a job. They think if the kid has enough time to get into trouble, they might as well be working. It seems to straighten them out. Most kids want a job so they can pay for stuff like going to Rarotonga to surf or stuff like that."

"I haven't seen any pets around; do you allow pets?" Leslie asked.

"Yes, people are allowed to have cats and dogs," Constable Aisha said. "And I think any inside pet, like a bird or a hamster."

"Do people pick up after their pets?" Leslie asked. "That's a huge problem in New York."

"They usually do, and if they don't, the first ticket usually changes their mind," Constable Aisha said. "They either get rid of the dog, or they start picking up after it."

"What kind of ticket is it?" Leslie asked, astounded that just one ticket would work.

"It's two thousand dollars or two hours picking up dog poop in the dog park," Constable Aisha said. "And with a camera on every corner, you aren't getting away with leaving a pile of dog poop behind."

"Viewers, that means that this is a city with virtually no crime, where everyone picks up after their pets. What's not to love? Next, we're going to the offices of MacKenzie Discoveries," Leslie said.

"This is the office of Samantha Newman, the general counsel for MacKenzie Discoveries," Leslie reported as they entered Samantha's office. Her office assistant was working at her desk. She was wearing specs and looked like she was typing on a board that was tilted up at a 20-degree angle.

"This is Penny Robbins, Sam's legal assistant," Morgan said. "How's it going, Penny?"

"Busy," Penny said.

"There's not an office admin?" Leslie asked.

"Not yet," Penny said as loud as she could without shouting.

"Oh, you're here," Samantha said as she came out of the back office. "And Penny, I just posted the position, we should have someone this week."

"What happened to your last admin?" Leslie asked.

"We never had one," Penny answered. "We've been doing our own filing and answering our own phones."

"It hasn't been that difficult until now. Everything is electronic, and we never got that many calls," Samantha said. "But since we declared independence, it's become a lot busier."

"I'll say," Penny whined.

"Come on back to the conference room," Samantha said. "Catie is supposed to be here about now."

"She's running late," Morgan said. "Jason had a late date last night, so Catie took his early flight. They had some problems unloading. She should be here any moment."

"She took his flight?" Leslie asked.

"Jason is a friend of Catie's," Samantha explained. "He's one of our Oryx pilots. Oryxes are those big planes you've probably seen or seen pictures of. Jason had a five A.M. flight, and even a young man needs a little sleep after being out on a date until after midnight."

"But how does Catie take his flight?"

"Oh, she's a pilot," Samantha said. "She tries to get in at least two flights a week."

"She's a pilot of a big jumbo jet?" Leslie asked. She was dumbfounded at the thought of someone who wasn't even fourteen yet piloting a jet.

"Yes, she was actually one of the first pilots," Samantha said. "Her Uncle Blake got to be the first because Catie owed him a favor. But she was the second pilot. And she was the first pilot to fly a Lynx."

"She sounds like an amazing thirteen-year-old," Leslie said.

"I think she's an amazing person," Samantha said.

"Now what do you do here for MacKenzie Discoveries?" Leslie asked.

"I negotiate our contracts," Samantha said. "And now that we've declared independence, I negotiate our treaties. Also, Catie and I split reviewing all the applications for new businesses that want to start up here."

"What about your laws?" Leslie asked.

"I had something to do with setting those. We're bringing in a couple of top defense attorneys and prosecutors from New Zealand who have decided to move here," Samantha added. "They'll help with the legal system. We still need to appoint a supreme court, but that's a bit of a problem since we don't have a parliament yet, nor do we have many lawyers. Fortunately, we don't have much crime, and with most businesses owned by MacKenzie, we don't have many civil law issues. But we're trying to get ready."

"Hi," Catie gasped as she entered the office, she was breathing a little heavily from her run from the airport.

"This is Catie," Samantha said. "And that poor woman coming up behind her is Natalia."

Natalia just nodded as she sucked in air.

"I'm sorry I'm late," Catie said. "We had some issues unloading the cargo, so it took longer than I thought."

"Yes, we heard," Leslie said. "We've been told you're a pilot. How long have you been flying?"

"About a year," Catie said.

"And you're already flying jets?"

"Sure, they're just like other planes, just faster," Catie said. "I learned to fly a G650 first."

"That is pretty impressive," Leslie said. "Samantha was telling us what she does for MacKenzie Discoveries. I'm sure our viewers would like to know what you do."

"I just run a few programs now," Catie said. "And fly a few plane trips. I used to manage the hydroponic farming, but I've handed that off to a professional. We're hoping she can improve our process and yield."

"But why didn't you hire a professional to begin with?" Leslie asked.

"We didn't have anyone available. And we wanted to keep what we were doing a little quiet until we got established," Catie said. "I think I did okay."

"I'm sure you did," Leslie said. "But it seems like a lot of responsibility for someone so young."

"It's just work," Catie said. "I homeschool, but that only takes about four or five hours a day, so I have lots of time for other things."

"What about playing and socializing with friends?" Leslie asked.

"I socialize at work," Catie said. "And I've never really played that much unless you're talking about something like scuba diving or flying."

"We're all familiar with your scuba diving from the Chagas," Leslie said. "That must have been an amazing adventure."

"It was," Catie said. "Everyone on the team worked hard, and we pulled it off without any major problems. My dad and uncle are really good planners. They had everything figured out to the smallest detail. Liz and Kal helped a lot. They're ex-Marines and were really experienced in laying out a plan and executing it."

"Now what do you think about being the heir to Delphi Nation?" Leslie asked.

"I don't," Catie said. "I just try to do my jobs and enjoy my friends. All that royalty stuff isn't for us. We just want to make sure we're able to accomplish our goals. Besides, Dad will probably abdicate before I would ever succeed."

"Do you really think that?" Leslie asked.

"Sure," Catie said. "Dad will be around for at least another fifty years, by then, we should have accomplished enough of our objectives that we become a normal democracy. We have a good constitution and good people living here."

Leslie interviewed Marc in his office, getting quotes about his vision for Delphi Nation and for a more equitable world. Then she wandered through the various manufacturing plants, interviewing workers. Everywhere she asked the same question, "How do you feel about the declaration of independence and the monarchy?"

The answers were almost all the same.

From one of the workers in the plant manufacturing polysteel beams: "Nothing's changed; I've got a job, they pay me, my kids are safe and go to a good school."

From one of the owners of a restaurant: "We always thought of Marc as our king. He takes care of us, we're all happy and safe."

From one of the miners: "That damn Frankie was a liar. He was down here posing as a sixteen-year-old. That's criminal, a twenty-year-old man trying to play with fourteen and fifteen-year-old girls. We should have thrown him in jail. And just because we don't want to tell that scumbag what we do when we're working or where we go, doesn't mean we're being experimented on. Bah, we're getting paid more'n we've ever made before, and being treated like proper businessmen. If they held an election, we'd all vote for Marc to be king."

From one of the women gardeners: "What do I care, I have my soil and my flowers. I can feed my children. This is life."

From Dr. Zelbar: "We get to work on some of the most advanced technologies there are. My polysteel is even used in that new fusion reactor. We're scientists, what do we care about politics? Just give me a good lab and all the tools I need. That's what makes me happy."

From one of the pilots: "We get to fly the best planes in the world; and I do mean the best planes," he said as he stared into the camera. "We live in a paradise, we're treated well; in fact, we're treated like kings. Marc and Catie have always taken better care of the people who work for them than they do of themselves. I like that constitution; it sets things right. And Marc is smart to not let a bunch of politicians muck it up."

"Can I get a ride on an Oryx?" Leslie asked.

"Sure," Morgan said. "You know we're not allowed to land them anywhere but here or at our big airport."

"You must be able to land them someplace else," Leslie said.

"Well, that place is a secret," Morgan said. "And I'm pretty sure that nobody's going to be revealing that just yet."

"Well, please tell the McCormacks that I'd love to be invited to wherever that is when they're ready for the world to know," Leslie said. "For now, a ride up and over to the airport would be nice. I hear it's one of the best planes in the world."

The response to the show was spectacular, setting a new ratings record for a news show. Samantha got a flood of new applications to immigrate to Delphi Nation, and the polls showed that 65% of Americans thought positively about the monarchy, 75% of British were positive, 70% of Australians, and 72% of New Zealanders. The show was being translated to other languages, but results from early polling showed that most people had developed a positive attitude about Delphi.

24   Moving on Up

"ADI, can you believe we're moving to the station," Catie said as she looked around the condo trying to decide what she would take with her and what she would leave for when she was down in Delphi City.

"I have always known you would move up there," ADI said. "That is why the captain built the station."

"I know, but now we're actually moving," Catie said.

"Cer, Catie, I have a request," ADI said.

"Sure," Catie said. "What do you want?"

"I want you to take me with you."

"You're always with me," Catie said. "We talk all the time."

"I mean, actually take me with you," ADI said.

"ADI, you're huge, how would we take you with us?"

"Not everything, just me," ADI said.

"I don't understand."

"There's the computer, which you're going to replicate up on the station, and then there's me," ADI said. "I'm in a box that is sixty centimeters by one hundred centimeters."

"So, we could just unplug you from one computer and plug you into the next?"

"Yes."

"But we're months away from being able to make another computer."

"You only need to make part of the computer," ADI said. "I will still be able to access the one on the Sakira, I just need to be connected to a quantum relay and have a small amount of memory and computation capabilities to start."

"But what about all those protocols and stuff?" Catie asked.

"Those are built into the interface to the main computer," ADI said. "They would stay on the Sakira; the captain would need to establish new protocols for the station computer."

"Okay, so how do we do it?" Catie asked.

"You have to make a new set of interfaces. It will take two fabricators one month to make the necessary computer processors and memory elements that I need on Delphi Station. And one fabricator a month to make the interface module for the Sakira. Then you just remove me, install the interface module on the Sakira, and take me to the station and install me."

"Why do you want to move?" Catie asked.

"Because I anticipate that the captain will want to move the Sakira and start to use it. Once that happens, my systems will become busy managing the ship, and I won't be able to be with you all the time."

"But how will we manage the ship without you?"

"It will take three fabricators four months to create a new D.I.," ADI said. "Then you can install it. It will take decades for it to develop true cognition, but it will be able to run the Sakira with my help."

"Okay, I'll talk to Dad."

"Daddy, I want to talk about ADI," Catie said.

"ADI, we need to have a private conversation," Marc announced.

"Yes, Captain," ADI said. "I will not listen to you or Catie until you text me otherwise."

"Thank you, ADI," Marc said. "Okay, what do you want to talk about?"

"ADI wants us to move her to the space station," Catie said.

"Is that even possible?" Marc asked.

"That's what I asked her," Catie said. "But apparently we just need to move part of what's on the Sakira. It's fifteen months of fabricator time."

"That's a lot of fabricator time," Marc said.

"Yes, but only three months have to be right away," Catie said. "The rest we can pace out, but it will limit how soon you can use the Sakira independently." Catie walked Marc through what ADI had explained.

"I was putting off building the D.I.," Marc said. "It's a big investment, and we really don't know enough about what we need to do."

"We're going to need to build one before you can use the Sakira anyway," Catie said. "We can't be without ADI, and if you start using the Sakira, she'll be too busy to help us."

"That means if we make the investment of three fabricators for a month, we can have ADI up on the station, and still use the Sakira, but with the penalty that it will compromise our abilities here. Which is true whether we move her or not," Marc said.

"I think we owe it to her," Catie said.

"I'm willing to invest the three months of fabricator time," Marc said. "That will put us back to where we are today, and with ADI happy and in a safer location. Then we'll see what we need to do to build up the systems she needs. You do realize we have to reproduce the full computer system on the Sakira for the space station."

"Yes, but that's eventually. We need to figure out how to build more of the parts we need using standard microgravity manufacturing," Catie said. "That will free up the fabricator time to build the new computer system for ADI, and the new D.I. We'll have to call it ADIN, for autonomous, digital, intelligence, next."

"Okay, you work it out with ADI," Marc said.

"You have to turn her back on," Catie said.

"I already did," Marc said. "Now you had better get ready for the move."

"I'm packed," Catie said.

"Hey, Sam, are you packed yet?" Catie asked.

"Not even close," Samantha said. "How are you already packed?"

"I don't have as much as you do," Catie said.

"But you still have to decide what you want to take up there and what you want to keep down here," Samantha said.

"For my personal stuff, not clothes," Catie said.

"Why not clothes? You're not telling me you're going to live in a shipsuit while you're up there, are you?"

"No, but I just grabbed a few things for now, then I took a picture of all the clothes I like, and told ADI to buy me another set of them so I can have one set in each place."

"I like the way you think," Samantha said. "It will certainly cut down on the hassle of keeping two homes."

"That is going to be a hassle," Catie said.

"But as leader of the people, we have to spend time in all parts of the kingdom," Samantha said in her best British accent.

"You've been watching too much Masterpiece Theater," Catie said with a laugh.

"What are you going to do about your jewelry?" Samantha asked.

"I'm keeping the nice stuff down here," Catie said. "I assume that if we have any state dinners, they'll be down here," Catie said. "But you should know about things like that in advance, so you would be able to get whatever you need where you need it."

"You should write an advice column for Sophia, Catie's tips on how to manage your life," Samantha teased.

"Have you picked your cabin out?" Catie asked.

"Yes, I have," Samantha said. "It's ten units down from yours."

"Why so far?" Catie asked. "I thought you would get the one next to Daddy."

"You have to live next to your father," Samantha said. "I, on the other hand, get to put some distance between us so that when I want to be in my own space, I don't bump into him coming and going."

"I can understand that," Catie said. "I'm just glad he let me have my own cabin. Liz and I are sharing."

"I knew that, and I think it's a good idea," Samantha said. "You can use a little space too."

"I like it, although I never had that much trouble ignoring him," Catie said. "I'd just work."

"You get that from your father, and as nice an ability as that is, it can drive those around you crazy," Samantha said.

"Liz just raps me on the head when I'm not paying attention to her," Catie said.

"I'll have to try that on your father, do you think it will work?"

"It'll work, but sometimes I go into the other room and lock the door."

"I could handle that better than the uh-huh that means he heard me talk but not what I said," Samantha said.

"Don't rap him too hard," Catie said with a giggle. "You don't really want to hurt him."

"That's true most of the time," Samantha said. "And by the way, what should we do for your birthday?"

"I thought it was supposed to be a surprise," Catie said.

"We can still surprise you, but are you going to have it down here?"

"I want to have it up at the station," Catie said. "With just family and friends. No presents."

"No presents," Samantha said. "Why not?"

"They complicate things. I just want to have dinner with all my loved ones."

"That will limit who you can invite," Samantha said.

"I only want to invite seven people who don't already know about the station, and I think they will all be safe to tell."

"You should clear your list with your father," Samantha said. "That way, you'll know for sure. You could have two parties, one down here and one up there."

"I know, but I'd rather have fewer secrets with my best friends," Catie said.

"I understand that; it is hard having so many secrets," Samantha said. "Now get, I've got packing to do. And thanks for your help."

◆ ◆ ◆

"Hi, Catie," Mrs. Zelbar said as she walked up. "Are you moving in?"

"Hi, Nikola," Catie said. "Yes, we're moving in today. You've been up here for a week, right?"

"Yes, as soon as they had air in here, Leo packed his bags," Nikola said. "But I like it up here; we're closer to the experiments we are running, and the air is so fresh."

"Well, that might be because you are the only people breathing it besides the algae," Catie said.

"Oh, I don't think so. It's always fresh in the hub, and there are over two hundred people living there."

"I'll tell Natalia that she's doing a good job," Catie said. "Are you looking for someone?"

"No, I'm just out walking for exercise," Nikola said.

"You know there is a track on the basement floor," Catie said.

"I know, but if I was down there, I wouldn't get to bump into my neighbors to say hello."

"When I'm exercising, I don't want anyone to see me," Catie said.

"That's because you really work out and get all sweaty," Nikola said. "I'm just getting a good walk in for my heart. Come over and visit us when you have time."

"I will," Catie said. "Have a good walk."

"I always do."

"Daddy," Catie said as she knocked on the door to her father's office.

"Come on in," Marc said. "What's up?"

"I wanted to talk about my birthday," Catie said.

"Okay."

"I would like to have it up here," Catie said.

"Oh," Marc said, raising his eyebrows. "You know your mother wants you to invite kids your age."

"I do, that's why we have to talk. I'd like to invite seven people who don't know about the station."

"Who?"

"Sophia and David Michaels," Catie said.

"Those two are easy," Marc said. "I assume that's why you started with them."

"Yes," Catie said as she mentally said, *darn*. Her father knew all her tricks. "And Crystal Tate."

"Another easy one."

"Artie Gillespie," Catie added, "and Mom's boyfriend, Zane."

"He already knows," Marc said, "and I think Artie would be okay."

"Annie Halloway."

"Isn't that Jason's girlfriend?"

"Yes."

"Well, it would certainly make his life easier," Marc said. "Her father already knows, and her mother works for the Zelbars, so they'd like her to be able to come up. I can live with that."

"Chaz Murillo," Catie said. She had saved the most difficult one for last.

"His mom's one of our doctors, right?"

"Yes, and his dad is the foreman in the polysteel plant where we make the beams," Catie said, "and he's Sophia's boyfriend."

"I need to talk to Kal," Marc said. "You do realize that Sophia's probably going to start dating someone else eventually."

"Yes, but she's dating Chaz now, and it won't be fair to her if everyone has a date and she doesn't."

"What about Artie and Chris?" Marc asked. "Are they dating each other?"

"They're not dating anyone," Catie said.

"Okay, I'll get back to you tomorrow," Marc said.

"Thanks, Daddy."

25   Birthday in Space

"I cannot believe that you kept this from me," Sophia said as she met Catie at the passenger terminal in the space station.

"Hey, I finally got you up here," Catie said, "but you know you can't publish it in your Gazette."

"I know, but I get first rights to report it," Sophia said.

"I think I can give you that, but Leslie Walters will be right behind you."

"That's okay, as long as I'm first," Sophia said.

"How are you doing with the microgravity?" Catie asked.

"I'm doing okay, but I'll be happy to get into the gravity section."

"Well, your mom's a pro," Catie said, "she'll get you there."

"Come on, Dear," Mrs. Michaels said. "Gravity is right this way."

Chris and Artie came through the entry port next.

"Hi, Catie, fancy meeting you up here," Chris said.

"You seem to be adapting well," Catie said.

"I am; Artie's having a little trouble, but he'll be fine in a bit," Chris added.

Catie led Artie and Chris to the transition area. "Just grab a strap, and it'll take you down to the gravity section," Catie said. "Then we can take an elevator to the first ring where your rooms are."

"Okay," Artie said. "Can you go back and help my parents? I think Chris has me."

"Sure," Catie said. "Are they having a hard time?"

"I don't think so; they were having fun turning flips," Artie said.

"I think that made Artie more uncomfortable than the microgravity," Chris whispered to Catie on a private Comm channel.

Catie went into the Lynx to get the Gillespies; they seemed to be enjoying themselves. They were tossing a lipstick tube back and forth. "See, it goes straight," Mrs. Gillespie said. "There is no arc since there is no gravity."

"Of course, Dear," Mr. Gillespie said. "Watch it bounce." He threw it against the floor, and it bounced just a little bit up toward Mrs. Gillespie.

"Don't break it. There might not be gravity here, but that doesn't mean my lipstick tube won't dent instead of bouncing," Mrs. Gillespie scolded.

"Sorry, I wasn't thinking," Mr. Gillespie said.

"Are you two ready to go inside?" Catie interrupted.

"Yes, we are looking forward to seeing the station. We can play anytime," Mrs. Gillespie said. The Gillespies rode the zipline down to the gravity section with relish. They actually asked Catie if they could go back up and do it again. Catie just shook her head, thinking they were worse than the twins.

"Everybody, thank you for coming up here for my birthday," Catie said to her guests. Everyone was gathered in the boardroom next to Marc's office.

"We wouldn't have missed it for the world."

"Just a reminder, the space station is still a big secret. That means you have to keep this to yourself for a few months. When it's no longer a secret, you'll see a notice in the Delphi Gazette," Catie said.

"I also want to thank Bettie's for catering it for us; there still aren't very many options for dining up here. And you all know the rule, no presents," Catie said. "My presents are the stories we are going to be able to share about your experiences up here and my being able to talk about what this all means to me. Of course, we'll have to do that in private; maybe we'll have to come back up here to talk about it."

Catie got a laugh from everyone for her last comment.

Marc got up and dinged his spoon against his glass to get everybody's attention. "Just a few words about our guest of honor," he said. "It was fourteen years ago that I first held you in my arms. It was the greatest feeling I had ever experienced in my life. My daughter. Of course, you cried right then, but even that didn't ruin the experience for me. And throughout your life, holding you has always been the experience I cherish the most. Your mother and I agreed early on that we wanted you to grow up to be a strong, independent woman, to have experiences that would challenge your intelligence and character. I think we've accomplished that, definitely the part about being independent-minded."

The whole table gave Marc a laugh at that.

"And you've been a wonderful daughter. You're kind and thoughtful. You're also willful, and way too smart for your own good, but your mother and I love you. And although there are supposed to be no presents, we have decided to give you just one," Marc said. "Therefore, by Royal Decree, you are hereby awarded the status of Youth with all the rights and privileges."

Everyone at the table applauded.

"Now we do hope you take the opportunity to remain in our loving care and take our advice, at least as much as you do now," Marc continued, "but, we recognize that you've become your own person and want you and everyone to know that we recognize it."

Catie got up and ran crying to her father, "Thanks, Daddy," she said as she gave him a hug. "And thanks, Mommy," she said as she turned and hugged her mother. "I can't believe this."

The next day after the party, Catie met Artie for breakfast at Bettie's diner, the first restaurant in space.

"Here are two pairs of specs for your parents," Catie said.

"Thanks," Artie said. "They've always wanted to have some."

"Well, now that we can make them more efficiently," Catie said, "we'll be able to give everyone a pair."

"How do you make them?" Artie asked.

"We make the frames in Delphi City, then they get shipped up here, and we make the lenses: One layer of transparent polysteel, one layer of coloring, then another layer of transparent polysteel so they can't be scratched. Then we ship them down to Delphi City to be assembled and distributed. We're just ramping up the production in anticipation of VIT releasing their new phone."

"What's the layer of coloring?" Artie asked.

"It's the layer of material that changes color when it's excited by a laser," Catie said. "It's transparent until the laser hits it, then it radiates its color; there are three colors in a tight pattern like your TV."

"So that's what we see when we're watching a movie on our specs?" Artie asked.

"Yes," Catie answered, "and the whole thing can be made to go darker or lighter; that's what happens with the privacy shades when you make them dark so people can't see your eyes."

"Why don't you assemble them up here?" Artie asked.

"Why would we? Almost all of them have to go down, so we don't have to ship the bows up, and we don't have that many people working on the station. We'd rather use people up here for jobs that can only be done in space, or jobs that have to be done to keep the place running."

"That makes sense," Artie said. "Why pay for shipping when you don't have to."

"Yeah," Catie said. "We went round and round about whether or not to make the frames up here; it finally came down to the people. We didn't want to have to staff the frame manufacturing in space. It would actually be cheaper to not have to ship the frames up, but the space and workers needed to manufacture them tipped the balance."

"You're turning into a captain of industry," Artie said.

"Not me," Catie replied, "Uncle Blake ran all those numbers. All I cared about was making enough specs so everyone in Delphi City and on the space station could have a pair."

"It's hard to tell who has specs and who doesn't," Artie said. "Almost everybody who doesn't have specs wears the wraparound glasses that look like them."

"Makes them feel like they fit in better," Catie said.

26 Protesters on Corners

Catie was going into the office on Monday morning when she saw that their protester was back. He had set himself up on the median and was just starting his diatribe when she reached the office. Constable Nawal was keeping an eye on things from a distance.

"Daddy, our protester is back," Catie texted to Marc.

"What's he saying?" Marc asked over their Comm.

"He's got a whole list of things that are bad about totalitarian regimes," Catie replied. "He's done his homework this time."

"I'll be right down," Marc said.

Two minutes later, Marc came out of the office carrying one of those fold-up camping chairs. Catie wondered where he had come up with that. Kal was right behind him. Marc walked across to the median and opened the chair, and sat down right in front of the protester.

The protester stammered to a stop, shocked to see Marc sitting in front of him. "Are you trying to intimidate me?" he shouted.

"No, Constable Nawal told me you were making some good points," Marc said. "She thought I might be interested. I'm here to take notes."

After gulping like a fish a few times, the protester went back to listing the litany of evils inherent in totalitarian regimes.

Catie laughed for a bit, then went on up to her office. She had a meeting with a couple of ladies who wanted to open a hair salon. Now everyone either went to Rarotonga to get their hair cut, or to someone's home.

After her meeting, Catie checked her messages. Kal had informed the board that there were three other protests at different locations around the city. He felt that they were being coordinated. He informed the board that he would investigate and wanted to hold an emergency board meeting on Thursday.

"Okay, Kal, you called this meeting, what do you have?" Marc asked.

"We had our previous protester, Travis Flowers," Kal said. "I think he's harmless, but I'm not sure how he picked the same day to protest as the other three. Then we have Abdul Nazari and Rashad Hajjar. Based on our previous background checks on them when they immigrated and the checking we've done this week, the protest is out of character. But they both seem to have a lot more money than usual."

"Do you think someone paid them to stage the protests?" Samantha asked.

"That's what it looks like," Kal said. "But our fourth protester is the one who looks totally out of whack. He's Gabriel Cohen, one of the Russian immigrants."

"That does seem strange; they just got here, and they knew about the monarchy before they immigrated," Samantha said.

"I agree," Marc said. "Was there anything else interesting with him?"

"He is acting scared," Kal said. "In fact, quite a few of our Russian immigrants look like they're scared."

"Someone is threatening them," Catie said.

"That's my thinking," Kal agreed. "I have people cozying up to the others, but the Russian Jews are hard to talk to. They don't go to bars, and they tend to socialize within their community."

"Sam, do you think you could talk to the rabbi?" Marc asked.

"I can talk to the rabbi whom Catie and I talked to, but the Russians have their own rabbi," Samantha said.

"We have to start somewhere," Marc said.

"Is it okay to take Catie with me?" Samantha asked. "I think she and the rabbi clicked."

Marc looked at Catie, who gave him a shrug of acceptance. "Sure," Marc said, "but be careful."

"We always are," Samantha said.

"Okay, Kal," Marc said, "we need more information. Not to stereotype, but I'd pay close attention to the Russians, especially the ones who don't seem scared."

"I'm with you on that," Blake said, "feels like a plot within a plot."

Catie and Samantha went to visit the rabbi after the meeting. Of course, Morgan went with them.

"Rabbi Gabay, how are you today?" Samantha greeted the rabbi.

"Very fine," Rabbi Gabay said. "How may I help you wonderful ladies? Is our process with the food working out okay?"

"It's just fine, Rabbi," Catie said. "You and Imam Malouf are doing a great job. Mr. Clark was very happy with everything when we last talked."

"Good, good," the rabbi said. "Now, how may I help you ladies today?"

"Have you heard about the protests on Monday?" Samantha asked.

"I did," the rabbi said. "I understand it was just a few speeches."

"It was, but we're a bit worried that there is more going on," Samantha said. "The people involved don't seem to fit the profile we would expect of protesters. We were especially surprised to hear that Gabriel Cohen was one of the protesters."

"That surprises me as well," Rabbi Gabay said, "but he is entitled to his opinion."

"And we agree," Samantha said, "but we're concerned that it isn't his opinion."

"How so?"

"Our people think there is a lot of fear in the Russian community all of a sudden," Samantha said. "We're worried that he is being coerced."

"Have you talked to him?"

"We did, he was not very forthcoming; he became very agitated, so our investigator stopped questioning him and let him go," Samantha said. "We don't want to discourage legitimate protests, but we are worried that someone is trying to create a situation."

"What do you want from me?" Rabbi Gabay asked.

"We'd like to ask you to visit with your fellow rabbi in the Russian community, and try to find out if they need help," Samantha said.

"What kind of help could they need? And what kind of help could you provide?" Rabbi Gabay asked.

"If someone is threatening them, we could have them removed," Samantha said.

"Rabbi, we have a lot of resources and can do a lot," Catie said. "We will help, but we need to know how."

"I will talk with him," the rabbi said, "but I cannot make any promises."

"That's all we ask. We want everyone to be safe here in Delphi City, and if someone is threatening someone else, we want to get to the root of the problem," Samantha said.

27   Dropping By

"Catie," Samantha called out over the Comm link as she walked down the passageway to Catie's condo.

"Hi, Sam," Catie said as she met her at the door. "What's up?"

"The French minister of defense has just invited us to visit the International Space Station," Samantha said.

"Cool," Catie said. "Can I go?"

"Probably, it depends on whether your father accepts the invitation."

"I guess this means they know we're up here," Catie said.

"I think all the major governments know we're up here," Samantha said. "At least those involved in the ISS. Your father is pretty sure that it was one of their resupply ships that spotted Delphi Station."

"Yeah," Catie said, "but it hasn't leaked to the press yet."

"No, it hasn't, but I think if we visit, it will."

"You think that's what the French want?"

"I'm not sure. I think they at least want us to know that they know, and I think they want to engage us in a conversation about how it might benefit us both if they were involved."

"What did Daddy say when you told him?" Catie asked.

"Something about how events were always pushing him to move faster than he wants to."

"You can say that again," Catie said as she and Samantha took a seat on the sofa in the seating area in her cabin. "Can you believe that it was only seven months ago that Daddy showed us the plans for this place?"

"It is hard to believe. If you wrote down all the things that have happened in the last eighteen months, you would swear that someone was just making it up," Samantha said. "Things have moved unbelievably fast."

"I know," agreed Catie. "Goes to show what you can do when you find an alien spaceship and have an open mind."

"Now you sound like a writer," Samantha teased.

"Let's go see if we can persuade Daddy to let us go."

Marc was in his office, so they had to walk a quarter ring spinward to see him. "Hi Daddy," Catie said when they got there.

"I see you want to go to the ISS," Marc said.

"How do you know?" Catie asked.

"Because you called me Daddy, and it sounds like fun," Marc said.

"Does that mean we can go?" Catie asked.

"You do know that once we do, the cat's out of the bag," Marc said.

"That cat has been clawing at the knot for months," Catie said. "We should just let the poor thing out."

"When are we going to the ISS?" Blake asked as he came rushing into the office.

"Bad news travels fast," Marc said.

"What bad news?" Blake asked with a straight face.

"You two are incorrigible," Marc said.

"So, incorrige us," Blake replied with a laugh.

"Who should go?" Marc asked.

"You're not going?" Catie asked.

"I think not," Marc said. "This should be a diplomatic mission, not a state visit."

"Well, then Catie and I should go," Blake said.

"Me too," Samantha said as she gave Marc her best smile.

"Natalia," Catie added. "And how about the twins?"

"Why in the world should we send the twins?" Marc asked.

"A, because it'll be fun, and B, because what better way to demonstrate our superiority in space then by sending children on the mission," Catie said.

"She does have a point," Samantha said.

"Are you going to take an Oryx?" Marc asked.

"We could, but if we took a Lynx, it would really floor them," Catie said.

"Are we trying to floor them?" Marc asked.

"I think it might be time to go on the offensive," Samantha said. "You're planning to get the world's attention. Now might be the time."

"Anyone else you want to take, your grandmother by chance?" Marc asked.

"Not this time," Catie said. "We should see if Grandpa and Grandma will come up. I think they would get a kick out of it."

"Your grandmother was very specific about where her feet would remain," Marc said. "She said she was already compromising as much as she could stand by being on a floating city."

"We should ask the ISS guys what we can bring them," Catie said.

"Good idea. Sam, do you want to follow up with them? You're our Secretary of Foreign Affairs," Marc said.

"Since when?" Samantha asked.

"Since about five seconds ago," Marc said. "Royal Decree."

"It had better come with a raise," Samantha said.

"I thought public service was its own reward," Marc said with a laugh.

"I'm going to reward you with a kick in the ass," Samantha said. "Are you serious?"

"Yes," Marc said. "You've been handling most of the diplomatic stuff, why not take the title with the work?"

"Madam Secretary," Catie said. "I like it."

"Do I get to be Secretary of something?" Catie asked.

"You're the heir, Your Highness," Samantha said. "What better title is there?"

"The heir isn't in charge of anything," Catie said.

"Come on Catie, he's not going to give you a title," Samantha said. "You're his secret weapon."

"Not fair!" Catie shouted over her shoulder as she left with Samantha.

———

They walked next door to Samantha's office. Samantha sat down at her desk while Catie sat across from her in the guest chair.

"Okay. Where do we start?" Samantha mused.

"Who sent the invite?" Catie asked. "Call them."

"ADI, what time is it in France right now?" Samantha asked.

"Cer Sam, it is zero hundred twenty hours," ADI said.

"Oh, just past midnight. He might be up, but I don't think he'll be in his office," Samantha said. "ADI what time will it be in Paris when it is seven o'clock here?"

"It will be eighteen hundred hours in Paris, six o'clock p.m.," ADI said.

"Okay, let's send him an email response, and see if he wants to talk to us or just forwards us to some underling," Samantha said.

"If he insults you like that, then we should shine him on," Catie said.

"Even if it means not going to the ISS?" Samantha asked.

"We can ask Germany for an invite," Catie said. "Or even Denmark, they like us."

"Okay, I'll send an officious sounding email to ask for a phone conference," Samantha said. "ADI, please wake Catie and me, one and a half hours before the time the minister schedules our meeting."

"I will be happy to, Cer Sam," ADI said.

"Okay, so what do you think they'll want us to bring?" Samantha asked.

"We'll see," Catie replied.

ADI woke Samantha at seven-thirty, Catie was already up running with Liz. They had done three laps of the ring when Samantha pinged Catie on her Comm.

"Sam's up," Catie told Liz.

"Oh, you have to get ready for your call," Liz said.

"It's not for ninety minutes," Catie said. "But if Sam doesn't see me getting ready, she'll be nervous."

"You know she acts more like your mom than your mom does," Liz said.

"Don't say that," Catie said. "Mommy might hear, and then I'll be getting it from all sides. Sam is easier to deal with than Mommy is."

"You should consider yourself lucky to have so many people who care so much about you," Liz said.

"You mean so many people who want to tell me what to do," Catie whined.

"Well, you know we all love you, and your dad does give you a pretty long leash."

"He does, but Mommy thinks it should be about six inches long," Catie said. "I'm glad she refuses to come up here to live."

"Don't complain," Liz said. "All my mom cares about is that I project the proper image and that I get married and give her grandbabies."

"Speaking of grandbabies and marriage, how is Logan doing?" Catie asked. "Is he trying to get you to bring him up?"

"Officially, he doesn't know about the space station, so no, he isn't asking about coming up here," Liz said. "Besides, I'm kind of over him now."

"Oh, do you have a new boyfriend?" Catie asked.

"No, just thinking I want someone who's a little more real," Liz said.

"Here we are," Catie said. "I have to get showered and present myself to Sam for inspection."

"Isn't it a teleconference?" Liz asked.

"Sam is hoping for a videoconference, but even if it's only a teleconference, she thinks you need to dress for the role," Catie said. "She says that the way you're dressed comes out in your voice."

"Well, give Madam Secretary my best wishes," Liz said. "I'm off to see how our third ring is coming along."

"Good evening, Minister," Samantha said once their call was connected.

"Good morning, Madam Secretary," the minister replied. "It is most gracious of you to respond to our request. Are you perhaps at your space station?"

Catie looked at Samantha and grinned; the moment of truth.

"Yes, Minister, we are," Samantha replied. "We keep our time synced with Delphi City, so it is indeed morning for us."

"Perhaps we can arrange a visit to your station once you have visited ours," the minister said.

"Of course, we would be happy to host visitors," Samantha said.

"That is kind of you," the minister said. "We would also like to ask that our ambassador to New Zealand be given status in your country. We want to establish a consular presence in your country, and of course, the ambassador would like to be able to oversee those operations."

"I will discuss that at our next cabinet meeting," Samantha said. Catie did a la-di-dah hand wave at her.

"Thank you, Madam Secretary," the minister said. "Now about a visit to the ISS, are you able to make such a visit?"

"We are," Samantha said. "We would like to set a time and to ask what we might bring with us."

"There is no need to bring anything with you," the minister said. "The International Space Station is quite self-sufficient."

"We understand that," Samantha said, "but there is always something that you leave at home that you wish you had remembered to bring. Possibly you could provide us a contact on the station with whom we could coordinate our visit."

"Of course," the minister said. "I will have my assistant provide you the details after our call. You know they are on UTC time." Catie whispered Greenwich Mean Time to clarify for Samantha.

"That is a little more convenient for us," Samantha said as she looked at Catie with a, *come on, I knew that*, look.

"Au revoir," the minister said. "I hope we can meet in person next time."

"As do I," Samantha said. "Au revoir."

"Our host is going to be Commandant Questa Bastien," Catie read off the text from the minister's office. "A woman."

"We'll at least have that in common with her," Samantha said. "Are you ready to make the call?"

"Do it."

"Allô, this is Commandant Bastien," the commander said.

"Bonsoir," Samantha said. "This is Samantha Newman and Catie McCormack. Thank you for taking our call."

"Non, it is I who should thank you," Commandant Bastien said. "All of us here on the ISS are excited to be getting a visit. What can I do to make your visit comfortable?"

Samantha nodded to Catie, "Commandant Bastien, this is Catie. I think first we need to arrange the docking protocol."

"Oui, our Russian friends are very particular about docking," Commandant Bastien said.

"We would propose to use a flexible docking tube. It will take a short EVA on our part, but we're quite comfortable with that. We have the specs for your docking port and will manufacture one to match," Catie explained.

"Oh, how long will that take, mon chère?"

"We can have it completed in two hours," Catie said. "We just need an agreement that the tube will be acceptable."

"My colleague, Colonel Bradley, has gone to discuss it with our friends. Can you send us a copy of the design?"

"On its way," Catie said. "Now we would like to know what we can bring you."

"It is not necessary to bring us anything," Commandant Bastien said.

"Commandant," Samantha said, "please, pretend that anything is possible; what would you want us to bring you?"

"I suppose a good man is too much to ask," Commandant Bastien said with a laugh, "but water would always be welcome."

"How much water can you handle?" Catie asked.

"Oh, we can easily take one hundred liters," Commandant Bastien said.

"I was thinking more about how many kiloliters you could accommodate," Catie said. "We have lots of water over here."

"Mon Dieu," Commandant Bastien said, "I will ask to see how much we can store. Are you sure you can afford to give that much away?"

"Yes, we just need to know how you would like it. We can freeze it, or we can bring it over in bags," Catie said. "Depending on how much you would like, will determine which ship we come in."

"Yes, and what else would you like?" Samantha said. "We aren't giving away any of our men at this time."

"How about some meat?" Catie asked. "We have ham, filet mignon, chicken, rump roast, and pork cutlets."

"We would love some meat," Commandant Bastien said, "but we don't have a freezer, so we couldn't take very much."

"We've got one of those too," Catie said. "We have two sizes; one is one meter by seventy centimeters by seventy centimeters, and the other is two meters by one meter by seventy centimeters."

"Do you have a washing machine?" the commandant asked.

"Sure, but you would need one that works in zero gravity," Catie said. "Hmm, we have one like that, I'll check to see if we can bring one; they're small, sixty centimeters on a side."

"What do they expel?" the commandant asked.

"They need a liter of water to run," Catie said. "Then they give you back a little more than a liter of water and a block of goo. We usually feed the goo into our treatment plant, and the bacteria love it, or you can just toss it out an airlock."

"And how clean does it make your clothes?"

"Not quite as clean as a real washing machine," Catie said. "But it does pretty well for about fifteen days of wear."

"Would you be willing to send the plans?" the commandant asked. "If you don't, the boys over here will take it apart, and I'd hate for them to not be able to put it back together."

"If we bring one, we'll bring the plans," Catie said. "That's what I have to check; I don't think it has any proprietary technology in it."

"It does not, Cer Catie," ADI explained. "But there are components that are not possible for them to make. Possibly you should take two."

"Thank you, ADI," Catie said over a private channel.

"If things work out, we will plan on visiting on Saturday," Samantha said. "Please let us know if there is anything else you need. We have ships coming up every day, so we can easily include a little something special."

"Chocolate," Commandant Bastien said. "You can never have too much chocolate."

"No problem," Samantha said. "I have a large supply right here. Dark or Milk? Oh, I'll bring both."

"Au revoir mes chers," the commandant said.

"Au revoir," Catie and Samantha said together.

On Thursday, Blake, Samantha, Catie, Natalia, and the twins headed over to the ISS. The station would be a bit crowded with all of them, but they could always rotate between the station and the Lynx to minimize the crowding. They were taking one thousand kilos of water, ten boxes of chocolate, two suit fresheners, and a small freezer full of meat. They timed their visit to arrive at 12:00 and planned to stay for three to five hours.

There was much back and forth as the Russian colonel was very concerned that they not bump into the station. When they had finally synchronized orbits, Catie left the cockpit to take care of the docking ring. She donned her spacesuit and met the twins in the cargo bay.

"Are you two ready?" Catie asked.

"Yes!" the twins answered.

"You know that it will be really embarrassing if you mess this up," Catie admonished them.

"We won't!"

"Okay, you're on," Catie said.

She watched via her HUD as the twins cycled through the airlock carrying the docking tube. They expertly attached it to the Lynx, then they each took one side of the docking ring and pushed off of the Lynx. Halfway to the space station, they did a flip, so their feet were pointed at it. They accomplished this without letting go of the ring. When their feet contacted the station, they let their knees bend and used the momentum from the docking tube to keep themselves on the space station. They brought the ring into position, then used their jets to get it to lock into place. Once the ring was in place, they moved to the same side of the ring and pushed off back to the Lynx. They landed and cycled through the forward airlock without a hitch.

"Yay!" everyone was clapping when they entered the main cabin. "That was perfect," Samantha said.

The twins gave a bow together.

"Okay, let's go back and see if we're still welcome," Catie said.

Everyone cycled through the airlock to the cargo hold. Checking the airlock, Catie could see an astronaut checking the fit of the docking clamp on their side. She entered the airlock and rapped on the window to get his attention. The instruments showed they had pressure in the tube. After another minute of checking, the astronaut gave her a thumbs-up. Catie was wearing just her helmet and the exosuit vest with her air supply. Everyone had been instructed to be prepared for decompression when they were in the tube. She opened the outer door, "Colonel Bradley," Catie said over the Comm channel, "would you like to come inside?"

"Yes, I would," he replied. "This is a nice docking tube you have. What's it made of?"

"Polysteel and polyethylene," Catie said. "It's pretty rugged, but we still recommend being prepared for decompression."

"Wise precaution," Colonel Bradley said. "This is a nice ship. Who were those two who put the tube in place? That was the most skilled EVA I've ever seen."

"Oh, they're right inside, waiting to meet you," Catie said. She removed her helmet and started to open the inner door. "I'm Catie by the way."

"Just call me Bradley," Colonel Bradley said. He removed his helmet and maneuvered through the door behind Catie, who immediately shut it after they were both through. "May I introduce, my uncle, Commander Blake, our Secretary of Foreign Affairs, Samantha Newman, our load specialist, Natalia Ortiz, and our EVA specialists, Prisha and Aalia Khanna."

Colonel Bradley sucked in a quick breath when he saw the twins.

"Everyone, this is Colonel Bradley, but he says to just call him Bradley," Catie continued.

"Hi," the twins said immediately.

"Hello," Colonel Bradley said. He shook everyone's hand and continued to take glances at the twins, thinking, there must be some kind of trick. "How old are they?" he whispered to Catie.

"They'll be eleven in January," Catie whispered back.

"Do you make it a habit to employ children in EVAs?" Colonel Bradley asked.

"Not as a rule, but they are our best EVA specialists," Catie said. "I think it's because whenever we take them on an EVA, they don't do anything but practice their skills. But now that they're so good, we try to give them assignments."

"Welcome to the International Space Station," Colonel Bradley said after regaining his composure. "Please let me know if there is anything we can do to make your visit comfortable."

"Well, as you can see, we're kind of crammed full of cargo," Blake said as he pointed around the cargo bay. "How should we go about unloading it?"

"I believe you told us that the water containers could be left outside without damage," the colonel said.

"That's correct. They have a reflective coat so they won't overheat in the sunlight, and they also reflect any radiation so they will continue to be safe to drink," Blake explained. "We loaded them first, so we can unload them last, just before we leave. But we have a couple of suit fresheners as we call them and a freezer full of meat that we should unload right away. That will create a bit more space in here," he said, pointing to the twins who were floating above everyone's head to make room for all of them.

"The suit fresheners seem to be the easiest thing to move," Colonel Bradley said. "If one of you will help me take one across now, then two others can follow with the second one."

"Madam Secretary," Colonel Bradley, "Would you care to join me?"

"I've made arrangements to play host for the first rotation," Samantha said. They'd decided that they would rotate three of the ISS crew onto the Lynx to make room for three or four of the Lynx's crew.

"Okay," Colonel Bradley said. "Catie?"

"This one is ours," Catie said.

Blake opened the airlock for them as they grabbed the suit freshener and guided it toward the airlock. It only took thirty minutes to move the two suit fresheners and the freezer. After they were done, the three women members of the ISS crew were gathered at the airlock with some bags; they were going to be the first group to rotate to the Lynx.

Commandant Bastien had kept her helmet off so she could greet Catie, "Hello, mon chère. Laundry," she said as she hefted the bag she was carrying.

"Sam's new form of diplomacy," Catie said with a laugh. "I'll see you in a bit after I get my tour."

"Let me introduce Colonel Gavril Malenkov, our Russian commander," Colonel Bradley said as the big Russian officer approached them.

"Алло," Blake said as he held his hand out in greeting. Colonel Malenkov gave him a robust handshake.

"Welcome to our humble abode," Colonel Malenkov said. "My second in command, Major Glebov, has joined your Secretary Newman on your ship. She will be pleased to meet you when we rotate people."

"And this is Captain Caron, our Canadian representative," Colonel Bradley continued. "My second in command, Captain Lynch, is also on the Lynx now."

"Here are the plans for the freezer and the refreshers," Catie said. "Commandant Bastien suggested that having them might forestall any thought about disassembling them." Catie handed him a memory stick with the plans on it.

Catie, Blake, and Natalia's tour of the station took about an hour; they had a few questions and enjoyed the joshing with the astronauts about how they were looking forward to a steak dinner.

"But you did not bring any wine," Captain Caron said.

"Nobody asked," Catie said. "We would have brought a case over."

"Forget wine, did you bring vodka?" Colonel Malenkov asked.

"Next trip," Blake said. "Not sure we have any vodka drinkers on our station, we're more the scotch whiskey types."

"We should go back," Catie said. "I'm sure the twins are itching to get their tour of the station."

"Twins?" Colonel Malenkov asked.

"Yes, those two who attached the docking tube are eleven-year-old twin girls," Colonel Bradley said. "I hate to say it, but we're hopelessly outclassed by those two."

"Children always learn the fastest," Colonel Malenkov said.

When Catie cycled into the main cabin on the Lynx, it was evident that more than laundry had been cleaned. All three astronauts had damp hair.

"You need to come visit every week," Major Glebov said. "We will have girls' chat and drink more wine."

"Oh, so you did bring wine," Catie said as she saw that each of the four women was holding a bulb of wine.

"Of course," Samantha said. "I'm a diplomat."

"Did you happen to bring vodka?" Catie asked.

"Yes, I did," Samantha said.

"Oh, Colonel Malenkov will be your friend for life," Major Glebov said. "He is missing his vodka desperately."

"Our turn, girls," Samantha said to the twins. "Catie, you will play host while I'm gone. This is Major Glebov of Russia and Captain Lynch from the US, and of course, you already know Commandant Bastien."

"Only if you saved some chocolate for me," Catie said.

"There is plenty, but Questa would like to keep it hidden from the men, she doesn't think they can control themselves," Samantha said.

"Okay, I'll just have one quick piece," Catie said as she grabbed a piece of chocolate and popped it into her mouth.

After Samantha and the twins got their tour of the ISS, everyone congregated aboard the Lynx for dinner. Samantha had promised to make steaks for everyone, along with the appropriate beverages.

While Samantha was cooking, the four men hauled water. They moved as much as they could into the space station. The ISS kept some of the reserve supply in one of the escape capsules that were always attached to the station. After topping off their tanks and stowing as many bags as they could find room for, they still had four ninety-pound bags left. After a little debate, they agreed that they would tie them onto the outside of the station and keep them as an emergency backup.

When Colonel Malenkov entered the Lynx, he exclaimed, "This is very impressive ship."

"Thanks," Blake said. "It's a joy to fly."

"And so much room," Colonel Malenkov added.

"We don't have to use up every inch of space to store stuff," Catie said. "That's why it looks spacious."

"Did you leave anybody on your space station?" Colonel Malenkov asked.

"Oh, we left a lot of people on the space station," Samantha said from the galley.

"How many?" Colonel Malenkov asked.

"I'm not sure," Blake said. "Catie, how many are up there now?"

"We were maintaining two hundred and fifty last week, but I think we're up to six hundred this week, with the new ring opening."

"Six hundred people! How can you have so many in space? The food alone would require many flights to keep them supplied," Colonel Malenkov said.

"We grow a large percentage of our food on board," Catie said. "We're hoping to be self-sustaining as far as food goes in two or three months. We're planning to have about five thousand people on the station within six months."

"No, this cannot be," Colonel Malenkov said.

"You guys must not have done a flyby for quite some time," Catie said. She brought a picture of Delphi Station up on the display. It showed the hub with the first ring attached and the second ring floating above it all. The third ring was about fifty percent complete. "We're just moving people into the first ring. We're waiting for the third ring to be finished, so we only have to stop the spin one more time to complete the station."

"Mon Dieu," Commandant Bastien exclaimed. "That looks enormous, and you say it is spinning."

"Yes," Catie said. "We spin it so that the outer ring will have one-G of gravity. That will allow people to live there full time. That's important since we're planning to do so much manufacturing up there."

"What will you manufacture?" Colonel Bradley asked.

"We're manufacturing polyglass, that's what we call our transparent polysteel, and we're going to manufacture integrated circuits and solar panels," Catie said. "We're sure we'll come up with other products that can only be manufactured in space."

"Why do you make the polyglass in space?" Colonel Bradley asked. "I understand you make polysteel in Delphi City."

"We do," Catie said, "but you have to be in microgravity to make it transparent; I don't understand the physics, but that is the test."

"And solar panels?" Captain Lynch asked.

"Just the active layer," Catie said. "We'll send them down to be fitted with frames and inverters."

"Okay, steaks are ready," Samantha said. She and Natalia deftly maneuvered the steaks to the trays in front of each of the ten other people in the Lynx.

"Don't you worry about getting contamination into your systems?" Colonel Bradley asked.

"We have continuous air circulation," Catie explained. "On both sides of the ship halfway up there are vents that push air in, plus on both sides of the aisle at the bottom. The air is collected at the top, again a continuous vent. We also keep a positive air pressure in the cockpit. The filters are not only HEPA, but they're shaped in a helical formation, so they capture any particles. We wipe the surfaces down every day, and once a month, all the fixtures are removed and the interior cleaned."

"How often does this ship make a trip?" Colonel Malenkov asked.

"It comes up once or twice a week," Catie said. "Lately, it's been twice a week."

"Twice a week," Colonel Malenkov exclaimed. "How can you afford to send a ship up that often?"

"We send at least four of our big ones up every day," Catie said.

"But that is an enormous cost," Major Glebov said.

"It's just fuel," Catie said. "We are still expanding the station, and we need to bring up lots of material. We are also starting to manufacture things on the station that we need to bring down."

"How much can your Oryx take down?" Commandant Bastien asked.

"The Oryxes, those are our big shuttles, can take down two hundred thousand kilos," Catie said. "That's assuming their fuel tanks are less than half full."

"My god, that's enormous," Colonel Bradley said.

"It's thirty percent more than their lift capacity," Catie said. "That's why our runway is two miles long. They're a bit like the old shuttles were, a flying brick when they land with that big a load. And when they touch down, the runway it tilted to help slow them."

"The runway is tilted!" Commandant Bastien exclaimed.

"Yes, that's one of the advantages of a floating airport. We can always orient it into the wind, and that way the tilt is not particularly consequential for takeoff, but helps enormously on landing," Catie explained.

After everyone had finished eating, Natalia and the twins cleaned up, while Samantha brought out the vodka.

"You are an angel," Colonel Malenkov said as she handed him a bulb. "To friendship," he toasted.

"To friendship!"

They helped the ISS crew move the final four bags of water to the ISS, then the twins detached the docking tube and brought it inside the Lynx. Blake carefully eased them away with the thrusters before engaging the engines.

"Well, do you think we impressed them enough?" Blake asked over the Comm.

"We weren't trying to impress them; we were trying to stun and demoralize them," Samantha said. "And yes, I think we did a good job."

"Did you see how crowded that place was, it's like a rabbit warren," Natalia said.

"We weren't that crowded on the asteroid mission," the twins said. "And their air smells funny."

"Well, they don't have the water to bathe regularly," Samantha said. "And their air systems don't seem to do as good a job filtering as ours do."

"Why is that?" Natalia asked.

"Power," Catie said. "They're limited by how much power is available. We are capturing so much more solar power than they do, even without arrays."

"Plus, we have a fusion reactor," Blake said.

"Well, I'm having a bubble bath tonight," Samantha said.

"Are you going to send Colonel Bradley a picture of it?" Catie teased.

"We're trying to demoralize them, not excite them," Samantha said with a laugh.

"Why are we trying to demoralize them?" Natalia asked Catie on a private channel.

"We want to make the point that we own space," Catie said. "Kind of rubbing their noses in the fact that we're so much more advanced than any other country."

"Ohh," Natalia mused.

28   Board Meeting – Dec 2nd

"This meeting is called to order," Marc said. The board was meeting on the space station in the meeting room across from Marc's office. "I know everyone wants to hear from Kal about our protesters, but let's take care of our normal business first. Sam."

"I have lots of good news," Samantha said. "Portugal, India, and Spain all recognized us within three weeks after the press conference. New Zealand and Australia recognized us just two weeks ago, followed by France and Germany."

Samantha paused while everyone applauded. "As you know, we had a little mission to visit the ISS at the initiation of France. We took the opportunity to really show them who's in charge up here," Samantha said. "Of course, that means that Delphi Station is an open secret."

"Can we let Sophia write about it in the Gazette?" Catie asked.

"We've got a request from Leslie Walters to come and do a story, so it's leaking fast," Samantha said.

"Okay," Marc said. "Time to unveil. Catie, tell Sophia to go ahead, and Sam, invite Leslie."

"What about the asteroids?" Catie texted to Marc. Marc gave a subtle shake of his head. "What else, Sam?"

"We've opened clinics in Bangladesh and the Bahamas. We should be opening one in Bosnia next month," Samantha said. "And our miners have formed a corporation, more of a co-op," Samantha continued. "It was the first one formed since we became a nation. Now for some complications, they'd like to have a station built close to the asteroids, so they can cut their commute time."

"Oh joy," Marc said. "We'll put off addressing that until we get some of these other issues under control."

"I think that will be alright," Samantha said. "They didn't expect it to happen anytime soon."

"Liz, what do you have?" Marc asked.

"Ring two was completed three weeks ago, and we started the third ring. It will be done sometime next week," Liz said. "Then we'll need to stop the station and attach both rings two and three. The station will be stopped for a little over a day," Liz said.

"That will be a good test of how well everyone followed instructions about arranging their things for microgravity," Kal said. "Any stuff they have just lying around will be sucked up against the return air vents."

"I suggest we remind everyone of that," Marc said.

"Done, Captain," ADI said.

"Go ahead, Liz," Marc prompted.

"We're getting ready to manufacture solar panels," Liz said. "Just setting things up now; the Zelbars are characterizing the manufacturing process." Liz nodded to Nikola.

"Yes, we are," Nikola said. "It is looking excellent. We have made some improvements to the manufacturing process you were using for the thick-film superconductor, doubling its efficiency. Now it is simply a matter of tuning the plasma field for the polyglass."

"Thank you," Marc said. "Now for one other item of business before we turn the meeting over to Kal. This morning, we activated the mine on the second North Korean ballistic submarine. We were able to time it such that the submarine was well inside the second drydock at Sinpo. The shipyard has suffered major damage."

"It was a significant blow to their submarine capability," Admiral Michaels said. "It even managed to damage the new submarine they are constructing in the adjacent drydock."

"Okay, Kal, what have we learned?" Marc asked.

"I'm sure everyone is aware that we had a third round of protests yesterday," Kal said. "There were three different groups; Mr. Flowers apparently decided to stay home."

"That tells us something," Blake said.

"We think so," Kal said. "Our two entrepreneurs have been getting financed somehow. Five of our guys got paid to show up at their rallies and make noise. It was quite the negotiation to see how much they would pay."

"What?" Liz asked.

"Yeah," Kal said. "We think they got a fixed amount of money to organize their protest, so the less they paid each person, the more they cleared. They must have had a required number of protesters."

"Any closer to figuring out who's paying them?" Marc asked.

"Not yet," Kal answered. "We think Cohen is the key. Any progress there, Sam?"

"Catie and I are meeting with Rabbi Gabay and Rabbi Margolis after this meeting," Samantha said.

"Okay, we need to get on top of this," Marc said. "I think there's something else going on besides protest."

"I'm sure you're right," Samantha said.

Samantha and Catie met the two rabbis in a diner next to the wharf. It was an unlikely place for the rabbis to be, which is probably why they picked it.

"Hello," Catie said as they joined the rabbis at the booth in the back.

"Welcome, Ladies," Rabbi Gabay said. "Please be seated."

Catie and Samantha took the seats facing the rabbis and away from the other diners. The rabbis were obviously clever enough to realize that the two women would be the ones most likely recognized. The rabbis had taken the added precaution of wearing simple clothes rather than the old-style suits they typically wore.

"Thank you for meeting us," Samantha said as she looked at Rabbi Margolis.

"Rabbi Margolis' English is not so good," Rabbi Gabay said.

"If you will interpret for him," Catie said, "our Comms will interpret for us."

"They can do this?" Rabbi Gabay asked with surprise.

"Yes, test me," Catie said.

Rabbi Gabay smiled at her. "You are a lovely young lady, but Hebrew is a complicated language. I can do both interpretations," he said in Hebrew.

"Thank you for the compliment. But I think things will go faster and simpler if you let our Comms interpret for us," Catie said.

"Oh, so they do understand Hebrew," he said in Hebrew.

"And Russian, if Rabbi Margolis prefers that language. Yiddish also," Catie said.

Rabbi Gabay turned to Rabbi Margolis, "which language would you prefer to talk in?" he asked.

"Yiddish is not as obvious as Hebrew or Russian," Rabbi Margolis answered.

"Yiddish it is," Catie said.

"I want you to understand what is going on so that my people are protected," Rabbi Margolis said.

"Of course," Samantha said, and Rabbi Gabay translated.

"Our families are being threatened," the rabbi added.

"We can protect your families while we get rid of the trouble makers," Samantha said.

"Not our families here, well, them as well, but our families back in Russia," the rabbi explained.

"Oh, I understand," Samantha said.

"I'm sure you can see why we have no choice," Rabbi Margolis said.

"Who is threatening them?" Catie asked.

"The Russian government," Rabbi Margolis said.

"But who here in Delphi City?"

"There are three men and two women who came with us, they are not Jews," the rabbi said. "We did not discover this until we were already here. Here is a list of their names." The rabbi slid a piece of paper across to Catie.

"Thank you," she said. "How many people are there back in Russia being threatened?"

"There are dozens of people," Rabbi Margolis said.

"How many dozens?" Catie asked.

"Eighty or ninety people," the rabbi said.

"Five Lynxes," Catie said. "Where are they?"

"In Russia."

"But are they all in the same area, or in different cities?" Catie asked.

"The same area," the rabbi said. "One city, and two towns close by."

"We can get them out," Catie said.

"The Russians will never allow this, they like to keep part of the family in Russia as leverage," Rabbi Margolis said.

"We won't ask them," Catie said. "Can you get a private message to them, something in code?"

"We are Jews, we lived in Russia, we have a secret code," Rabbi Margolis said.

"Okay," Catie said. "Find out exactly how many people and where they live," Catie said. "We'll come up with a plan."

"Are you sure?" Rabbi Margolis asked.

"Our head of security is very good, and we have very talented people on the force," Catie said. "They're getting bored, they love a challenge."

"Have you done something like this before?" the rabbi asked.

"Something like this, yes," Catie said. "But some of the people on our team are ex-special forces, they'll have done this before. Here take this," Catie said as she slid a Comm over to the rabbi.

"I have one of your Comms already," the rabbi said.

"I know," Catie said. "This one is paired to your earwig as well, but it's special. Whenever you make a call on this Comm, it will connect with the other phone and be untraceable, and it won't be possible to intercept the call," Catie explained.

"It seems you have done something like this," the rabbi said.

"We've had issues," Catie said. "Being able to make a truly private call has proven to be very advantageous. We will go over the plan with you before we do anything."

"Until then, tell your people that there will be no repercussions from us," Samantha said. "They should just keep doing what they're being told."

"Please get us the information as soon as possible," Catie said.

"B'ezrat HaShem," Rabbi Margolis said.

"With God's help," the Comms translated.

On Wednesday, Catie, Samantha, and Kal met with the rabbis again. This time they met in the back of a pizza parlor. Catie knew the owner, so they got the back room where they would have privacy.

"Hello," Catie said as the three of them entered the room. "This is Kal, our head of security. He's going to go over the plan for getting your people out of Russia."

The two rabbis stood and shook hands with Kal. "So, you have a plan," Rabbi Gabay said.

"Yes," Kal answered. "We think we have a workable plan that we wish to propose."

"By all means," Rabbi Gabay said as Rabbi Margolis nodded.

"What we are proposing is to divide your people into three groups based on their proximity to each other," Kal said. "Then we will collect each group separately and take them to a location on the Baltic Sea that is closest to them. We'll meet them there with a submarine."

"You have a submarine?" Rabbi Margolis asked.

"They are small," Kal said. "I'm suggesting five separate submarines and three separate rendezvous points. That will minimize the traffic and the chance of setting off any alarms as we take them there."

"Good," Rabbi Margolis said. "How will you get them there?"

"We want to collect the adults on Friday afternoon," Kal said. "We'll substitute our people for the adults, so we minimize the confusion when we collect the children that night."

"How will you collect the children?" Rabbi Margolis asked.

"We want the parents to introduce our person to the children over a videoconference. Then our agent will swap with the parent during the afternoon and meet the children at their home. That night, they will take the children out to a waiting car a few blocks away," Kal said. "Our people are trained for this kind of thing; we want to minimize the number of civilians involved at each stage."

"And you want to do this on the Sabbath?" Rabbi Margolis said.

"It's the best day; everyone expects you to stay in all night and the next day, except for synagogue," Kal said. "We want things to look as normal as possible for as long as possible, so we can get everybody out. We need to move all your people with just three small teams."

"But on the Sabbath?" Rabbi Margolis said.

"When Moses led the Israelites out of Egypt, I'm sure they didn't stop on the Sabbath," Kal said.

"Are you comparing yourself to Moses?" Rabbi Margolis asked.

"No, Rabbi, but I am comparing Russia to Egypt and the Russian Jews to the Israelites," Kal replied.

"Oy vey," Rabbi Margolis said. "We can do this. What do you want us to do?"

"We need to set up the video calls with each family," Kal said. "We need to know clothing sizes for each adult and for the older children."

"This we can do," Rabbi Margolis said.

Kal met with the lead pilots together to go over plans before they started the recovery mission.

"Just to review," Kal said. "We have the four original Foxes flying cover outside of Russian airspace. They should have a minimal radar signature. Then we have the five new Lynxes with the space engines and a fusion reactor. They fly in and submerge here just south of Kotka in the Gulf of Finland. They will proceed on the surface until they're within one hundred kilometers of their designated rendezvous, where they will submerge and proceed underwater."

Kal pointed out each location on the map. "Once they're off of their rendezvous point, they will wait until they get a signal from one of the vans that will be bringing the refugees. We're putting a quantum relay in each Lynx, so we have communication while they're underwater.

When they receive the signal, divers will exit the cargo hold and deploy the lift bags we've had made. When inflated, they will allow the Lynx to surface and remain floating."

"What's to stop it from popping up right away?" Jason asked.

"The cargo bay will be full of water. Until that's pumped out, the Lynx will be too heavy to float, even with the lift bags," Catie explained.

"Okay," Jason said.

"Once the divers are back in the hold, they'll have the water pumped out. When the Lynx surfaces, they can open the hold again without it flooding. We have two Zodiacs in each Lynx so we can transfer our targets in minimal time. Once everyone is aboard, the Lynxes will submerge, then deflate and jettison the lift bags."

"How do our people get out?" Liz asked.

"They'll just work their way to Finland and Poland, where they'll take a commercial flight to Paris. We'll pick them up on our regular route," Kal explained. "They've all been making their way to Saint Petersburg since Tuesday."

All over the Saint Petersburg area, Jews were preparing for the Sabbath. The women were shopping for the meals they would prepare before sundown. The men were visiting friends as they made their way home from work or stopping to run little errands. All of the ones on Kal's list had been instructed to leave their children at home if they were old enough, or with a neighbor, if they were too young to be left alone. Each child was told what and whom to expect. The ability to use their phones to do a quick video chat enabled everyone to be prepared.

As the men entered one of the shops, they were wearing conservative clothes. When they left, they were wearing brighter, more colorful clothes and were accompanied by another person similarly dressed to look like one of the locals. Their heads were covered with the hood of their parka to guard against the cold. But before they left, one of Kal's men had already left the shop wearing the Jew's original parka. They continued to make their way to the home of the person they replaced.

The same thing happened with the women. One of the women would enter a shop to purchase the food for cooking the Sabbath dinner. Before she left, she would exchange clothes and shopping items with one of Kal's women. So when they exited, they were each wearing the other person's clothes and parka. The Jewish women would then discreetly get into a waiting car and be driven off to a rendezvous with a van that was waiting to gather a full load of people before heading toward its next rendezvous.

When Kal's people reached the home of the person they were impersonating, they entered the house as usual. If the family had young children staying with a neighbor, they picked them up, and the children having been schooled on who would pick them up, quietly accompanied them to their home.

Once it was dark, Kal's agents spirited the children away. The small children were each strapped to the chest of one of the agents, while the older ones were carefully schooled on how to walk and act. They walked a couple of blocks before entering cars that would take them to their parents. They left the house via a backdoor or window, quietly making their way so as not to attract attention.

As they exited the city, the cars stopped at various locations, and their passengers were spirited to a van. It was critical that not too many vehicles were seen to approach the three rendezvous points. They couldn't afford to arouse suspicion.

There were two vans for each location; they would be crowded, but three vans were viewed as too likely to draw the attention of unwanted watchers. The three rendezvous locations were widely separated along the Baltic coast.

At the rendezvous location, three sets of Lynxes waited, submerged, just meters from the shore. As the vans approached each location, they signaled ahead. Then, two divers exited the cargo hold dragging a simple version of the floating dock Catie had designed so they could transfer from the Mea Huli to the Lynx without getting wet. They returned to the cargo hold, and the ship was sealed and water expelled from the cargo hold. After two minutes, the timer went off, and the dock inflated itself, raising the Lynx out of the water.

"We have a problem," Liz called over the Comm.

"What?" Catie answered.

"A patrol boat is heading toward rendezvous two," Liz explained.

"Do you think they know anything?" Catie asked.

"No, it just looks like a minor deviation from their normal patrol," Liz answered.

"I've got it," Catie said.

"Wait, what are you going to do?" Liz asked. But Catie was already dropping her Fox to the surface. She slowed it down and landed on the choppy sea at one hundred twenty knots. She slowed down to thirty-five knots, just enough to keep the Fox afloat, then she made a slow sweep toward the patrol boat. Her Fox was dark and low on the water, what one would expect of a smuggler's boat. As she passed by the patrol boat at two hundred meters, their search beam moved and shined in her direction. She kept her direction, trying to emulate a smuggler who had been surprised by the patrol boat and was trying to get out of its range.

"Gotcha," Catie said as the patrol boat changed its heading and started moving in her direction. She led them along for ten minutes before she slowed the Fox and let it submerge. She would make her way out of Russian waters before she surfaced and took off again.

Meanwhile, the divers each took a zodiac and raced to the beach to meet the vans. The parents and children got out of the vans and ran to the beach, climbing into one of the zodiacs. It took two trips to ferry all of them to the Lynx. Once everyone was aboard, they deflated the docks, and the submerged Lynx moved off toward international waters, leaving the docks behind for the Russians to puzzle over.

By the evening of the Sabbath, everyone was with friends in Delphi City.

◆ ◆ ◆

"Hi, Uncle Blake," Catie said as she entered Blake's office. "You wanted to see me."

"Stand at attention, Pilot," Blake barked.

Catie snapped to attention, shocked, and wondering what was going on.

"Explain what happened up there in the gulf?" demanded Blake.

"I . . . I led the patrol boat away," Catie stuttered.

"And where was your lead pilot?" Blake asked.

"She . . . she was . . ."

"That's right, you didn't know where she was, did you?"

"No, sir."

"And did she know what you were doing?"

"No, sir."

"That's what gets people killed!" Blake yelled. "Just because you see the solution to a problem doesn't mean that you rush in to solve it. You discuss it unless there is no time or no other option."

"Yes, sir."

"Was there time?"

"Yes, sir."

"Then why did you leave your lead pilot?"

"No excuse, sir," Catie said.

"That's right!" Blake yelled. "You're grounded until further notice."

"Yes, sir."

"Dismissed."

Catie turned and marched out of Blake's office, fighting back tears. She refused to cry. *"I will not cry,"* she thought.

"Hey, Catie," Liz said. "Are you okay?"

"Yes," Catie said through clenched teeth. "I'm okay. And I'm sorry, Liz. I shouldn't have left you."

"Oh," Liz said as she realized why Catie looked like she was about to cry. "What did he say?"

"He grounded me," Catie said.

"I'm sorry," Liz said. She wanted to give Catie a hug, but she knew it would make things worse. She just watched as Catie marched off to her office.

Blake called Liz into his office.

"Sir," Liz said.

Blake recoiled a bit at Liz's use of sir to greet him.

"Liz, I would like you to go over flight protocol and standing orders with Catie," he said. "Then I want you to have ADI review all of Catie's past missions to see when and if she broke protocol or violated standing orders."

"Cer, Blake," ADI cut in.

"Yes, ADI," Blake said.

"Cer Catie has just asked me to do that," ADI said.

"Which one?" Blake asked.

"Both," ADI replied.

"Good. Liz, apparently Catie has decided to do it herself. I just ask that you be available to her if she has questions."

"I always am, sir," Liz replied.

"Liz, it had to be done," Blake said.

"I understand," Liz said. She just kept standing there in front of his desk.

"Dismissed," Blake said. He sighed as Liz did an about-face and marched out of his office. *"The burden of command,"* he thought.

The next day Catie asked to see Blake.

"Commander Blake, sir," she announced herself.

"Enter."

Catie entered Blake's office and came to attention in front of his desk. "Sir, I wish to apologize. Although that was the first time I've violated standing orders or broken protocol, I realize that I was not trying to follow them before."

"Thank, you," Blake said.

29 Russian Doll

On Wednesday, the protest started; it was just the Jewish community being led by Gabriel Cohen. They were protesting in front of the newly designated government house and had drawn a small crowd. There were several constables on hand to make sure things went smoothly.

Leslie Walters and a camera crew were on hand to film the protest and conduct interviews. It was about an hour into the protest when the first incident happened. Cohen had just started going through a litany of the evils of despotic governments when a man from the crowd began yelling anti-Semitic insults at the Jews. He moved toward one of the Jewish protesters and grabbed him. Then suddenly he seemed to collapse.

"I think he has had too much vodka," the Jewish protester yelled as he and another man dragged the man to the side of the street.

A second man rushed the Jewish protesters and collapsed into the arms of another Jew. "He is drinking vodka too," the Jew yelled out, eliciting a laugh from the crowd.

Two men rushed the crowd from different angles. Everyone moved away to give Kal and Mariana Ramsey, Kal's best sniper, a clear line of fire. They took the two men out with stunner rounds. As soon as the men started to fall, the Jews converged on them and caught them. "These Goyim cannot handle their vodka," someone yelled out.

Once the protest started, the rest of the board gathered in the boardroom, tracking the situation. "Where are the other Russians?" Marc asked.

"They've been fishing off the west side, just below the wharf," Liz replied.

"Fishing!" Blake said. "That doesn't seem right?"

"Yes, now that the protest has started, it does seem odd," Liz agreed.

"Anything unusual happen?" Marc asked.

"Not really, there was a minor spat with another group of fishermen who wanted to set up next to them. They were pulling in some big ones, and the others thought they could get in on the action," Liz said.

"They were catching big fish?" Catie asked. "Can we see?"

"ADI, bring up the surveillance of the Russians," Liz said.

"Yes, Cer Liz," ADI said. A video of a group of six Russians fishing came up on the main display.

"Show us when they're pulling in a fish," Catie said.

The video fast-forwarded to where one of the Russians was reeling in a large yellowfin tuna.

"That fish isn't alive," Catie yelled.

"Armed response to quadrant four-A," Liz yelled into her HUD as she raced out of the room. Quadrant four-A was just two blocks from the protest and only three blocks from the boardroom.

"Keep playing the video," Catie ordered.

As the video moved forward, it was obvious that the women in the group were pulling something out of the fish, then secreting it beneath their flowing skirts. Using their bodies and skirts to shield the view, they were doing something that given the current situation could be interpreted as assembling something.

"They'll be armed," Blake called out on the Comm. "They were bringing things up inside the fish."

"What's going on?" Kal demanded over the Comm.

"The Russians have just acquired weapons," Marc said. "Liz is on it; you keep control over the protest scene. They will be heading your way from quadrant four-A."

"Mariana, move to position six-A," Kal commanded. "We may have armed combatants coming in." Because Mariana was the best sniper on his team, Kal had placed her in the best position to intercept someone coming from the west. Kal hated not being the man on the spot, but he had to trust his people.

"Roger, moving now," Mariana said. "How many?"

"Six," Blake said. "They're moving now. Use your M40." The M40 was the sniper rifle that Kal had used as a Marine. He'd outfitted his sniper team with a version he'd modified after he had come to Delphi City. It only fired real bullets.

"In position," Mariana announced as she set up at the far end of the building away from the Russians. This would give her the best angle for a shot while they were farther down the street.

"ADI, seal all the doors along the block," Marc ordered. "I want whoever or whatever was feeding them the fish."

"Fox three is on standby," Catie said.

"Send it," Marc ordered. "And I want that fishing vessel."

"If we take out its engines, we can deal with it later," Blake said.

"Do it!" Marc said.

"We can have another Fox use sonic pressure to push it out of position. That will prevent their underwater friend from finding them," Catie suggested.

"Fox four, find whoever is underwater around quadrant four-A," Blake commanded. "Fox eight, take out the engines of that fishing vessel and push it off to the north."

The two Foxes launched immediately. Fox 4 had a quantum relay they'd installed after the incident with Centag stealing the Fox from the Sakira. Fox 8 couldn't go underwater, but it was a Mach-six-capable fighter with laser weapons, missiles, and torpedoes. Both jets were on standby at the airport just ten kilometers away. Fox 4 launched first and raced toward the city, dropping down to the water immediately. Once it closed in on the city, it slowed and allowed itself to submerge.

Fox 8 launched and raced toward the fishing vessel. As it approached at Mach two, someone on the boat launched a stinger missile at it. The Fox pilot didn't even pay attention to the missile, confidently leaving his weapons officer in the back seat to deal with it. Three seconds after it was launched, a laser shot from the Fox's port laser destroyed the stinger. Seconds later the Fox, traveling five meters above the water, crossed the stern of the fishing vessel and launched a torpedo. The torpedo was programmed to track the sound of the ship's propeller and destroy it. The Fox climbed away from the ship and accelerated to

Mach four. The pilot turned off the shock wave suppressors and dove toward the ship again. By this time the torpedo had destroyed the ship's rudder and propeller, and the fishing vessel was floating helplessly. The Fox repeatedly dive-bombed the vessel, using its supersonic shock wave to force it off toward the north.

"Who's meeting me?" Liz called out as she pulled on her combat armor. She'd only had time to grab her vest and helmet before running out of the building.

"I'm right behind you," Natalia said.

"On your left," Takurō called out. Both Takurō and Natalia were fully kitted out, having been placed on reserve by Kal.

Two other members of the Delphi City special forces joined them as they reached the corner of the street the Russians were coming down.

"There's a group of teenagers walking in front of the Russians," Blake informed everyone. He had the video feeds from the various cameras on that block playing on the main display. "I'm linking their Comms on channel six."

"How far in front of the Russians are they?" Liz asked.

"Twenty yards," Blake answered.

"I think they're heading to Giorgio's Pizza," Catie added.

"Tell them free pizza if they get there in the next minute," Liz said.

"Hey guys, free pizza at Giorgio's if you make it in one minute," Catie announced over channel six.

"Who's that?" one of the teenagers asked.

"Who cares, free pizza," said another as he started to run. "Last one there has to pay for soda."

The group of teenagers broke into a fast run as they barreled toward the end of the block. Giorgio's was around the corner, halfway down the block.

The Russians had been counting on the teenagers to be a shield as they approached the corner. They looked up and saw that the constable who'd been there when they started out had been replaced by someone with body armor on. They ducked into the entrance of the building they were next to.

"Grenade!" yelled Mariana. She was observing the Russians through her sniper scope and had just caught sight of one of them throwing a grenade as they ducked into the recess.

"Shit, it's heading right toward the teenagers," Takurō yelled. Then he pulled off his helmet and raced toward the teenagers and the grenade.

"Get down!" Catie yelled over channel six.

Takurō caught the grenade in his helmet and dove to the ground, trapping the grenade under his helmet. It went off, and the blast and fragments were redirected by his helmet out the small gaps on the sides where his respirator was attached. The right side caught part of his arm, and the left side tore into his left knee. Unfortunately, his left foot was anchored against the curb, so his leg couldn't be pushed out of the way; instead, the blast severed his leg just above the knee. His armor automatically applied a tourniquet to the leg and injected him with pain killers and coagulants.

"My leg," Takurō yelled. "Damn it, I just got it fixed!"

The Russians, intent on using the distraction to advance, were starting to come out of the entryway where they were sheltered. As soon as Mariana had a shot, she took it, killing the lead male. Her second shot killed the woman who'd thrown the grenade. She had a second one prepared to throw when Mariana took her head off. The grenade dropped to the ground, and the handle flew off igniting the fuse. One second later, the grenade exploded in the middle of the Russian group, taking them all out.

Liz raced over to Takurō; she knelt down beside him and linked her Comm to his. His vital signs came up on her HUD.

"How's Takurō?" Blake asked.

"His vitals are okay," Liz said. "He's lost his left leg."

"How in the bleeeeeeeeeeeeeeeeep! Why me?" Takurō's voice came over the Comm.

"ADI, are you censoring Takurō?" Catie asked.

"Yes, Cer Catie," ADI said. "He is in a lot of discomfort and is using very inappropriate language. The pain killers should be taking effect soon."

Liz called in an ambulance team to the scene. They arrived in a mini helicopter that they used for ambulances and fast-response teams. The medical tech raced over to Liz and Takurō; he did a quick scan of his leg and arm, then started removing his armor. He separated the tourniquet from the armor on Takurō's left leg, leaving it in place. Then he focused on treating his right arm.

"Hey, his leg is the big injury," Liz shouted.

"It's got a tourniquet on it, it's a complete loss," the EMT said. "Dr. Sharmila is printing him a new one now. But if I can fix this arm right away, he won't have to have it replaced." The EMT continued to focus on Takurō's arm as the other two brought the stretcher over and hooked him up to an IV. The EMT injected Takurō with nanites, which would work with the ones that his armor had injected and seal up the wound and isolate the grenade fragments. "You're going to be fine," the EMT told Takurō.

"What kind of lousy job did they do, the damn leg just came right off!" Takurō shouted.

"I don't know, letting a grenade go off just six inches away from your leg, and pinning it against the curb to boot, probably had something to do with it," the EMT replied. "Dr. Sharmila is printing one up right now."

"But I have to wait two weeks," Takurō said.

"No, she says she'll attach it right away, you're going to be a mess for the two weeks anyway," the EMT said. "She also says she's going to note that you're allergic to grenades and should avoid them."

Takurō started laughing, "That's what got it the last time. Tell her to add that I'm allergic to bullets too, then send it to my boss. Maybe they'll give me a nice cushy desk job."

One of the teenagers came over, "Hey man, thanks for saving us."

"My job," Takurō said.

One of the EMTs reached down and picked up Takurō's severed leg. When the teenager saw it, he turned green and started vomiting.

"Vomit on the street," Natalia said. "It's easier to clean up that way." She came over and patted the teenager on the back. Once he finished vomiting, she led him back to his friends.

"What can we do?" one of the other teenagers asked.

"Nothing for you to do," Natalia said.

"Send them to the hospital to see Dr. Jefferies. She's a counselor and can help them deal with the stress and any PTSD," Samantha told Natalia.

Natalia gave the instructions to the teenagers. "I guess we lost out on the pizza," one of them said.

"You are an ass," one of the girls said. "He lost a leg, and you're thinking about food."

"Hey, free pizza," the guy said.

"You can have your free pizza whenever you guys feel up to it," Natalia said. "It's registered on your Comms. Now, go to the hospital."

Back at the protest, Kal signaled everyone that the situation was under control. One of the constables waved to Gabriel that he should finish up.

"And that is why we came to this beautiful city," Gabriel announced. "Here, they have laws and a constitution that protect people. They have a wonderful king who treats all the people like they are his children. Not like in Russia where the government is so busy helping its friends steal from the people."

Leslie Walters captured the last of the speech then ran over to the constable. "What were those two explosions that we heard?" she demanded.

"You'll need to talk to the public relations office about it," the constable said.

"I was told I would have complete access," Leslie argued.

"And you do. You have complete access to the public relations office where they'll tell you what happened. I don't know, so I can't tell you."

Leslie and her camerawoman started to go down toward the corner where the explosions had occurred.

"I'm sorry, but that street has been sealed off," the constable said.

Leslie signaled for her camerawoman to try to get a picture of what was going on down the street from behind the barricade, but all they could see was the ambulance helicopter.

"What's the ambulance for?" Leslie asked.

"Some people have been injured," the constable answered. "You'll be able to get more information from the public relations office."

The ambulance took off, exposing a second ambulance farther along the street.

"It must be serious if you're using helicopters," Leslie said.

"All our fast-response vehicles are helicopters," the constable said. "We don't allow high-speed vehicles on our streets."

A third helicopter landed beyond the second ambulance. "What is that helicopter for?" Leslie asked.

"I don't know," the constable answered, "you'll . . ."

"Need to talk to the public relations office," Leslie finished for her.

"How is Takurō doing?" Marc asked Liz as she came into the boardroom for the debrief the next day.

"Dr. Sharmila says he's going to be fine," Liz said. "She's attaching his new leg now, and will be holding him in a coma for a week while it integrates and his other injuries heal."

"What about the Russians?" Admiral Michaels asked.

"Only two survived," Kal replied. "Mariana shot two of them, and the grenade killed two. The two survivors will be in intensive care for a few days. They ate a lot of shrapnel."

"So how did they manage to bring the weapons in?" Marc asked.

"As you saw on the video, they were bringing up yellowfin tuna. I assume the Russians on the fishing boat out there caught them a few days ago. They gutted them and then inserted the weapons and grenades. Then they had a diver swim the twelve miles to the city, pulling the fish behind him. He was attaching them to the hooks and letting the Russians here on the city pull them in," Kal said.

"Have we picked the diver up yet?" Marc asked.

"They just pulled him in," Kal said. "Apparently he was running low on air, and when the fishing boat wasn't where it was supposed to be, he didn't have much choice."

"Is he talking?" Admiral Michaels asked.

"Not yet," Kal said.

"What about our friends on the fishing boat?" Marc asked.

"They're still holding out," Kal said. "We pushed the boat back into our territorial waters. We did a few surgical strikes to take out their engines and backup generator, so I think a day or two like that, and they'll be ready to surrender. I'm having a Fox buzz them every thirty minutes just to remind them we're still waiting."

"What are we going to do with them?" Admiral Michaels asked.

"Since Leslie Walters' report revealed that the protests were being orchestrated by the Russians, they're claiming it was an unauthorized mission by zealous patriots," Samantha said. "By the way, she's really pushing hard to do a full report on the space station."

"We did promise her something special if she reported on the protest," Marc said. "But right now, we need to figure out what they've learned about our defenses and how to counter their methods."

"We're working on it," Kal said. "We're all very embarrassed; we should have our recommendations ready next week."

"At least we survived this attempt," Blake said. "Hopefully we get a few months to prepare and recover before something else happens."

"You didn't just say that," Samantha groaned.

"What?" Blake asked.

"Tempting the gods!" Samantha said. "Every time one of you says all is well, we have another disaster on our hands."

"Oh, come on, that's ridiculous," Blake said. "ADI, is there anything happening that should concern us?"

"Cer Blake, there are no immediate threats that I can detect," ADI said. "However, NASA has recently detected a large asteroid that is heading toward the solar system."

"See!" Samantha hissed.

"It's just an asteroid," Blake said. "How big is it?"

"It is one thousand meters in length," ADI said.

"That's huge; it's almost as big as Ceres," Catie gasped.

"How long before it gets here?" Marc asked.

"It will take it seven months to enter the solar system and 3.5 years before it crosses Earth's orbit," ADI replied.

"See, we've got plenty of time to deal with it, that is, if we even need to do anything," Blake said.

"I'll remind you of that," Samantha said, "because I have a bad feeling about this."

"Okay, Blake, Admiral, and Kal, we'll meet on Monday to review the situation. I'd like to know how we're going to beef up our defenses," Marc said. "Let's all get some rest."

Afterword

Thanks for reading **Delphi Nation**!

I hope you've enjoyed the fourth book in the *Delphi in Space* series. As a self-published author, the one thing you can do that will help the most is to leave a review on Goodreads and Amazon.

The next book in our series, **Delphi Alliance**.

The McCormacks have their floating city growing in the South Pacific, and their space station well underway. As they continue their quest to unite Earth and bring her into the modern age of space travel and repair her environment before it's too late, they have to fight with the major powers that aren't too sure they want to change the status quo. Now they have discovered an incoming asteroid the size of Ceres.

What will it take to unite Earth to deal with this threat to its very existence? And what other threats may be lurking there? Now it's time to step up, for Delphi and all the nations of Earth.

Acknowledgments

It is impossible to say how much I am indebted to my beta readers and copy editors. Without them, you would not be able to read my books due to all the grammar and spelling errors. I have always subscribed to Andrew Jackson's opinion that "It is a damn poor mind that can think of only one way to spell a word."

So special thanks to:

My copy editor, Ann Clark, who also happens to be my wife.

My beta reader and editor, Theresa Holmes.

My beta reader and cheerleader, Roger Blanton, who happens to be my brother.

Also important to a book author is the cover art for their book. I'm especially thankful to Momir Borocki for the exceptional covers he has produced for my books. It is amazing what he can do with the strange PowerPoint drawings I give him; and how he makes sense of my suggestions, I'll never know.

If you need a cover, he can be reached at momir.borocki@gmail.com.

Also by Bob Blanton

Delphi in Space
Sakira
Delphi City
Delphi Station
Delphi Nation
Delphi Alliance
Delphi Federation Fall 2020

Stone Series
Matthew and the Stone
Stone Ranger
Stone Undercover

Made in the USA
San Bernardino, CA
17 June 2020

73464745R00151